PURSUIT OF THE BOLD

BOLD TRILOGY #1

JAMIE MCFARLANE

FICKLE DRAGON PUBLISHING, LLC

PREFACE

FREE DOWNLOAD

Sign up for the author's New Releases mailing list and get free copies of the novellas; *Pete, Popeye and Olive* and *Life of a Miner*.

To get started, please visit:

http://www.fickledragon.com/keep-in-touch

PROLOGUE

One of the difficulties of writing a long running series is getting people back up to speed with characters they may have forgotten. I have two resources available for this. The first is a glossary at the end of this book. In this glossary, I have descriptions of the major characters. The second is on my website at fickledragon.com/privateer-tales-characters. And, don't worry, neither resource is required. I'll introduce each character as you run into them, just like you'd expect.

Writing a trilogy is a new experience for me and I wasn't exactly sure what I was getting into when I started this venture. I can say that so far it has been very rewarding. I've enjoyed the ability to develop a much longer story and work through a full arc instead of a single story. Don't worry, though. I stand first in line for my dislike of cliffhangars. Each installment of the Bold Trilogy is a complete story with a satisfying end. You'll no doubt have an idea as to where the next book is going, but of course, it will be another story entirely.

Happy Reading!

Jamie

Chapter 1

JOYS OF LEADERSHIP

PETERSBURG STATION OVER PLANET ZURI,
SANTALOO SYSTEM

"Frak, Liam, exactly what do you have against *Intrepid*?" Nick's voice came over the comms. "You could have at least recovered the pieces; those were brand new engines."

The quick cadence of my best friend and business partner's voice brought a smile to my face. For a ten-day, *Intrepid* had been sitting in the primary repair bay of Petersburg Station, which was in its permanent home over the planet Zuri in the Santaloo System. Nick and the brightly-colored, frog-faced alien Jester Ripples were finishing the rebuild of the heavy struts that would hold two of *Intrepid's* powerful engines.

"Look out!" Merrie, a young and extremely talented engineer, shouted just after striking a frozen iron pipe with a four-kilogram sledge. I looked over in time to see a wash of aged bilge water stream toward me as the ten-centimeter-diameter pipe broke loose from its fitting. I attempted to spin away but was caught in the shoulder by the frigid slime.

"That is disgusting," Sendrei Buhari, the former Naval gunnery officer we'd rescued from planet Cradle, complained in his deep baritone voice. I turned to find that while I'd taken a glancing blow, he'd taken the pressurized black water full in the back. Worse yet, Sendrei had turned at Merrie's call and a portion of the sludge had also caught him in the face.

"Oh, I'm so sorry," Merrie, often the smartest person in the room and always the most impatient, pushed her sledge onto a magnetic clamp, flitted over and dabbed at the gunk on his face. "I thought that might free the pipe, but I had no idea the contents were under pressure."

Sendrei took the towel from her hand and continued cleaning. "An unfortunate eventuality of working in a bilge." The heavily muscled, ebony-skinned gunnery officer had once been enslaved for more than ten stans by the bug-aliens we knew as Kroerak and was generally unflappable.

"Why don't you head up and get cleaned off," I said. "Send Semper down if you see her."

"I have arrived, Liam Commodore." Semper was Felio, a humanoid species with feline characteristics, including fur that covered the entire body, retractable claws, and a tail. For whatever reason, Semper, like most Felio, had difficulty placing a person's title in front of their name.

"Merrie finally got this beast free," I said, laying my hand on the heavy pipe that floated in zero-gravity.

Semper was unable to pull her wider-than-usual cat eyes away from Sendrei, her long tail twitching anxiously. "Buhari Sir, you are covered in fouled waters."

"And so will you be. There appears to be more than enough to go around." Sendrei chuckled as he gracefully pushed off and glided upward through the tangle of piping.

"There is malodor," Semper said, turning her attention to the long seventy-kilogram pipe I had marked for recycling in Merrie's forge atop Petersburg station. Even in zero-g, a special touch was required to move an object which out-massed you. Semper, however, had adapted to ship-board life and maneuvered it expertly.

I shook my head. "I swear. You and Sendrei compete for understatement."

"Sendrei Buhari is superior in this," Semper said as she continued guiding the pipe upward.

I caught a humorous glint in Merrie's eyes as we exchanged glances. In addition to not understanding titles, Semper was notoriously slow to pick up on humor. This trait was something that gave me no end of entertainment and in Merrie, I shared a co-conspirator.

The bilge in which we stood belonged to our largest and one of our most recently acquired ships — *Hornblower*. Originally called *Sangilak,* we'd captured the 20,000 tonne cruiser from a pesky lizard-chinned Pogona pirate named Belvakuski. And while it was generally considered bad luck to rename a ship, I figured we were well within our rights. We were not only modernizing the light cruiser, but were upgrading it to be better classed as a standard cruiser.

"Commodore, your attention is required in the engine room." Commander Greg Munay's voice came over the ship's comm.

While Munay had originally been one of my most ardent and outspoken critics, he'd changed his tune when the *Intrepid* crew had seized *Sangilak,* now named *Hornblower,* rescuing him and eighteen other Mars Protectorate from Genteresk pirates. A younger version of myself would have held past behavior against the man, punishing or at least ignoring him. Even now, trying as hard as I could, I was unable to completely forget that Munay had once seen it as his right to threaten the seizure of *Intrepid* if I didn't do as he demanded.

"On my way, Greg," I answered. I had issues using his previous Mars Protectorate title as it signified rank that did not fit within our current structure.

"Are you good to keep going?" I asked Merrie.

"Amon is on his way. These pipes are made from old steel," she replied. Merrie's husband, Amon, was a blacksmith by trade. "He will be better at disassembly than we are."

"Are you sure he'll be okay?" I asked, pushing off the hull, aiming for the hatch five meters above our position. Amon had virtually no instincts when it came to moving around in low gravity and he preferred to stay out of confined spaces like a ship's bilge.

"Don't coddle him," Merrie said. "He's a big boy."

"Don't worry," I raised an eyebrow as I passed in front of her. "I'll leave that entirely to you."

"You are a wicked man, Liam Hoffen."

Hornblower was by far the largest ship I'd ever been on. There were entire decks I'd spent no more than a few minutes on while passing through. The ship's design had more in common with an ancient seafaring battleship than any modern spaceship I'd been in, military or otherwise. Just about every system was manual and good operation of the ship required a minimum crew complement of one hundred, twenty sailors. *Hornblower* could comfortably hold a couple thousand crew, provided they didn't mind sleeping on the rusted decks without much access to any sort of facilities.

Like all aspects of the ship upgrade, the bilge refit was a massive undertaking. I'd worked with Nick on the redesign and we'd agreed to a plan that would completely replace clear water, grey water, and black water systems throughout. For now, we would save considerable effort by not plumbing the middle seven decks and instead stub off the main supplies and waste at each of those decks. There'd been some talk of installing a smaller system, thereby lowering the ship's crew capacity. In the end, I'd made the call to fully build out the bilge. Most of the human labor was in the removal of the older system components, anyway.

With Munay's influence, Nick had been able to procure the IP (intellectual property) for naval hull repair bots. The bots' sole purpose was to grind, weld, repair and paint interior metal surfaces. They weren't particularly good at replacing missing sections of hull plating, nor could they restore bracing. However, they could cut holes in bulkheads and build up mounting brackets for power, atmo, and the three different types of water. Left to their own devices, a fleet of these little bots would work tirelessly to bring the ship's hard spaces up to the Navy's high standards.

Once we were done with the little machines, Nick was sure he'd be able to sell them for three times what we'd invested. The problem was fitting them into his production schedule. In the sixty-some days we'd been out chasing the Kroerak, Nick had piled up orders for twelve hundred stevedore bots and was struggling to expand manufacturing capacity to meet the demand. Even so, we both knew that pursuit of the Kroerak was critical and the short-term switch in bot production, while not a great financial decision, would get our small fleet back into the hunt more quickly.

"Cap, where are you headed?" Marny, our chief of security, caught me as I arc-jetted aft to where Munay had requested my presence.

"Munay has a problem in the engine room. Walk with me," I said dropping to the deck. The gravity had been turned up to .3g in the upper decks.

"Sounds expensive," she chortled.

I nodded with a lopsided grin. Between Nick's manufacturing orders and the repairs of *Hornblower* and *Intrepid,* we were burning resources like someone had dumped an oxygen tank on 'em. "Might have been cheaper to just make a new ship," I quipped.

"Given any thought to manufacturing shells?" she asked. "Belvakuski's armory was nearly depleted."

"Your boyfriend would have my head if I asked him to manufacture one more thing," I said.

"Why is it Nick-my-boyfriend when you don't want to discuss difficult issues and otherwise he's your best friend?"

"I'm going to consider that question asked and answered."

"We also need to find a source for fuel," she said. "*Hornblower's* engines are like sieves. We burned over half of our stock just getting home."

"Doesn't Merrie have a line on a cluster of asteroids with trapped hydrogen in the silicate?"

"Yes, but someone needs to go get it," Marny said.

I was purposely trying to avoid several issues and Marny knew it. I'd slowly but surely discovered that immediate, urgent issues often got in front of the more strategic. Marny was reminding me that I couldn't afford to ignore ordnance or fuel.

"Copy. The bilge project is moving without me. I can take on the munition and fuel issues now," I said. "According to Merrie, we're running short on iron. I'll have to talk to Hog and see if the York settlement has any more folks who'd like to stake a mining claim."

Marny stopped me by grabbing my arm. "You're getting pulled thin, Cap." An Earther, Marny was physically imposing with broad strong shoulders and heavily banded musculature. While Earthers were typically larger than spacers, her proportions were out of the ordinary. Instead of shying away from her size, however, she'd embraced it and kept herself in top physical shape. It was a running joke amongst the crew that I had a crush on her. I'd be dishonest to suggest otherwise, but I would categorize my feelings more as ... intrigued. "No reason for you to be working the bilge. You need to take higher-priority items. Lean on us harder and spread the load."

"It's hard to let go of some things," I said. "Merrie has a good handle on the project. She's going to turn Amon and a dozen recruits from York loose on clearing the cast iron pipe. Even so, we're looking at two more ten-day just to clear it all out. The good news is with new waste and supply pipe, we're going to drop over a hundred tonnes of mass."

"About the munitions," Marny continued patiently. "There's good news and bad."

"I'm all about good news. Let's hear that first," I said.

"I located a source on Abasi Prime for munitions," she said. "They have the capacity to manufacture shells that will fit *Hornblower's* 400mm, 250mm and 75mm kinetic cannons."

"And the bad news?"

"Six million credits for a full loadout."

I whistled. I was used to expensive ordnance, but six million beat my personal high-water mark by at least twenty times.

"How in the frak did Belvakuski arm this ship?" I asked. "She made decent money as a pirate, but that's insane."

"She has no 400mm or 250mm shells in the armory," Marny answered. "I had my AI replay data streams from her return fire on the Kroerak cruiser. She only fired eight 250mm shells and there were no 400mm shells fired at all."

"Sure. Explains why she only went after smaller fish. A 75mm shell is more than enough to get your attention, especially if you believe she'll follow it up with something bigger," I said. "I'll be honest, though, I'm not about to push off into the Dark Frontier without a full load. We'll come up with the money somehow, even if we have to delay for a few months."

"Commodore Hoffen." Commander Greg Munay and three Mars Protectorate officers snapped to attention as Marny and I entered the starboard engine room. To the best of my knowledge, none of the officers who had been captured by Belvakuski had resigned their commissions to Mars Protectorate, nor were they about to abandon their mission to locate the Kroerak or secondarily, bring injury to the Kroerak war apparatus. Instead, Munay and the men in his command had decided we were their best chance to defeat those bugs. They had all sworn their allegiance to me, something I knew Munay had communicated to Mars Protectorate and had not backed away from.

"Please go about your business," I replied. "Seems like we should work on loosening military discipline a little, don't you think, Greg?"

"No sir, I don't," he replied, unflinchingly. If there was a type of soldier with 'all the right stuff,' Greg Munay was it. His greying sideburns, weathered face, and flinty stare left no doubt about the character that lay underneath; one of loyalty, duty, respect, selfless service, honor, integrity, and personal courage. He was always in command and never without a strong sense of purpose. "Way I see it, we're going to need to bring on a lot more crew to launch this fleet of yours. You'll require every bit of discipline we can muster and then some."

"You requested I come up?" I asked, looking around the cramped compartment where all the panels had been removed from the walls. Wires, cables and conduit fell untidily from the openings and it didn't take an AI to recognize that the systems we were looking at were antiquated – by centuries.

"We have good news, not so good news, and bad," he said.

I caught Marny's eye and she grinned. After asking her for the good news first, I wasn't about to repeat that mistake with Munay. "Give it to me straight, Greg," I said. "Bad news first."

"Senior Engineer Hawthorn, would you explain your assessment to the commodore?" Munay asked, turning to a man I'd met only briefly in passing. I studied the man for a moment. He had reddish brown hair that was cut short and a thin line of hair that followed his jawline.

"The engines are shot, Commodore." My AI flashed up the man's full name – Adrian Hawthorn, graduated with honors from the Naval Academy on Mars. His field of study had been propulsion systems. I raised my eyebrows. Nothing like an expert opinion.

"Define shot," I said. "Belvakuski seemed to do pretty well with them."

Hawthorn's brief smile disappeared as he acknowledged my grasp of the obvious. "Unfortunately, the Genteresk did not keep tight maintenance records so we are only able to make assumptions based on forensic inspection, but I believe this ship regularly experienced engine failure while underway. The number of recent repairs in this section," he waved his hand at a jumble of wires and components that hung arbitrarily to the starboard, "is actually stressing the connective material to the point that if you were to place any pressure on the hanging components, they would likely become detached."

"Control circuits should be something we can manufacture relatively easily," I said. "Do you just need time on the replicator?"

Hawthorn shook his head negatively. "This is just one example. I ran a calculation. To bring the two engines to minimal level of operation would require over two months of constant production from the replicator currently in Loose Nuts' possession. And even that ignores the necessity of redundant systems."

I sighed. It was an accepted fact that engine, navigation, and life support systems required at least a single redundancy. "That's the bad news, right?" I asked. "You're not about to tell me we need to scrap the engines too, are you?"

The man's eyebrows shot up and he nodded his head, smiling reassuringly. I suspected he hadn't appreciated being given the task of telling me about the systems. "No, not at all. That was the *really* bad news," he said enthusiastically. "The Pogona engine design is ingenious and with attention, we could more than double output and increase efficiency by a factor of six. The thing is, they've been so poorly maintained, that they're choking with too much fuel forced down their throats. It'll take work and we'll have to manufacture parts, but they're definitely keepers. She'll never be a racer, but I think you'll be surprised what a difference good maintenance will make."

"Could you get started on the engines while we come up with a way to manufacture new control circuits?" I asked.

Hawthorn looked from me back to Munay, who nodded his agreement. "Aye, aye. We'll get right on it," Hawthorn answered. I wasn't sure if he was answering to me or Munay.

Marny, on the other hand, wasn't quite as quick to let it go. "Lieutenant Hawthorn," she asked with her raised, command voice, while stepping into Hawthorn's personal space. "Would you explain the chain of command aboard *Hornblower* as you understand it?"

"Um," he stammered, looking nervously from Marny to Munay.

"Hawthorn! Are you ignoring a superior officer's question while she's standing in your face?" Marny's voice filled the entire room and I cringed.

"I guess I assumed we still reported to Commander Munay," he said, sweat forming on his brow as his attention snapped back to Marny.

"Stand down, Gunny," Munay said calmly. "We're all after the same thing here."

Marny spun on her heel and I could have sworn that fire was about to shoot out of her eyes. "*Mister* Munay, out of respect for your years of service to Mars Protectorate, I'll keep this short and to the point. There is no chain of command that doesn't end at Liam Hoffen. If you or Mr. Hawthorn can't get on board with that, I am positive there are any number of jobs in civilian life on planet Zuri that either of you would be well suited for. Are we clear?"

Munay raised an eyebrow as he looked from Marny to me and I answered his unasked question. "It's easy enough, Greg. You swore an oath to me, but perhaps you have unfinished business with Mars Protectorate that needs your attention. I'd love to have your assistance, but I'm not going to have my orders questioned and I won't be put in a position where I question the loyalty of *my* crew."

"You can't do this without us," he said evenly.

"Maybe not," I said. My HUD showed that Marny had formed a tactical team channel and that Tabby would arrive at our position in twenty seconds. "That was not my question. You need to know that I will shoot, or order shot, any crew that participate in mutiny. I'm surprised I need to explain this to you."

Soft footsteps landed on the deck behind me and my HUD showed that Tabby, my fiancée and all-around bad-ass best friend, had arrived. With her by my side, I truly had nothing to fear. In short, she was considerably faster and stronger than any human should be, thanks to reconstruction by the Navy's best doctors. Tabby had lost most of her limbs when the Naval ship she was on was destroyed by pirates. She'd also had an unusual reaction to the synthetic tendons and muscles, only increasing her speed, strength and agility.

"You don't need to escalate this," Munay said. "It was a simple mistake."

"Glad to hear it," I said.

"You don't need to escalate this, *Sir!*" Marny corrected.

Munay pursed his lips in a small frown. "Sir. I apologize for my insolent behavior," he said. Anger flashed in his eyes, but to his credit he kept his voice even. "As I have not formally discussed rank with you, I apparently made assumptions that are onerous and have directed Mr. Hawthorn inappropriately. I remain dedicated to the pledge I made on *Hornblower's* deck after the Battle of Kameldeep. Although I am no longer in a position to speak for the other Mars Protectorate personnel, I believe my statement holds true for each of us. I ask that you find the fault in this misunderstanding to be my own and not hold Mr. Hawthorn accountable."

"Thank you," I said. "Are we good, Marny?" I asked.

"We are," she said. "I will communicate a formal chain of command to all personnel, so we can avoid confusion. Will that be acceptable, *Mister* Munay?"

"Yes, Ma'am," he replied.

Chapter 2

PISCIVORU

Sklisk awoke and flicked the tip of his tongue from his mouth, tasting the humid air of his rocky nest. The smell of his mate, Jaelisk, next to him and their brood only a few arm lengths away filled him with pride. It was the responsibility of every Piscivoru to grow a strong family, and their boys – Baelisk and Boerisk – had brought honor to his line.

Reaching over Jaelisk, Sklisk twisted and stretched, just able to touch their nest's rocky ceiling. Grasping with first one clawed hand and then the other, he lifted his torso and twisted so his stomach was flat against the warm rock. Turning his ankles, he locked onto the wall with clawed feet and crawled quietly to the edge of the family's nest. Preferring a vertical orientation, he rounded onto the cavern's sheer face, careful not to drag his tail across his mate.

"Skli, where are you going?" Jaelisk's voice was nothing more than a whisper on the pale blue vapors rising from the deep pools six counts of fall beneath him.

"I seek morning sustenance and to rid myself of this skin," he hissed back quietly, not wanting to wake the overly active Baelisk and Boerisk.

"I wanna come."

"I wanna come."

Sklisk's secondary eyelids blinked in understanding at the failure of his stated objective. He sighed as his boys skittered out onto the wall from their rocky beds, their tongues flicking excitedly, tasting the air. An armlength-and-a-half long, with torsos not much wider than the base of his tail, they were only six cycles grown.

Now that his sons were awake, Sklisk knew there was no fight to be won. He would have to find another private moment to scrape the weathered skin from his body. Piscivoru never stopped growing. It was perfectly natural to outgrow one's skin, but considered a sign of immaturity to be seen peeling away the dead skin. So much so, that he'd never seen more than a slight pouch that was loose on Jaelisk. The deep brown along her back, the dusty-tan of her stomach, and the fiery-red top scales were always smooth beneath his touch.

"Boys, give your father a moment to tend to his needs," Jaelisk said, sliding onto the wall with her family. "Sklisk, I will take them to water's edge and collect pouches for our journey."

Sklisk blinked his translucent eyelids at his mate in appreciation. The boys would do as she said as they knew she would brook few arguments.

"Aw, do we have to? Can't we go to the quarry before school? All the broodlings are doing it," Baelisk argued.

Sklisk winced, his lids shuttering fast, twice. Baelisk was a strong-spirited child and seemed to demand that all lessons be learned more than once. Faster than could be tracked, Jaelisk's tail lashed out and detached the boy from the cavern wall. With nothing to hold him, he fell toward the luminescent blue pools, tumbling in the humid air.

Jaelisk released her hold and straightened her body to fall after him. Unlike the tumbling boy, she fell in a line as straight as spider's silk, overtaking her son as he rushed toward the waters below, pushing him into position. Sklisk flicked his tongue nervously as he followed their progress into the warm waters.

"Ohh, he was almost bug guts," Boerisk said, impressed, as he scurried downward after them.

Sklisk knew it was an exaggeration. Tumbling for a six count would be painful upon entering the waters, but nowhere near fatal. The lower nests were given to pairings because of that very reason, as it wasn't uncommon for broodlings to become detached as they grew.

Releasing his grasp on the rock face, Sklisk aligned himself to grab Boerisk as he passed.

"Dad, stop," Boerisk complained as he arrested Sklisk's fall for only a moment before being torn from the wall. "I think you broke my claw."

Sklisk closed all three eyelids as he straightened out and entered the waters. A moment later, he opened the outer two and paused to enjoy the underwater grotto's brilliant blue crystals. He rushed along, propelling himself by quickly swishing his strong body and tail from side to side. Taking advantage of his surroundings, he slid behind an outcropping of jagged crystals and felt the satisfying scrape as hard-to-reach skin peeled away from between his shoulder blades and lower neck.

"Ooh, gross," Baelisk said, vibrating his tongue in the water to communicate.

"You look like such a delicious little grub," Sklisk said and flicked his powerful tail, turning to chase the already-fleeing troublemaker. The child squirted through the underwater grotto and turned toward a hole no more than two hand-breadths wide. If Baelisk was allowed to enter such a small space, Sklisk would not be able to follow. Fortunately, as fast as the boy was, Sklisk was faster. An expert swimmer, he caught his son only moments before losing him to the grotto's many hidey-holes. Sklisk raked his claws down the light-brown scales which ran along the boy's back. The move both served to stop the boy and convey Sklisk's affection.

"Don't eat me, big pokey monster," Baelisk trilled in delight.

Sklisk reached around and jabbed the boy's soft stomach scales with sharpened claws and was rewarded with a tiny bubble of air escaping from one of the boy's nostrils.

"Stop – I'm gassing," Baelisk complained, still giggling and trailing a thin line of bubbles.

The Piscivoru had the capacity to stay submerged for upwards of twenty minutes if they conserved captured air within their lungs. Exertion reduced this time considerably as did 'gassing,' which simply meant releasing the oxygen they'd captured. Unlike other oxygen breathers, this species separated oxygen from the atmosphere and stored it for later use.

"Okay," Sklisk agreed, releasing his often orneriest of sons. "Why don't you come with me to the kill. We will bring morning sustenance for Boer and mother." He caught his wife's eye as she swam past and acknowledged his plan with a subtle flick of her tongue, no more than a claw's width out of her mouth.

"Really?" Baelisk asked.

It was unusual to take a juvenile so far up in the caverns, but Sklisk and Jaelisk were leaving on a clan mission that might take as long as a full count of moon cycles. The boys would need to know how to retrieve daily food and Baelisk was the best-equipped for the task.

"Only if you can catch me," Sklisk said and turned abruptly, following the path of a bubble to the pool's surface.

He waited at the water's edge for only a moment before Baelisk broke the surface and leapt onto the wall. The two raced up the sheer face, rocketing past their home and climbing well past the danger zone of ten-second falls. Of course, any decent Piscivoru knew that when falling from any distance, safety could be found by angling back toward the safety of the rock face.

"How far up is the kill?" Baelisk asked curiously.

"Ten hands of the bug warriors managed to reach the second lock," Sklisk answered.

"Engirisk says we should use our numbers and not count by hands," Baelisk said, referring to a technically minded elder who taught the young and old alike.

"Very well, how many bugs are ten hands?"

"Fifty, father. That is so easy. But how did the bugs make it past the first lock? I thought their shells were too wide."

"They used great machines to break through, Baelisk," Sklisk answered. "But you have nothing to fear. It took them forty cycles to pass through the first and it will take them another forty to pass the second. If they do, we bury the grotto and hide within the great under."

"Frielisk says something has made the bug warriors angry and that they are attacking more than ever before. Why do they wish to kill us?"

"They fear the Iskstar," he explained. "Before our eyes glowed with the Iskstar and we lived beneath the ground, we had a great civilization that lived beneath the yellow sun. Our ancestors lived peacefully in nests they built with our own great machines. There were multitudes and multitudes of our peoples and we were safe and happy."

"But then the bug warriors came and attacked the people who lived beneath the sun," Baelisk said, repeating the lore that had been told to him time and time again. "And our great machines could not defend the peoples. And we had to hide in the ground and be protected by the Iskstar."

"You listen well, Baelisk," Sklisk said, inwardly amused by his impatient son's highly shortened rendition of the last five hundred cycles of the Piscivoru species. Baelisk had heard the stories and eaten of the bug meat, but he had never seen the vast ruined cities nor the great bug armies that were intensely focused on rooting them out.

They continued to squeeze through the upper passages, quietly greeting those they passed with blinks and tongue flicks. For as long as Sklisk could remember, the bug warriors had dug in his home world's stony ground, looking for the remnants of the once powerful Piscivoru. Great care had been taken to lead these bugs away from the shattered civilization that lived under the protection of the Iskstar. The warrior's presence at the second lock was worrisome as it showed the bugs were closer than ever before.

"They're so big," Baelisk said, stopping at the edge of the rubble field where the bug warriors still lay. Even his father was not as long from forehead to tip of tail as a bug warrior. "How do they run?"

"They stand vertically, as all Piscivoru used to," Sklisk said, pushing off the ground and raising onto his back legs so he stood straight. "Now we must hurry. You will be late for school."

Sklisk pulled a glowing blue long-bladed dagger from the belt he wore around his waist, and sliced into a bug warrior's armor. He found it ironic that the very monsters that sought to destroy his people, were in fact most delicious. Working quickly, he slabbed enough food for Boerisk and Baelisk to survive for ten moon cycles. His Iskstar blade found no resistance in the alien bug's carapace as he cut. For a moment, he felt sorry for the bug who would feed his family. It had died beneath the ground far from home. His clan would devour its body and no trace of it would ever be found. It seemed pointless, although he appreciated its contribution to his family's health.

"They are fearsome looking," Baelisk said, touching the tip of the bug's pincer with his open hand. " Its claws are very sharp. I would not enjoy fighting with it."

Sklisk turned his Iskstar blade over in his hand and held the handle out to Baelisk. "When we are gone, you are responsible for retrieving food for our family. You will defend your brother first and then our clan. We stand together ..."

Baelisk looked nervously at his father and then back to the dagger. "So that we may all live." He finished his father's statement solemnly, accepting the blade.

"Jaelisk, Sklisk, your bravery brings life to our people," the aged leader known as Noelisk said as the young couple stood in front of the small gathering of leaders. "A hand of moon cycles past, bug warriors broke through the second lock. Even though we destroyed those invaders, we know they have passed the scent of our ancestral home back to those that seek to destroy us."

Sklisk blinked his eyelid in acknowledgement. The information was not new, but he understood Noelisk and the older Piscivoru found comfort in formality.

"If this were not enough, the soul of Engirisk's machine has returned to the sun where it was born. While I do not adhere to Engirisk's teachings, I cannot deny the effectiveness of his machine's capacity to draw away the bug's advance. The people ask that you venture to the ancient city and find what Engirisk requests. Do you understand what is asked of you?"

Sklisk blinked again. There was a subtle cultural war being waged within the remnant of Piscivoru. Among the several thousand souls, a growing percentage seemed to be reverting to a more animalistic state, preferring to live wild and free and to communicate with gestures over spoken language. Noelisk was one of those types and both Jaelisk and Sklisk were sympathetic, to a degree. There was little value in the education Engirisk and his faction had brought to the people. Life below was simple and with the constant threat of the bug warriors, hoping for a better life seemed to be folly.

"Should we not just collapse the upper passages?" Jaelisk asked. "What has walking above given us beyond death?"

Engirisk flicked his tongue, showing his desire to answer Jaelisk's question. "You are right to question, Jaelisk. I do not believe the Kroo Ack would stop attacking us even if we were to seal ourselves to the under. My machines are effective at leading the Kroo Ack away, and without them I believe the bugs will clear passage to the Iskstar grotto within one hundred fifty moon cycles. The Kroo Ack are as numerous as drops of water in the under. I do not ask that you choose education. I only ask that you restore my capability to deceive them."

Jaelisk flicked her tongue in agitation. She was one of the growing faction that preferred a simpler life. For the peace of his family, Sklisk had avoided conflicting with her other than to send Baelisk and Boerisk to Engirisk's school.

"We offer life to our people," Sklisk answered.

Noelisk stood on weary hind legs and picked two objects from the table. At each end of the arm-length weapons, glowing blue Isktar crystals had been attached. Sklisk and Jaelisk accepted the weapons as they bowed their heads.

"Taste of my device," Engirisk said, holding a small, flat device out to them. Obediently, they both ran their tongues across the alien device. "You will take this machine and follow its instructions only when you have entered the ruined city. The machine is not all-seeing and you must protect it while it is within your possession. It is fragile and must be cared for. Its loss would be devastating. It will help you locate the parts I require for my machines."

"We understand, Engirisk," Sklisk answered. He'd spent time in Engirisk's school and knew the operation of the machine. It had often sparked his imagination of a greater life, living beneath the warm sun. He knew it to be Engirisk's prized possession and the gravity of the moment weighed on him.

"Baelisk and Boerisk will be cared for should you not return," Noelisk said, leaning his broad snout onto Jaelisk's so their foreheads met.

"You bring comfort in trial," she responded.

"Go quickly, my friends," Engirisk said. "The Kroo Ack were driven back but they will return very soon."

Sklisk stowed the weapon he'd been given in a pouch that ran along his side. Engirisk's machine was more difficult to stow, as it was fragile and could not withstand the rigors of scraping through rock passages. With Engirisk's help, he strapped it to his stomach.

Jaelisk flicked her tongue, its vibration communicating her desire to move. Sklisk found no further reason to hesitate and fell to the ground, digging his claws into the stone as he propelled down the unfamiliar passages that led to the above.

As they skittered forward, he stopped only long enough to test the markers left behind by the people's scouts. A map of taste markers had been provided and he knew they were in for a long run.

"Why does he insist on calling them Kroo Ack," Jaelisk asked, still agitated from the meeting.

"That is their ancient name."

"We give them honor by using it. They are simply bugs. Food," she said.

"You speak truth," he said, not wanting to rile her further.

"I will feed on fresh Kroo Ack under the moons of our ancestor's homes. I will sing death to these Kroo Ack who threaten my family and my people," she said, twisting through the passages.

Sklisk flicked his tongue in acknowledgement. Both he and Jaelisk were adept with the warrior's staffs. The bug warriors had difficulty striking low targets and were also vulnerable to an up-striking Piscivoru. While he'd never engaged with the bugs, he had talked at length with the scouts that often cleared the passages and collected foods.

"I taste the above," Jaelisk said after a long run. "Let us refresh before we enter. We cannot know when we will next rest."

The scent of the above was thick within the passage and intensified with every arm's length they traveled. Taking Jaelisk's suggestion, they stopped. Each drew on their water pouch and bit off a small portion of the bug warrior's shell they'd brought. Sklisk relished the sweet taste of the shell as it cracked and crumbled under the fantastic pressure of his bite.

"We go, Jaelisk," he said. "Do not hesitate. I am with you and we will prevail."

With caution, the couple climbed the final two hundred meters to the surface and onto the side of a mountain overlooking a deep valley. Even with only the light from the three moons overhead, Sklisk had to lower the unused second eyelid to shield against its brightness. The weathered rock was cold against his belly and he searched the vertical face for bug warriors but found none. Engirisk had taught that the bug warriors could not traverse a vertical surface, but he would leave little to chance while in Jaelisk's company and on such an important mission.

"Did our people really build all of that?" Jaelisk's voice held awe, something Sklisk had never heard from her before. He followed her gaze into the valley below them. Tall rectangular structures dotted the landscape, some seemed to stand as high as the side of the mountain where they rested.

"Engirisk says many thousands of cities like this were filled with the people," Sklisk said.

"It feels like a dream," Jaelisk said. "I cannot understand how this could be."

"The Kroo Ack came and killed the people. Engirisk said we did not know of Iskstar's power over the Kroo Ack. He says if our ancestors had, they would have defeated this enemy."

"I will see Engirisk's machine," Jaelisk said. "I will listen to its instructions."

"We were to wait until we reached the city," Sklisk said.

"There is no enemy near," Jaelisk said.

Sklisk blinked agreement, pulled the machine from its pouch, and tapped the clear surface as he had learned in school. A dim glow indicated that the machine was operational.

"Hold the reading pad so that it points at the city," a disembodied voice instructed.

Jaelisk pulled the machine from Sklisk's hand and pointed it at the city, with the screen showing upward.

"Do not be that way, Jaelisk. I attended school. You did not," Sklisk said. "Bring it back so you can look at the flat part with your eyes."

"That is stupid. I followed its instructions," she said, handing the device back to Sklisk.

Sklisk accepted the machine and turned it so the screen faced them. A glowing arrow appeared on the screen and pointed into the center of the city. Without further instructions the pad zoomed in on the location and showed a low building that had substantial plant life growing out of it.

"Kroerak technology is capable of locating signals of this device. It is advised that you power down and evacuate the immediate vicinity. Please move to location identified before powering up again."

With nothing more to say, the device turned itself off.

"Kroo Ack will find us?" Jaelisk asked.

Just before a horrific crashing sound, Sklisk sensed several large objects streaking toward the mountain face to which they held fast. Something struck no more than arm's length above their heads and the entire mountain shook under the impact. From nowhere, long spikes had embedded themselves into the mountain. A moment later, the wall they clung to shattered beneath their hands. Instinctively, Sklisk grabbed for the crumbling wall. The face of the mountain, however had broken off and with the dislodged slabs of rock, he tumbled toward the darkened valley below.

Chapter 3

CRACK IN THE ARMOR

"Are those new armor-glass ovens?" I asked as Marny, Tabby, and I arc-jetted across the two-hundred meters of open space separating *Hornblower's* aft section from Petersburg Station. My eye had caught a row of new machinery on the bottom side of the station.

"Merrie is up to eight kilns and still can't keep up with demand," Tabby said. "Did you know she hired four more full-timers from the York settlement?"

"Not surprising. Her revenues went way up over the last five ten-days," I said. "Really that's true for all of Petersburg. Mom and Katherine are killing it."

The progress on Petersburg Station had continued at an incredible rate under the command of my mother, Silver Hoffen, and her partner, Katherine LeGrande. Once just an oversized, shoe-shaped hunk of iron and silicate, the asteroid had undergone countless hours of refitting over the last three stans (Earth standard years). We had hollowed it out and transformed it into a modern space station. I say 'we' in the most generous sense. While I might have put the right people in charge, I had little interest in building a station, mining, or anything else that kept me from sailing.

Even so, the transformation of rock into station had been a win-

win, as every meter of iron removed was turned into the highly profitable steel products now managed by Merrie and her husband, Amon. Almost equally valuable, the silicate, generally just waste on most mining operations, was utilized in the manufacture of armor glass. Back in the Milky Way, armor glass was an inexpensive commodity. In the Dwingeloo galaxy, however, our glass was cutting-edge and a much stronger product than anything else available. As a result, our glass ovens operated at full capacity, every meter of product spoken for even before it cooled.

"You're going to need to give Munay a command," Marny said, obviously still thinking about our recent conflict.

"Are you psychotic?" I asked. "You just dressed him down in front of his old crew. It had to be humiliating. That's all they're going to talk about. If anything, I think we just made him an enemy."

"No, she's right," Tabby said. "Munay's a natural leader – his crew stayed loyal to their mission even when they were sure it was going to be their last."

"Look, I'm not the one who just blew him up!" I said. "For frak sake, Marny accused him of mutiny. I was the one in damage control, trying not to let things get out of control."

"You did good, Cap," Marny said, unperturbed. "And thanks for the promotion to Executive Officer."

First to reach the station's air-lock, she sailed through the translucent pressure barrier. Grabbing a long bar on the bulkhead, she twisted around so her feet met the deck as she passed through into full station gravity of .7g. I smiled as I recalled how clumsily she had operated in zero-g when we'd first met.

"XO?" As usual, I had missed something. Tabby and I set down in the brightly painted hallway behind her.

"I wondered when you would get to that." Tabby turned to Marny, pulling her helmet off and freeing her long, amber braid.

"You don't mind?" Marny asked. "It was either you or me."

"Hah! Appreciate the vote of confidence, but that's not my style," Tabby said. "I'd have knocked Munay's block off back there."

"You did plan to let me know, though, right?" I asked. I wasn't really surprised by the exchange as Marny had always been my XO if not in title, in practice.

Tabby slapped my butt. "I think she just did, Sweetcheeks."

Passing through a hard air-lock door, we'd entered on the Promenade level where many of the station's activities took place. In addition to the meeting room where we were headed, the level included workout facilities, a running track, pod-ball court and most notably, a water feature. On one end of the huge space, a waterfall cascaded down the rock face, emptied into a stream that ran next to the central corridor, and ended in a pond that held the station's reserve water. Seeded by our Norigan friends, lush aquatic plants thrived along every inch of the park-like space, providing both a spectacular visual attraction as well as helping to filter and clean the station's water and atmosphere.

A splashing sound caught my attention as Jester Ripples' bulbous head broke the surface of the reclamation pond. With a powerful thrust of his flat wide feet, he swam across the water, jumped onto the deck, and ran toward us. I held out my arms so he could climb up and wrap his spindly legs around me, as was his custom.

"I thought you were working on *Intrepid* with Nick," I said. "How'd you get here so quickly?"

"Jester Ripples and Nicholas James arrived only 240 seconds before Liam Hoffen," he answered. "Nicholas James said it was okay for Jester Ripples to swim until Liam Hoffen arrived. I attempted to convince Nicholas James to have his meeting within the cool waters of promenade, but Nicholas James did not believe it was a good meeting room."

"He's stuffy like that," I said, rubbing a finger along the soft, red fur on the ridge over his eyes. To look at the aquatic little alien, most would think his skin covering was frog-like – that is, rubbery. Oddly, even though Jester Ripples' epidermis was shiny, the texture more closely resembled cat fur.

"Nicholas James is annoyed that the engines of *Intrepid* were destroyed. He complains of the expense in replacing them," Jester Ripples said. I could hear the tension in his voice. Conflict with enemies was something Norigans were fine with, however, conflict within the family was not acceptable.

"He sure is," Nick said, as the four of us entered the meeting room. "The engine you lost will cost forty million to replace. And the one you broke beyond recognition, about half that."

"You know as well as I do that we didn't have much of a choice. They had Jonathan and Sendrei. It's hard to put a value on our friends' lives," I said.

He wasn't done with me. "If you'd recovered the pieces, we might have been able to rebuild them."

"I know. I'm sorry," I said. "Getting home was pretty high on our priority list."

"I believe we have a solution." I had to blink twice to believe what I was seeing. The sentient collective we called Jonathan had just walked into the conference room. The unbelievable part was that I knew his body had been destroyed on the Kroerak Cruiser. Since then, the fourteen-hundred-thirty-eight sentients that made up the collective we called Jonathan had been residing within the cruiser's circuitry.

I stepped forward to embrace Jonathan, but my arms passed through empty space. "What in Jupiter?"

"Ah, yes, Liam," Jonathan answered. "As we are no longer within humanity's jurisdiction, we have unburdened ourselves from the confines of the human-looking shell with which you identify our beings."

"A hologram?" I asked.

"A reasonable perceptive leap," he said. "We were not comfortable within the Kroerak ship. I tasked the industrial replicator within Nicholas's manufacturing plant to create this vessel. It was a simple matter to add a holographic projector to maintain the familiar visage. Your desire to embrace us was confirmation that our decision was appropriate."

"So, you believe if we can't touch you, we won't think you're real?"

"Touch is secondary only to visual perception for most humans," Jonathan explained patiently. "If you were neither able to see or feel us, we believe it would strain our ability to communicate effectively."

"Which model did you go with?" Nick asked.

Instead of describing their current form, Jonathan simply turned off the projector that displayed the image of a meter-and-three-quarter-tall human male. Floating at about chest height was a fist-sized black sphere. Atop the sphere, sat a mini version of Jonathan with his legs hanging off the side. "We find this form to be efficient for life aboard the station. We have also produced a humanoid form as well."

"You suggested there's a solution to our engine problem?"

We moved to sit around the table that was centered in the room.

"We have been in contact with Thomas Anino. We described the issues related to *Intrepid's* engines and he has transmitted plans for a replicator hive capable of manufacturing the requisite parts," Jonathan said.

Thomas Anino was the inventor of the Trans Location technology that allowed travel through fold-space, greatly reducing transit times over vast distances. That particular invention was also what had allowed the Kroerak to find Earth. Generally, I viewed Anino as a benefactor, but I maintained a wary distance. He tended to think of us as his employees instead of partners.

"Hive?" I asked.

"It is an invention of Thomas's own design," Jonathan said. "We will first utilize the manufacturing replicator on the surface of Zuri to produce a Class-F industrial replicator. This achievement will require significant capital investment, which we have estimated to be within Loose Nuts' capacity. With this new replicator we will improve by four hundred percent the manufacture of both construction and stevedore bots."

"How does that get us engines?" I asked. We currently had a single industrial replicator that was Class-E and it was capable of creating many of the parts required to repair one of *Intrepid's* engines. It was, however, nowhere near big enough to actually manufacture the engine.

"It's a cart-and-horse problem. We don't have enough capital to build the replicator hive yet, but by increasing our output, we'll be able to bring on revenue at a much faster rate," Nick said. "Jonathan, when did Anino do this? I just talked to him yesterday and he didn't bring it up."

"Perhaps you have forgotten. We possess a crystal that keeps us in direct communication. We formulated the plan upon entering this room. The replicator's plans are still being transmitted," The crystals Jonathan referred to were quantum communication crystals able to instantly transmit vibrations from one crystal to its twin, even between galaxies.

"I'd have thought it would take more effort to convince him to give up a hive replicator," Nick said. "That is worth more than five *Intrepids.*"

"Thomas has placed restrictions on its use."

"That's more like it," I said. His statement confirmed a bias I had regarding Anino. He was always first in line to provide just enough to get us into trouble, but never enough to make us comfortable.

"As you know, a replicator hive could cause a significant imbalance of trade in this region," Jonathan said. "We share a belief with Thomas that, given free reign of a hive's manufacturing capacity, Loose Nuts would attract much unwanted attention. We fear this may have already occurred with the stevedore and construction robots."

I started to speak but Nick cut me off. "That'll work, although I'm more worried about the type of attention we're attracting with a Kroerak cruiser sitting off our station than I am with a surplus of package handling robots."

"This was also discussed," Jonathan said. "Our commentary is not meant as criticism."

"We know," I said. "It's more than a little annoying to be held back."

"Thomas has made it clear that capital acquisition is critical and that we should facilitate prosperity," Jonathan said.

A knock at the door drew our attention and our main big-ship pilot, Ada, poked her head into the room. We'd been sailing with Ada Chen for what seemed like forever, having met when her mother's freighter had come under attack by pirates. Arriving too late to prevent her mom's death, we'd managed to find Ada's life-pod among the debris. We hadn't originally intended to bring her on as crew, but it turned out she was a great fit for our team.

"We're meeting in here?" she asked with a bright smile.

"Come on in." I motioned to her and was surprised to see Greg Munay close on her heels.

"We're just waiting on Sendrei," Marny said.

Sendrei hustled his large frame into the room, closing the door behind him. "I'm here."

"Are you sure you want me here?" Munay looked straight at Marny, his voice carrying a slight edge.

"You were right when you pointed out that we need you, Greg," she replied calmly. "In this room, rank is set aside. We will talk freely."

"You embarrassed me in front of my crew," Munay complained. "It was unprofessional to dress me down like a boot."

"Good, let's get this on the table," Marny said. I watched as all the other people in the room, besides Jonathan and Tabby, suddenly discovered an interesting spot on the table in front of them. "First, some ground rules. As of today, I am XO. As such, it is my responsibility to enforce discipline. Don't confuse my invitation to speak your mind as weakness, Greg. Today, in front of crew, you refused to acknowledge chain of command. I'm confident you would have severely enforced discipline if that had happened on any of your ships. Am I wrong?"

"You are not wrong," Munay said, although it was clear he still wasn't sold. "We also had not discussed rank and were working through a problem."

"Agreed," Marny said. "Which is why I haven't sought disciplinary action. It remains a fact that you were aboard a Loose Nuts ship, addressing the captain – someone I had just heard you refer to as Commodore."

Munay pursed his lips and nodded his head in acknowledgement. "That's a fair statement."

"Can you see why I was concerned?"

"Bringing in Masters with a blaster rifle and talking of mutiny was a bit over the top," Munay said. "Don't you agree?"

"I'll concede that I see your point," Marny answered. "I will also admit I was looking for an opportunity to publicly put you back in your seat. I need the Mars Protectorate officers to have no question about who is in charge."

Munay chuckled and for the first time a smile made it to his face. "I believe you have spent too much time in the presence of Admiral Buckshot Alderson. It is a confident person who exposes her plan so boldly. I appreciate your candor. I might have done the same in your position."

Audibly, I breathed a sigh of relief. The tension between Marny and Munay had me on edge.

"Now that we have that out of the way, what are we doing, Cap?" Marny asked.

For a moment, I felt hijacked. She'd told me we'd be doing a strategic session, but I hadn't realized it was up to me to come up with the agenda. My mind spun with possibilities as the people in the room stared at me.

"Sack up, Hoffen," Tabby whispered. "You got this."

I looked over to Tabby. Her cheeks had very light freckles that could only be seen in the right light. For whatever reason, seeing them always took me back to Colony-40 where we'd grown up. I could see the girl I'd fallen in love with and nearly lost to pirates. I could easily get lost in her green eyes, but I knew she'd beat me if I did.

"First things first," I said, moving past my split-second reverie. "Greg, I'd like to promote you to captain of *Hornblower* and task you with its repair and preparation to readiness. You will report to no one beyond Marny or myself and you will accept Marny's orders as if they were my own. To that end, we will transfer crew into and out of your command at our discretion, although with your foreknowledge and with discussion. Further, the rest of Loose Nuts falls outside of your command, including *Gaylen Brighton*, *Fleet Afoot*, *Intrepid*, and the Kroerak cruiser."

"I accept the commission with gratitude," Munay said. "I will endeavor to fulfill my duties with honor."

"We have limited access to capital and human resources," I said. "It's an impossible task."

"I have faith in the impossible."

"Second, we're taking on the mission Admiral Sterra gave to the brave men and women of the Hermes class sloops that were destroyed," I said. "Simply put, we endeavor to find the Kroerak home world and a mechanism in which to destroy it or them."

Sendrei raised his plastic cup from the table. "Hear, hear!"

He was joined by the rest of the command team with a salute.

"How will Liam Hoffen defeat the Kroerak?" Jester Ripples asked.

"I have absolutely no idea," I said. "I was hoping Jonathan and Sendrei learned something of value while aboard the Kroerak cruiser. Jonathan?"

"I do not believe everyone at this table is aware of what transpired. I will summarize. Ninety days previous, Loose Nuts discovered a Kroerak vessel buried beneath the soils of Zuri. As many of you know, the discovery was a significant surprise. While seated within the mobile unit humans refer to as a Stryker, Sendrei Buhari and I became aware of an open port along the side of this Kroerak vessel.

"It was an opportunity that ninety-eight percent of us decided could not be overlooked and we acted decisively to move from the Stryker vehicle to board the Kroerak vessel. We were surprised when we realized that Sendrei Buhari had followed us aboard, just as we were surprised when the vessel abruptly departed from the surface of Zuri.

"Initially, our concerns were solely for the survival of Sendrei. As we learned, the interior of a Kroerak cruiser is much different than that of a human ship. The systems are primarily biological and have very few mechanical parts. We identified that these systems are maintained by seven vastly different species, all of which have been enslaved by the Kroerak. Fortunately for Sendrei, there is little that resembles security within the vessel, although there were certainly predators. We quickly discovered that survival for Sendrei was simply a matter of finding an appropriate location to hide and a mechanism for extracting nutrients and water from the environment."

"When we came aboard, the noble controlled our thoughts," Tabby said. "Is that why Sendrei took off his suit? So she couldn't find him?"

"Partially correct," Jonathan answered. "Sendrei's long exposure to the Kroerak while on the planet Cradle made him very difficult for the noble to control. The nobles have an inherent ability to track mechanical technology. By removing his suit, Sendrei became virtually invisible to the noble as long as he did not physically get too close."

"So, when Liam distracted the Kroerak by singing, Jonathan was able to get further into the system undetected," Tabby summarized. "I'd always wondered how that worked out."

"Quite correct, Tabby. It is ironic. The Kroerak noble was both afraid of and quite jealous of humanity. She had been separated from her peers for two human centuries and longed for intelligent discourse. Even as she sought to purge us from her control systems, she dialogued with us, asking a never-ending series of questions, curious of life outside the bounds of her mission. We found it significant that she had the capacity to communicate over galactic distances with other Kroerak nobles, but lacked the will to disobey the order to focus solely on mission."

"I'm having trouble feeling sorry for her," I said.

"She sleeps forever," Sendrei said. "I would send her to her grave a second time if given the chance."

"Any clues on where they're from or how we might defeat them?" Marny asked.

"Many clues," Jonathan said. "Very little information. We believe that if we were to track the slave species aboard the cruiser, we might discover where the Kroerak came from. It is not perfect, but the species were not likely born on the same planet or system as the Kroerak. Their location would teach us much."

"You have something else," I said. I'd played enough poker with Jonathan to sense when he was holding an ace. My ability to read them drove his fourteen-hundred-thirty-eight entities nutty trying to figure out what clues they were giving off. To be honest, I had no idea. "What is it? It's juicy, I can tell."

"You sense this?" Jonathan asked. "We wish to understand how you know we have withheld information."

I smiled, knowing it would drive them bat-shite crazy for a while. "And?" I raised my eyebrows.

"There is a species they fear more than humans," he said.

"Damn straight!" Munay said. "Who and where are they? We need to ally ourselves with this species."

"They are known as Piscivoru," Jonathan said. "From what I was able to learn from the noble, the Kroerak brought the Piscivoru civilization to complete ruin. Once numbering in the billions, the Kroerak believe only twenty thousand remain. The Piscivoru are an unremarkable reptilian, humanoid species of average intelligence, much like humanity."

"Except the reptilian thing," Tabby interjected.

"Yes, of course," Jonathan agreed. "Originally living peacefully in expansive cities on their home world, the civilization fell quickly when the Kroerak invaded. A small remnant escaped far underground, where they apparently discovered an ancient weapon called the Iskstar, something the Kroerak fear beyond all else."

I shrugged as Jonathan looked at me. "What's an Iskstar?"

He continued. "The noble did not describe the Iskstar. It is forbidden to even name the weapon, and she had already broken this rule. Fortunately for the Kroerak, the Piscivoru only discovered this Iskstar after their civilization had been ruined. It is a widely held belief within Kroerak that this Piscivoru remnant will be their ruin. The fear expressed by this noble bordered on terror."

My comm channel chimed and Mom's face appeared on my HUD. She was using a high priority channel to contact me.

"Hold on, it's Mom. Something's going on," I said and accepted her comm request. "Mom, I'm patching you into a meeting we're having. What's going on? "

On the wall, Mom and Katherine LeGrande appeared. They were both sitting in the station's command center.

"We have an incoming Abasi battleship, *Thunder Awakes*" she said. "They were polite, but insistent on a lockdown of local space within fifty kilometers of Petersburg Station and positive turret control of our defensive guns."

"Sorry," I said. "I should probably have warned you. Mshindi Prime contacted me about the Kroerak ship and *Hornblower*. She'll hold a prize court aboard *Thunder Awakes* when they arrive."

"We didn't talk with Prime, but rather with Mshindi Second," Katherine answered. "She also mentioned something about a challenge issued by Tabitha?"

"She did?" Tabby perked up, not normally one for meetings. "Are they fielding a team?"

"Mshindi Tertiary asked me to carefully convey the following – 'your ears will lay flat in shame at your defeat beneath her paws.'"

"She did not!" Tabby squealed in delight.

"I believe she was rather agitated – her tail was twitching," Katherine said. "Now we've got to go. Apparently, we have dignitaries inbound."

Chapter 4

STAR FIRE

Sklisk twisted as he fell, pushing against the rocks. It was at least a twelve-count fall and neither he nor Jaelisk could survive that impact. He smelled Jaelisk's fear and confusion on the wind and recognized she must be hurt to be emitting those warnings. It was a simple matter to orient on her. He flattened his narrow body into the wind and ran across the rocks that fell with him.

Falling was a natural part of Piscivoru life, just as was using their flat-sided tails to propel against the winds. Sklisk ran into Jaelisk's tumbling body and grabbed onto her. Where they touched, her body was wet, smelling of her life essence. Subconsciously he recognized she had received great injury, but he knew better than to focus on anything beyond survival, as no injury would compete with the impact received on the rocks below.

Jaelisk thrashed against his grasp and Sklisk flicked his tongue across his mate's nose to calm her. With powerful legs, he turned her back toward the mountain and flicked his tail. In confusion, Jaelisk snapped her head back into his chest and for a moment they separated. Sklisk grabbed her once again and bit into her shoulder as he pushed them toward the mountain's face.

Having successfully separated from the tumbling boulders, Sklisk pushed Jaelisk toward a bluff they were falling past. Just missing the outcropping, Sklisk continued to fall as Jaelisk contacted the edge. Her sudden impact on the rock pulled her from him and he turned his focus to his own survival.

Falling faster than ever before, Sklisk knew he'd given up his opportunity for a safe landing to Jaelisk. It was a worthy objective, but he would need to use all the skills he'd learned as a broodling to survive, especially without the pools of the Iskstar grotto to provide a safety net.

Desperately, he scanned the mountainside that rushed to greet him while spreading his limbs to slow his fall. A plan hatched as he located the flattened face of massive rocks that nestled into the mountain just out of reach. To land against the gently sloping vertical face of the flattened rocks would slow him in a not-so-controlled slide, but first he had to reach them. Knowing the cost he was about to pay, he swished his tail, pushing himself into the mountain and colliding with an overhang. Pain as he had never felt before blossomed in every fiber of his being and he felt his life energy ebb. Ricocheting, he impacted the mountain a second time, this time a cruel twist to his body snapped clarity back to his focus.

The twin impacts, while planned, hadn't slowed him greatly, but instead tossed him toward the flat-iron boulders lying against the mountain. Mentally, he braced for a third impact and groaned in agony even as he flattened his stomach wide and held his limbs to his sides, assuring that the energy of his landing would spread to as much of his body as possible.

Upon contact, he dug claws into the rock surface. His side and leg were injured, but the inertia of his fall lessened. Dull rock points dug at his underbelly as he slid. A poorly placed rock caught him perfectly at his knee, breaking his contact with the rock. Scrabbling wildly in the air, he reached for the mountain.

An unfamiliar smell reached his nose as what felt like thousands of cloths whipped across his body. Turning, he discovered he'd fallen into a massive plant. It slowed his momentum as he snapped stalks which grew thicker the closer he got to its center. Grabbing at the thin outer stalks, he was unable to find purchase until his stomach violently struck a stalk that was thicker than his arm. The stalk did not snap but bent as it absorbed the remainder of his fall's energy.

His trip, however, was not finished. The flexible stalk reversed its path and flung him off. Falling once again, Sklisk grabbed for purchase as he cartwheeled through the plant's structure. Finally, as if it were annoyed with him, the plant ejected him entirely, depositing him into the heavy, low growing vegetation beneath its broad canopy.

Afraid that any movement on his part would result in a fresh round of insults to his battered body, Sklisk lay still. As his thoughts settled, he took stock of his multitude of injuries. Blood was on his long tongue; he'd bitten into it at some point, clipping a chunk off the tip. Moving the long digits of his fingers and toes, he discovered several badly damaged joints making movement difficult.

He rolled onto his stomach and checked for the Iskstar staff, not surprised that it had become dislodged. He remembered falling against it when pinging off the rocks along the mountainside. He crawled slowly through the debris and undergrowth, his confidence growing with each stride. Unfortunately, the pain in his digits also grew with each step. He would have to ignore the pain as finding and helping Jaelisk was paramount.

Moving more quickly, Sklisk startled a rodent which skittered underfoot. It had been a long time since he'd seen another living species and he mentally chastised himself for being startled. Of course there would be life on the surface of their home world. The bug warriors only sought to destroy Piscivoru and had little care for small native animals.

Sklisk reached the base of the mountain and began climbing. Flicking his tongue, he tasted the wind for Jaelisk and found nothing. He'd had little time to survey the mountain while careening down its side, but retracing his path wasn't difficult. Falling was mostly a vertical affair and it was easy to make out the tall flat-iron boulders that soared above. He wasn't far from where Jaelisk should be. The dry earth and rock felt strange beneath his claws as he climbed. Why it should feel so foreign, he wasn't sure, for his home was actually within this same mountain. His people had always talked about 'the above,' but no story could come close to what he was experiencing.

The familiar smell of Iskstar caught in his nose as he skittered across a ledge and discovered the location of his staff. Relieved, Sklisk recovered the Iskstar, placed it back in his pouch and continued to climb, ignoring the complaints of his injured joints.

The smell of Jaelisk's blood on the wind was worrying as he closed in on her location. The smell became so strong, Sklisk began to fear his mate had not survived. He raced into the plume of heady scents, discovering a thick trail of blood and his mate's body lying precariously at the edge of a cliff, unconscious. He panicked. Jaelisk's arm had been severed at the joint and was still oozing blood. Without hesitation, he pulled a cloth from his pouch and wrapped it tightly around the wound.

Pulling her to a more comfortable position, Sklisk flicked his tongue across her face. While she'd lost a lot of blood, her hearts beat a strong vibration within her torso. He'd lost most of his pack during the fall, but Jaelisk's items had been strewn along the blood trail. Knowing she would not recover without water, he laid her gently against the rocks and went about gathering her possessions.

When he pushed a water skin to her mouth and dribbled water along the thick inner jawbone, his hearts thrilled as her tongue moved in response. After giving her a long drink, he searched her pack and found the salve used on wounds. Carefully, he rewrapped her stub, this time applying the medicine first.

"What has happened?" Jaelisk's voice caught him off guard and he moved so he was close to her face. He peered into her glowing blue eyes, attempting to determine her level of alertness. She had always been strong, and Sklisk felt he could see this strength through the pain.

"We were attacked and fell from the mountain," he said. "Your arm is removed."

"My Iskstar staff?" she asked.

"It is recovered," he said. "I have not found Engirisk's machine."

"It is good you did not venture without me," she said, reaching into the pouch at her neck with her uninjured arm and extracting the machine.

Sklisk accepted the machine from her and inspected it. It had taken substantial damage from the fall, its transparent surface spider-webbed with cracks. He didn't dare power it up.

"I smell bug warriors below," Jaelisk said. "Can you not?"

"I bit my tongue," Sklisk admitted, shaking his head. In normal circumstances, biting off one's tongue was simply embarrassing; the flesh was soft and easily severed. Unlike Jaelisk's arm, his tongue would regrow.

"What a sorry pair of heroes we turned out to be," Jaelisk said. "I have no arm and you no tongue."

"We are alive, dear mate. I am pleased to be a sorry hero if I am allowed life," Sklisk said, flicking his damaged tongue out and catching the scent of bug warriors. "I will return in a moment."

"Be careful. You have never fought a real bug warrior before. They are dangerous," she said.

Sklisk had no response. She was right, but that did not change what needed to be done. He shifted the Iskstar staff to his back, dropped to all fours, and scurried toward the scent of the warriors.

At first, he was confused as he looked down at the single bug that clumsily attempted to climb up the rock. The bug's pincers were clearly strong as the rocks seemed to scream as it clamped on and pulled. The pincers had very little capacity to grip and for each movement forward, the bug slid backwards.

Sklisk felt guilt as he ran down the face of the mountain to be below the bug warrior. He was certain the warrior could sense his approach, but the bug was unable to maneuver or adjust its path in the rocky terrain. He was almost disappointed at how easily the bug fell to his staff. Sklisk slipped the glowing blue end of the Iskstar into the bug's back, sliding easily through its body. Sklisk found two more bugs twenty arm lengths below and with buoyed confidence he dropped between them, slicing through their legs and causing both to fall helplessly away from the mountain.

On the way back, Sklisk carefully carved a particularly delectable portion from the fallen warrior and hustled to where Jaelisk lay.

"You are now a Piscivoru warrior," she said proudly, accepting the meat.

"Are you able to walk?" Sklisk asked. "Perhaps we should try to re-enter the passageway back to the under."

"I feel pain, but I would not stop our mission," she said. "We will go forward until we are unable."

Together they worked their way to the base of the mountain and slipped into the thick undergrowth. While it pained Sklisk to see his mate hobble on three legs, he knew she would find offense if he attempted to help. He must accept her sacrifice. Even hobbled as she was, they moved more quickly over the ground than they ever could in the vertical standing position favored by some like Engirisk.

"The city seemed so close while we were on the mountain," Sklisk said as they moved forward.

"We are not accustomed to viewing from such a distance," Jaelisk answered. Sklisk noticed that his mate had slowed her pace. The strain of moving on only three legs and the wounds of the evening were finally taking their toll.

"We will stop and rest," Sklisk said. "Engirisk warned that the bright star over Picis gives advantage to the bug warriors and we are to only move while it is behind our home planet."

"Are those not stars?" Jaelisk asked. "I do not find them to be over bright."

"We will trust Engirisk in this," Sklisk said. "You will rest beside this large plant and I will climb it so that I might find an appropriate nest for us."

"Do not coddle me, Sklisk."

"I would not."

All along their path to the city, Sklisk had been forced to maneuver around the densely-packed vegetation, consisting mainly of the giant cylindrical stalks. The sparsely-leafed plant rose high into the sky, moving gently in the air above the surface. He grabbed the rough outer sheath of the closest stalk and began to climb. The ascent was easier than Sklisk anticipated, his claws effortlessly piercing the rough outer material of the plant. He climbed until the stalk thinned and swayed beneath his weight.

A dim glow on the horizon was something Sklisk hadn't expected and he filed the information for later consideration. It appeared a great fire was burning, but at such distance it could not possibly cause them harm. Looking toward the city, he discovered they'd made significant progress and were only a thousand arm lengths from the small rectangular structures that rose into the sky. Why hadn't he paid more attention to the image of their destination on Engirisk's machine? Sklisk's mind jumbled the information he'd gathered since their mission began. For the moment, he would prioritize finding shelter for the oncoming star rise. Engirisk's teachings had been vague as to the star's effect, beyond that the bug warriors would more easily locate them. Blinking his eyelids, he resolved to follow Engirisk's instructions more thoroughly, as opening the machine on the side of the mountain had very nearly gotten them killed.

Jaelisk greeted him as he joined her on the ground. "What have you discovered?"

"There is a great fire burning in the distance."

"I smell no fire," she answered.

"The fire is quite far. Also, I have located a nest of our ancestors where we will rest for star rise."

The two continued through the thinning undergrowth toward the building Sklisk had located.

"What is all of this?" Jaelisk asked as they moved through a tangle of jagged red-brown bars protruding from broken blocks of rock. "I taste iron, but what would make it long and straight?"

"Our ancestors once used iron to build their nests," Sklisk said. "Engirisk teaches this in his class. We stand atop the nests that fell to the Kroo Ack, when our people were pushed to the safety of the Iskstar grotto."

"Do you really believe the Piscivoru were as numerous as the drops of water within the grotto?"

Sklisk placed his hand against the side of the building he'd identified. The building's skin was pocked from age but was still firm and his claws bit into it easily. He allowed Jaelisk's question to hang for a moment, preferring to secure their nest for the rest period. From his observation site in the tall plant, he'd underestimated the height of the structure and together they climbed over seventy arm lengths.

They carefully avoided disturbing the unseen occupants of the building, knowing that fleeing animals would attract as much attention as unwarranted noise. As he climbed, Sklisk worked around damage to the building and more than once discovered his claws gripped only loose material. Idly, he wondered how much longer the structure would stand as a testament to the long-forgotten civilization.

"It is hollow," Jaelisk hissed as they reached the top and climbed over the edge. Indeed, the center of the roof had collapsed long ago, and for a moment they peered into the building's depths. As they scanned the gloom, it became clear that parts of the roof and subsequent floors hadn't completely fallen in. Small ragged ledges and random patches of flat rock remained attached to the outside walls.

"That is good," Sklisk said. "We will not be surprised as we rest."

They carefully moved to a corner of the roof that felt secure and as they had for much of their adult life, curled together.

"I saw the fire as we climbed," Jaelisk said. "It is so large that I am surprised I have not smelled of it yet."

"I do believe our ancestors were numerous," Sklisk said, suddenly suspicious as to what the fire might be. "There are none within our clan beyond Engirisk that could conceive of making a structure as large as where we lay. And I do not believe there is a fire."

"You speak nonsense," Jaelisk said. "We have both seen it with our eyes. There is no other explanation. But I believe we are safe, and so you will sleep." As excited as Sklisk was with all the new experiences, as soon as Jaelisk's breathing evened out, he lost his hold on consciousness and joined her in rest.

For several hours he slept deeply and without dreams. It wasn't until later that his nightmares found him. He helplessly looked on as the bug warriors opened the passageways to the grotto, murdering his friends. He saw his sons, Boerisk and Baelisk, as they were taken from him and could feel Jaelisk slipping from his arms.

Sklisk's body jerked and consciousness permeated his being. What he'd just seen hadn't been real, except that Jaelisk was indeed missing. His hearts hammered inside his torso as he prepared to defend himself. Flicking his wounded tongue, he searched for his mate, finally locating her on the opposite side of the building. Sensing that he'd awakened, she turned to him, blinking a greeting.

It was only when he realized she was safe that he recognized the difference in their surroundings. Jaelisk was bathed in a bright, yellow light that illuminated the entire sky. Instead of inky blackness and a starfield, the sky was a brilliant light blue. Sniffing the air, he searched for the fire they'd feared before falling asleep. Still not detecting any hint of fire, Sklisk accepted what he'd suspected: that they were experiencing the starlight of Picis.

"How could we give this up?" Jaelisk asked wistfully as he joined her at the side of the crumbling building. She looked across the ruined city at a bright amber ball that disappeared behind tall structures which appeared to be in no better shape than the one on which they stood.

"Engirisk taught that the star of Picis was on fire," Sklisk said. "I thought he was talking like he did when speaking poetry."

"I would give my life that our people could live once again in the above," Jaelisk said.

"There is no reason to talk like this," Sklisk said. "We will find Engirisk's devices and bring them back to him. It is just a matter of finding his building."

"His building will not be difficult to locate," Jaelisk lifted her one good arm and pointed forty degrees off the setting star. "It is right there."

He followed where her arm pointed and was surprised to discover a building shaped very much like the one he'd seen on Engirisk's flat device. His hearts fell as his eyes drifted across a teaming mass of bug warriors that filled the flat spaces around the building and for thousands of arm lengths in every direction.

"All is lost," Sklisk said. "There is no hope."

Jaelisk reached out and grabbed his hand with her own. "We cannot give up."

Chapter 5

PRIZE COURT

"What do the Abasi want with the ships?" Ada asked. "It's not like we captured any of them in Abasi space."

"I think it's more a matter of maintaining our Letter of Marque, which is under Abasi law," I answered. "Assuming they don't declare that we provoked the battle, our Letter of Marque provides for either a market-based buy-out or an outright award of the ships. Technically, they could refuse to award *Hornblower* and *Fleet Afoot* as prizes and buy them out from us. Same is true of the Kroerak cruiser."

Ada shook her head. "That letter gives them a lot of power."

"Don't underestimate the value of sailing under the Abasi flag within Confederation of Planets space," I said.

"I don't," Ada answered. "We've yet to see a government that isn't willing to take what it wants in the name of what's best for the people."

"You're right, Ada," I said. "It's possible they'll deny our claim on the Kroerak cruiser. We should have a market value in mind for it and a way to justify that value."

"If you don't mind," Munay interjected, "I believe Mars Protectorate would like a say in the disposition of a fully functioning enemy craft."

"I talked with Admiral Sterra on the matter," I said. The admission caused Munay's eyebrow to raise. I hadn't made the quantum communication crystal connecting us to Mars Protectorate readily available to him. "I offered the ship to her and she declined. Apparently, they captured a sufficient number of damaged Kroerak vessels. Also, there is no practical way to send a ship back to the Milky Way."

"I think it's worse than Liam says," Nick said. "There's no way Abasi will allow us to keep a Kroerak cruiser in their space. News of its presence is on every major regional news feed. Even as we speak, there are three ships inbound that have expressed interest in visiting the cruiser. I'm not sure it's the type of attention anyone wants. Abasi won't want its citizens getting nervous about the Kroerak coming back for their ship."

"Beyond financial, is there strategic value in the cruiser?" I asked. "I'm not sure if it's well known, but we used the last of its weapons and have no mechanism for regenerating them. On the positive, its hull is darn near impenetrable. We could mount turrets on the skin. Who could stop us?"

"Its fuel use is ridiculous," Nick said, poking a hole in my excitement.

"Doesn't burn that much more than *Hornblower*," I said, defensively.

Nick grinned, knowing I'd eventually come around. "*Hornblower's* engines leak more fuel than they use. I don't think that's your best argument."

"It has to have value," I insisted.

"Our analysis is that the Kroerak vessel has limited strategic value to Loose Nuts," Jonathan said. "The systems are in decay and without the noble to direct regeneration, we have no reasonable mechanism for maintenance. We propose you use the ship as a source of much needed capital."

"And *Hornblower*? Don't tell me you want to get rid of her, too," I said, giving Nick the stink-eye.

He chuckled at my poor attempt at intimidation. "*Hornblower* is a piece of junk. For what we'll invest in repairs, we could buy a much newer ship about half her size with modern systems."

"She's the only ship we have that has any chance of standing up to a Kroerak ship," I said.

"If you'll beg my pardon," Munay said. "Your analysis is too simplistic. Even with the proposed improvements to armor, *Hornblower* is no match for the alien cruisers, much less their battleships. That said, with improvements to the engines, I believe she could survive prolonged exposure to limited groups of their smaller ships."

"*Intrepid* survived. Do you believe *Hornblower* has tactical advantage over *Intrepid* against Kroerak?" I asked.

"It would depend on the mission. *Intrepid's* primary value is speed," Munay responded. "Properly equipped, *Hornblower* could be expected to thin a group of frigate-classed Kroerak. It could also provide cover against a cruiser, but only for a short period of time. In your history of encounters, you have experienced both types of engagements. You survived through both luck and brilliant tactical maneuvering. *Hornblower* could significantly enhance your odds in certain types of encounters."

"I'd like the minutes to reflect that Gregory Munay referred to my maneuvers as brilliant," I said, smiling broadly.

"I think he led with luck," Ada said. "And just remember who was sailing that ship, Liam."

"Brilliance is discovering an opportunity that most would not see. This team has done that time and time again," Munay said. "Luck is a poor description for a repeatable process. In war college, we talk about recognizing the brilliance in battle and separating it from favorable conditions. Many times, the best results come from a combination of both."

"Any chance Abasi will try to claim *Fleet Afoot* and *Gaylon Brighton?*" Ada asked me.

"I hope not."

THE ARRIVAL of the Abasi battleship *Thunder Awakes* was a spectacle Tabby and I wanted to observe from Petersburg Station's command center with Mom and Katherine. As it drew closer, the blocky ship shined brightly with the reflected light of Santaloo's white star. It wasn't lost on me that there was a certain amount of saber rattling going on. Some caution was justified since both the Kroerak vessel and *Hornblower* were at least partially operational. However, the Abasi's message here was clear: don't forget who's boss.

The Abasi was a coalition-styled government that represented the interests of the Felio. The feline-featured humanoid species was composed of hundreds of powerful Houses, the top twenty or so of which led the coalition. We'd first encountered the Abasi after our trip through the wormhole from Mhina and found a powerful ally in House Mshindi.

Of course, powerful ally or not, House Mshindi wasn't about to give us any special treatment. What I appreciated, however, was that the species placed a high value on honor. Their society was also a meritocracy based on physical prowess in battle, which strongly favored the female of their species. Tabby and Marny, not surprisingly, had both earned their respect and deference – something I was quite willing to take advantage of.

"Incoming comm – *Thunder Awakes*," Katherine LeGrande announced. We'd spent the last twenty minutes watching the battleship adjust until they matched our orbit around planet Zuri. The station had already granted the battleship control of our defensive cannons, which was part of the price we paid for setting up shop in Abasi-controlled space.

Mom stepped toward the armored glass separating the command center from space and looked out at the ship. With feet shoulder-width apart and hands clasped behind her back, she prepared to address the ship, nodding to her partner to open the comm.

"Greetings to House Mshindi," she said, more formally than I'd have expected. "Petersburg Station is honored by your presence."

"Greetings to Loose Nuts." A projection of Mshindi Prime standing on the bridge of *Thunder Awakes* showed on the glass, the AI sizing and aligning the Felio head of house so that Mom was looking directly at her. "I convey appreciation at your acceptance of agreed-upon security protocol. I request the presence of Liam, Captain of *Intrepid* for the purpose of executing our duties as Prize Court."

"It is good to see you ready for the hunt, Adahy," I said, using Mshindi Prime's given name. I might not have, but Jonathan, who was observing from elsewhere in the station, prompted me to, given her use of my first name. "I would bring three with me if that is acceptable."

Mshindi Prime's whiskers twitched but her tail didn't flick. I wasn't exactly sure if I'd caused agitation, but I knew that less words with the matriarch were better than more.

"Such is your right. I have dispatched a shuttle for your transportation. My communication desists."

"Please pardon my interruption, Mshindi Prime. I would address one more item," Mom said, recognizing that she was about to lose communication.

"It is permitted."

"I would like to invite Mshindi Prime and her command crew for a reception after your proceedings," Mom said. "We're quite proud of our station and would enjoy welcoming House Mshindi in a warmer setting."

Mshindi's whiskers twitched again but Mom stood still, waiting patiently for a response. "House Mshindi accepts a hospitable offer," Mshindi Prime said, placing her fist low on her chest, just above her solar plexus, and bowing slightly. "A functionary, Keenjaho, will contact Hoffen Silver for coordination."

"Not much for conversation, that one," Mom said, when the comm abruptly terminated.

"Not as far as I've ever seen," I said. "Tabby, you ready?"

"You're just taking me as arm candy, aren't you?" she asked as we exited the command center on the way to where the shuttle would pick us up. I'd decided earlier to take Tabby, Nick, and Jonathan along.

"Up to you, as long as you don't mind me going alone onto a

female dominated ship where they wear the equivalent of swimming suits," I said. It was a gross overstatement on the clothing. Most Felio preferred less clothing primarily due to their fur-covered bodies. As a result, their uniform covered only the necessary bits, and even then, not particularly well. I'd be lying if I didn't admit that I found it all rather, well, you know ... intriguing.

"You can glance, but Gunjway will be an apt description of you if you pay those hussies too much attention," Tabby said. I smiled at her use of the term Gunjway, the Felio word for a neutered male, which was about the worst insult a Felio could level.

Tabby and I were joined by Jonathan and Nick as we turned onto the ramp that led to the airlock. Knowing that Jonathan's body was projected, I inspected him more diligently than I had previously. The disguise was nearly perfect, but I finally discovered small imperfections where light interrupted the projection. Without foreknowledge, however, I'd have had no reason to disbelieve what my eyes were seeing.

Our timing was just about perfect, the Abasi shuttle arriving only a few seconds after the four of us loaded into the airlock.

"Are you apprehensive, Liam?" Jonathan asked. "We believe much relies on your successful negotiation."

"No pressure." Tabby laughed as she allowed her hand to stray from where it rested on my hip onto my butt, giving me an affectionate squeeze.

"Such was not our intent," Jonathan said. "We are unable to observe outward signs of stress."

I shrugged, then casually pulled Tabby's hand back to my waist. "It's a different kind of stress. We've been shot at enough that I'm not overly worried when arguing about the disposition of ships. I don't see it as a good sign that Mshindi Prime sailed all the way from Tamu system, though."

Our conversation was cut short when the red-furred face of Mshindi Tertiary showed in the airlock window. Noting that the air pressure had equalized and the panel showed three green chevrons, I placed my hand on the security pad, allowing the station door to open.

"Masters Warrior," Mshindi Tertiary growled, just as the doors disappeared into the bulkhead. "You best sharpen your claws. There is no challenge I will turn from."

"Majida," Tabby replied, stepping around me, extending her arm so her forearm crossed in front of her chest. "Do you understand the challenge court? I don't want any excuses."

Mshindi Tertiary pulled her lips back, allowing fangs to slip out and hang over her lower lip. She mirrored Tabby's position and bumped forearms in a greeting I'd never seen from the Felio in the past. "There will be no excuses. My people have a similar test, only we use a live stargenos as the prey to be. Will you use Bertrand Chief as your second?"

"I will not," Tabby answered. "My boy, Liam, is all I'll need to pluck the whiskers from your haunches."

Mshindi Tertiary chuffed, her eyes flaring at Tabby's response. "You curse as only a Felio could. Saliva moistens my fangs in anticipation."

"You guys need a minute?" I asked. "I was under the impression we were on our way to an important meeting."

Mshindi slid her gaze away from Tabby and thumped her paw onto her chest. For whatever reason, she'd never liked me much and her treatment bordered on insult. "Greetings, Hoffen Captain. It is talk that you desire and it is to this meeting we will hurry." Her tone conveyed little respect, but I was fine with that. "I am not sure how you survive the chatter, Masters Warrior. I do find the clean shaven one to be friendly to the eyes, though."

I looked to Tabby incredulously as she just smiled and followed Mshindi Tertiary onto the shuttle where a male Felio gestured to open seating.

"Hoffen Captain, a refreshing drink is offered." The male Felio who spoke had thick brown fur that surrounded his head and neck. Near his chin, the fur had been cut short with a geometric design shaved into it.

I accepted a pouch which I was pleased to discover was filled with fresh water. "What is this challenge you're talking about?" I asked, looking at Tabby.

"Don't worry your pretty little head," Tabby answered, obviously enjoying the tension Mshindi Tertiary had created. "I told Majida about pod-ball and challenged her to a couple of games. Semper was telling me about how they have a similar game they play as kits, either one-on-one or two-on-two. I guess they can get pretty rough. You in?"

"Frak, yeah. It'll be a vacation from the whooping you're always handing out," I said, glancing at Mshindi Tertiary who was staring at me. I believed I could hear a low growl emanating from the Felio as I spoke.

"A feisty mate is delightful," she said, addressing no one in particular as she moved past us to the pilot's chair.

"You think that's why she's smack-talking me – trying to get me fired up?" I asked in a low voice. "I don't think she likes me very much."

"I think you're reading her wrong," Tabby whispered back. "You might want to be careful around her. I think she'd jump you if she could."

"Ooh," I said, looking at the back of the Felio. From where I sat, I could just see where her uniform wasn't completely covering as much as most human females considered necessary and my mind jumped to things it shouldn't.

"You're such a horndog," Tabby said, slugging me painfully in the shoulder. I feigned ignorance with a shrug. I'd been caught, no sense in making it worse.

Fortunately, the trip to *Thunder Awakes* was short and Mshindi Tertiary set the shuttle down in a wide landing bay near the center of the ship.

"You will accompany Mshindi Second to your meeting," she said. "Do not worry, Liam Captain, I will endeavor not to damage your carastan-smoothed skin overly when we battle."

My AI showed that there was no direct translation for the word carastan. It roughly meant pretty, but was only used when talking about a male's underbelly.

I was saved from having to respond as the shuttle doors opened and Zakia, Mshindi Second, strode purposefully up the ramp. With considerably more deference, she raised her paw to her lower chest and bowed toward me. I bowed slightly, not bringing my hand to my solar plexus, but instead holding it out for a handshake, which she honored.

"Captain Liam Hoffen, it is indeed pleasurable to see you once again in the fur," she said, not catching her faux pas. "I have heard great tales of your adventures and they appear to be confirmed by the proximity of a Kroerak vessel and the Genteresk ship, *Sangilak*. I am sorry to inspect the damage done to the sleek warship, *Intrepid*."

I wrapped a free arm around her and we hugged briefly. My relationship with Zakia was much different than with Majida. Only a few standard years older than her sister, Zakia seemed to genuinely enjoy our interaction, although we'd spent quite a bit more time together, including a nasty battle with Kroerak.

"There's always a price to pay where Genteresk are concerned," I said, referring to a particularly dastardly tribe of Pogona pirates.

"You should know," she said. "The pirate Belvakuski was found guilty of conspiring with a mortal enemy of Abasi. She was executed four days previous."

"That was quick," I said as she led us through the ship's passageways.

As we walked, every Felio we passed pulled out of our way and gave us a wide berth. This behavior seemed equivalent to the Abasi stationary drill command for attention, which was simply a ready pose with feet at shoulder width.

"Justice comes quickly to those who would throw in with the Kroerak," she said. "It was discovered her people had been aligned with Kroerak and were supplying dead to the site on Zuri where the Kroerak vessel was trapped beneath the ground."

"Geez," I said. "Talk about not getting the bigger picture."

Zakia stopped for a moment outside a large door that was inset into a wood-framed bulkhead. "A most apt turn of phrase. A bigger view might be more accurate, but such is the nature of our translation units," she said, nodding to a male crew member who stood at attention next to the door controls. In response, he turned to the panel, causing the door to open, and exposing a room already filled with a score of Felio.

Following Zakia, I recognized the common setup: an open floor separated from a gallery of seating by a wooden railing and a table with two shallow wells. Each well contained a fist-sized bag; one painted white and the other black.

"Do you wish counsel?" Zakia asked. "You are allowed a single companion at your side."

"Are we allowed communication with our other companions?" I asked.

"It is allowed," she answered.

"We have sufficient counsel. Tabby will join me," I said. We'd already discussed the seating and agreed that Tabby's presence sent the right message.

Zakia stiffened as a good portion of the gallery rose and joined her at attention. The four of us turned to see Mshindi Prime, flanked by two powerful looking Felio guards, enter the room. I couldn't help but be intimidated by the feral vibe I got from her guard.

"Captain Liam Hoffen, mate Tabitha Masters, Nicholas James and Jonathan – friends of Abasi and honored among House Mshindi – I offer welcome," she said. Behind us we could hear chuffs as her faithful acknowledged the greeting.

"We are honored by your presence, Mshindi Prime, first of House Mshindi, friend of humanity, and mighty warrior," I answered, using a prepared line Jonathan had helped me cook up. It must have been acceptable because I heard appreciative chuffs around the room.

"There is much to discuss, and time favors the enemy," she said, still looking at me. My AI informed me that she was using a common Felio idiom, generally used to indicate a desire to move a conversation along. "Are you prepared to defend your prize claims under the terms of the Letter of Marque provided by Abasi?"

"No sense letting grass grow beneath our feet," I said. "We are ready."

She smiled as I suspected her HUD was showing her the closely matching human idiom. "In preparation, I state the Abasi find no claim required upon the ships known as *Fleet Afoot* and *Gaylon Brighton*. Both are recorded as belonging to humanity and are outside of the scope of our discussion.

"As there is disagreement, it is to this court that we will rule on the disposition of *Sangilak* and the captured Kroerak cruiser. Gundi Second has requested first words on *Sangilak,* a motion I permit."

I breathed out a quiet sigh as both Lindia, Gundi Second, and Badru, Gundi Fourth, approached a portion of the rail that separated the gallery from the open court. I knew Badru strongly opposed anything that increased humanity's standing in the system and did not appreciate the new role we'd taken in protecting their shipping lanes.

"Badru, Gundi Fourth, will speak for House Gundi," Lindia said.

Badru stepped forward and glowered at me as he spoke. "It is a simple matter. Four days previous we executed a pirate that plagued the merchants of Santaloo star system. We cannot trust these furless creatures. They have shown a clever capacity for surprise attack and they fight without honor. If the ship *Sangilak* is granted, we will trade a Pogona pirate for a human pirate."

"What say you, Liam Hoffen?" Mshindi Prime asked.

I waited a few moments while Nick pushed a few messages onto my HUD. He'd picked up on an interesting conflict in Badru's statement and I knew just how I wanted to argue.

"We have shown nothing but deference and respect for Abasi, even when they facilitated the dishonorable theft of our ship *Intrepid* by Strix," I said. "Not only did we act with honor after this disgrace, but we went further out of our way to restore honor to your long-dead ancestors."

Badru started to talk, but I cut him off. "If I accept your argument, it would seem to me that you are saying House Gundi would prefer to weaken an ally that fights with honor on behalf of Felio."

"You speak with lies dripping from your teeth," Badru said. "You seek to only enrich yourselves. We will regret that day we allowed humans to occupy our system."

"And you're positioning an argument you know you can't possibly win," I said, gambling that I understood where he was headed. "Our Letter of Marque is quite clear on the disposition of *Sangilak*. Either grant payment of value or transfer the ship. Your chattering is nonproductive and is simply a prelude to the arguments you wish to have regarding the Kroerak cruiser. Is honesty something only the female Felio possess?"

"Easy tiger," Tabby said under her breath. "That's an enemy for life you're creating there."

"Do you challenge me in front of this court?" Badru asked, his anger getting the better of him for a moment.

"I will not stand here and have my entire species dishonored by a fourth-ranked cur," I said, my ire momentarily shorting out reason. "If you wish a challenge, I will have no trouble opening you with my blade. And thank you for being plain spoken; I prefer to be able to recognize my enemies. I'll leave the challenge to you, Badru. I assume this is not how all of the honorable House Gundi feel? I recall their defense of humanity as quite vigorous."

"A moment to confer, Mshindi?" Lindia, Gundi Second, asked before Badru could respond.

"It is allowed," she said, gazing back at me with a look on her face I didn't recognize.

We all watched as House Gundi conferred in low tones that sounded less than friendly. After a few moments, Gundi Second walked away from the speaking platform and sat down.

"Badru, do you have further words?" Mshindi Prime asked.

"House Gundi respectfully declines further comment," he said, not making eye contact with either her or me.

"House Perasti has offered comments on *Sangilak*," Mshindi Prime said.

A female I'd seen before but couldn't name replaced Badru at the speaking podium. She looked much like the powerful guard that crouched within easy reach of Mshindi Prime.

"Thank you, honored of Mshindi," the Felio said. "It is I, Mpenda, Tertiary of House Perasti. We fully support the title transfer of *Sangilak* to Loose Nuts. Upon review of their interaction with the pirate Belvakuski, we find them to have operated within the legal guidelines of the Letter of Marque in both spirit and action. Further, we find no value in the pathetic vessel known as *Sangilak* and wish our human friends fortune in discovering a value unseen by this House."

"Thank you, Mpenda. Are there more who would oppose recognition of *Sangilak* as property of Loose Nuts?" Mshindi Prime addressed the room, looking around the gallery, waiting for any response. "A vote is required. Acceptance is to transfer. Rejection is to purchase *Sangilak* for its value of one-hundred ninety million credits Abasi."

I nodded. There was a lot we could do with that much money and part of me wished they would vote against the transfer. Pensively we waited while a stream of voters passed in front of us. The vote was almost unanimous for transfer, with the exception of House Gundi which abstained.

"As for the Kroerak cruiser," Mshindi Prime pushed, growing impatient at the proceeding which was dragging. "It is commonly agreed among the Abasi houses that under the Letter of Marque we have no jurisdiction over this vessel. This alien ship was obtained in a system that is not within Abasi control. Further, Loose Nuts caused this enemy ship to be removed from Zuri, much to the benefit of Abasi." She stopped and looked at me. I could tell she had more to say, but wasn't sure she wanted to get into it.

"I feel you have a 'but' coming," I said, perhaps a little more casually than I should have. "I'd prefer if you said what you were thinking, my friend."

Her whiskers twitched, as did her tail, and I hoped I hadn't offended her. "Very well. Many of the houses have argued that we should seize this vessel. It is argued the vessel is a danger to Abasi simply by its existence. This is a truth that hides a lie."

An uncomfortable murmur spread through the gallery as she spoke.

"The witnesses will quiet," she said, clearly not interested in brooking further discussion. "In working with human government, I discovered that it is acceptable to openly admit to issues that have no obvious solution. Captain Hoffen, I ask that you transfer this vessel to Abasi control for the benefit of the Abasi people. Its existence demonstrates a truth that agitates our populace and challenges peace."

My heart fell. It was exactly the type of argument I was easily sucked into. She'd laid her cards on the table and asked for a favor. I recalled being on the other side of the table as I asked her to consider coming to humanity's aid. With little hesitation she had stepped forward, knowing that to enter the fight meant certain death for many in her house. There was a lot more than money at stake in this conversation.

"Done."

Chapter 6

MATCH POINT

"Liam!" Tabby whispered harshly. "You can't just give that cruiser away."

"I have to," I whispered back. "Hold on."

Mshindi Prime stepped forward, turning quietly to face us and maintaining eye contact with me. Over the next few minutes, the voices in the room began to hush, until all eyes were on their leader. Finally, Mshindi Prime spoke.

"You freely offer this enemy vessel to Abasi because Mshindi Prime requests?" she asked, her voice incredulous. "Why would you associate no value?"

"Humans have an ideal that many subscribe to. We desire to do the right thing for the right reasons," I replied. "You are correct. The value of the Kroerak vessel to Loose Nuts is substantial. It represents much needed capital that we would use to build our company and restore the fleet with which we pursue Kroerak. The fact is, however, when humanity called to Abasi for help, Abasi responded with honor and sacrifice. How can we turn away from House Mshindi when it requests the same? The simple answer is that turning the Kroerak vessel over to Abasi is the right thing. Our sacrifice is financial and not the blood of our people. It is a poor gesture at best, but it is what we have to give."

"As it is freely given, we accept this most noble action," she said.

A chuff from the galley caught my attention and I looked over to see that Mshindi Second stood with paw to her chest. A moment later, Mshindi Tertiary also stood, chuffing and saluting. The action was soon mimicked by the remainder of the gallery.

"That was some expensive sucking up," Tabby whispered, as we looked out over the assembled Felio. My eyes landed on Badru. While he stood, I noticed he did not have his hand on his chest and if he could have burned a hole in me with his eyes, I'd have certainly been on fire.

"Mshindi Prime," a voice called out once the crowd quieted.

At the raised bar where speakers were allowed, Perasti Tertiary stood.

"House Perasti is recognized," Mshindi Prime answered.

"House Perasti wishes to know how Hoffen Liam and Loose Nuts intend to pursue Kroerak."

"The question is allowed," Mshindi Prime answered. "Loose Nuts is advised an answer is not compelled."

"We pursue Kroerak with the purpose to uncover their origins and discover their weakness. Simply put, they are humanity's mortal enemy. As for details; the history and efficacy of our pursuit is widely known. To our future plans, we will first rebuild. Beyond that, further details would not be wisely shared in a public forum."

"You accuse Abasi of aiding Kroerak?" Badru spat as he jumped to his feet.

"House Gundi is not recognized," Mshindi Prime said. "You are not required to answer."

"I don't mind answering," I said. "Badru, your statement shows a fallacy of logic. Abasi have shown great disdain for Kroerak. I do not question this. Yet I have no basis of understanding as to how broadly the comments made in this court would be shared. I mean no offense."

"What you mean and what you communicate are at odds," Badru said, still angry.

"Are there further comments?" Mshindi Prime asked. She didn't wait long before she continued. "This court desists."

Nick and Jonathan walked up to us and I had a gnawing in the pit of my stomach as I anticipated Nick's rebuke.

"Three out of four isn't bad," Nick said.

"A most noble gesture, Liam," Jonathan said. "We would discuss with you the logical path used to reach this decision, although, not at this moment."

"Really?" I asked, looking at Nick. "You're not pissed?"

"Adahy could have seized the Kroerak ship," he said. "She went way out on a limb. Asking for money would have changed our relationship with House Mshindi. Frankly, it made me proud that you understood the long-term value of our relationship with the Abasi as being greater than that ship."

"Many pardons," Mshindi Second interrupted. "I have been asked to convey a request for meeting with Mshindi Prime. Will you accept?"

"Of course." I looked and discovered that Mshindi Prime had disappeared.

"She is this way," Zakia said, leading us from the courtroom and up one level. As with previous trips onto *Thunder Awakes*, I was impressed by the level of fit and finish. Every detail of the ship was perfect, and I wondered if other Houses were similarly able to maintain their ships.

The room we entered was spare compared even to the passageways. A plain unvarnished wooden table sat atop low-napped carpet and was surrounded by wooden stools with low backs. The only ornamentation in the room was a landscape mural showing a hunting party of Felio wearing little clothing, chasing through the tall grass after a large-tusked animal.

We'd no more entered the room when Mshindi Prime, Perasti Prime, and the elderly Gundi Prime appeared from a panel in the wall I hadn't previously seen. I found it surprising that the other heads of Houses were aboard, but had not appeared in the prize court.

"Please sit," Mshindi Prime said in her usual abrupt manner. "There is much to do and to that I will delay greetings for the ceremony on Petersburg Station. Liam, do you recognize my companions?"

"Of course," I answered. "We are honored by the foresight of Busara and the clarity of Onyesha, firsts of House Perasti and Gundi." I'd spent some time researching the heads of each Abasi house and was happy I was able to properly use the information.

Both nodded and gave quiet chuffs of appreciation at the recognition.

"Let us be as plain-spoken as the furnishings of this room," Mshindi Prime said. "How will Loose Nuts pursue Kroerak?"

"Do I have the promise that you will neither stand in our way nor share this information beyond this circle?" I asked.

"There can be no promise for the first, but information will be kept tightly among only our most trusted. As leaders, we are aware of the dangers of information finding its way to our enemies," she said. "Let it be known we have no desire to hinder efforts against a most difficult enemy."

On my HUD, green ready checks showed next to Nick and Tabby's names, indicating their acceptance of my continuing.

"There is an ancient species known to the Kroerak as Piscivoru. The Piscivoru were at one time as numerous as Felio, Pogona, or even humanity. Five centuries past, the Kroerak began feeding on this species and ended up wiping them out. We have learned that the Kroerak fear this species because it possesses a weapon that does great damage to Kroerak," I said. "We quest to find this species."

"And yet you say this species was wiped out," Onyesha said. "Do you believe this weapon still exists?"

"We have reason to believe a remnant of this species still lives," Jonathan said. "While aboard the Kroerak vessel, we communicated with a Kroerak noble, which communicated its fear."

"This is the noble that sat beneath the soil of planet Zuri below us?" Busara asked.

"It is the same," Jonathan answered.

"It would seem this noble was out of communication for two centuries," she said, actually using timespan terms common to Felio, and translated by my AI. "This information is suspect."

"We learned that Kroerak nobles are capable of communication across galactic distances," Jonathan said. "They utilized the sunken vessel to secretly track the progress of Felio. We also discovered the Genteresk were complicit in providing aid to this ship and its inhabitants."

"Aid?" the wizened Onyesha asked. "These are inflammatory words with significant implications. I do not believe this."

"You asked for information," I said. "It is to you to determine its validity."

"We would transmit the dialog that exposes this information," Jonathan said, nonplussed.

"Honored Onyesha, no one accuses," Mshindi Prime said. "I do not believe Liam Hoffen has an understanding of previous, spurious accusations that House Gundi gave Genteresk traders lax oversight in Abasi space."

The old Felio's tail twitched and she glowered at Jonathan, but didn't say anything further.

"Our Houses will provide aid to Loose Nuts for the purpose of pursuing Kroerak," Mshindi Prime said. "In return we require detailed reporting of events and discovery. Loose Nuts is a fragile House that can be broken. It would not do that the information discovered be lost."

"What kind of aid?" I asked.

"Loans that do not require repayment for many generations and bear little interest. Access to ordnance manufactory at significant discounts."

"How much capitalization?" Nick asked. "To do this right, we need two hundred million credits."

A low growl was heard emanating from Mshindi Prime as she locked eyes with Nick. "Nicholas James, you are easily underestimated. I will grant one hundred million and I require an accounting that shows the expenses are attributed correctly to the objective."

"Easily accomplished," Nick said. "We're constructing a manufacturing plant for the purpose of rebuilding the engines of *Intrepid* and *Hornblower*. We need the capital to procure raw materials and pay for labor. We plan to add fuel production capability. These will have immediate, short-term impact on our capacity to continue our quest. Don't be fooled, though. For humanity to survive in this galaxy, we need a real foothold. I fully intend to use this capital for purposes beyond the mission Liam outlined. We have no desire to enter an agreement that hinders these secondary objectives."

"I would be disappointed if you did not," Mshindi Prime said. "Our only restriction is that the capital we provide be used for this objective. Ancillary benefit to Loose Nuts is acceptable."

THE RECEPTION MOM and Katherine hosted on Petersburg Station was nothing short of a blow-out. They'd gone all in, hiring our good friends from the human settlement of York, Patty and Hog Hagerson, to cater the event and even brought a local band from the nearby Pogona city, Azima, up to provide entertainment.

"Are you sure you're okay with what went down in the prize court?" I asked Tabby as we smiled politely at passersby.

"Not initially, but I think it worked out in the end," she said. "Don't get me wrong. Abasi are good allies, but we've given them a lot of power over us."

"It's no different than Mars Protectorate," I said. "They set out the rules and we had to abide by them."

"It's entirely different," she argued. "Mars Protectorate had a duty to protect its citizens."

I nodded, not wanting to argue. "I hear you."

It was at this moment that Majida, Mshindi Tertiary, or third in House Mshindi, approached. To be completely honest, her revealing outfit was the first thing that drew my eye. She'd softened her look somewhat by allowing her long hair to flow down her back, but she was still every bit the wolf, regardless of the sheep's clothing she might wear.

"I would have thought the pretty Hoffen Liam would be chattering amongst the shiny peoples," she said, pulling a glass of sparkling wine from a passing waiter. "Do you cower next to your mate for protection?"

I decided to take a different tack with her, having not made any progress in the past. "You look very nice, Majida. I did not realize your hair was quite so long on your back." From Semper, I'd learned that Felio enjoyed talking about their fur and that it was a safe conversation.

She smoothed her hair and a gleam brightened her eyes. "I understand human-Felio mating is quite pleasurable for both. I would find interest in play with both of you."

I opened my mouth to respond, but Tabby cut me off. "Not going to happen, and you should know, I'm done with this conversation. Stop making suggestions to my mate or we will find ourselves in combat – no matter the dignitaries in attendance."

"Ooh, I can almost see your fangs, Tabitha Masters," Majida said, a purring sound underlying her voice. "I find you most attractive."

"Stop this, Majida," Tabby said. "Our only contact will be in combat or on the challenge court."

A feral grin played across Majida's lips. "I accept. It is to you to choose the challenge."

"All this hot hussy routine was to get me to challenge you?" Tabby asked, unbelieving. Majida tipped her head to the side and looked away. It was clear that exactly what Tabby had said was true. "We'd talked about pod-ball already. This was unnecessary, but fine; I choose two-on-two pod-ball."

"Accepted. I have read of your game and demand that personal contact is no foul, only blood drawn results in penalty."

Tabby stepped into Majida's personal space and looked down into her eyes. "Those rules are for your protection, Majida, not mine."

"Majida!" Zakia, Mshindi Second, appeared, having worked her way through the party to us. "What is the meaning of this?"

"Masters Tabitha levied challenge. It has been accepted," she said.

"Tabitha Masters is not bound by our traditions," Zakia said. "You will withdraw and apologize, Majida."

"I cannot," Majida said. "Ask Masters Tabitha if she wishes withdrawal."

"Not even a little. This one needs a lesson in keeping her paws off what is mine," Tabby said, jabbing a finger into Majida's chest. "Put the word out. We'll meet on the Petersburg court in thirty minutes. Bring your anti-gravity suit. You're going to need it."

WHEN TABBY and I slipped away to get ready, news of the match spread quickly. I wouldn't have expected it to be quite such a big deal, but when we walked down the passageway to the courts, I was surprised by the milling crowd.

"Do us proud, Tabby," a woman I didn't recognize said as we passed.

"Show 'em what we're made of," another added.

"Why aren't they in the stands?" Tabby asked as we jostled our way through the final few meters.

The excitement was contagious and caused my stomach to sour with adrenaline. Mentally, I chastised myself; I'd been in plenty of real combat situations and shouldn't feel this way. I shouldn't have been surprised that station workers from the only human settlement in this galaxy, York, were heavily invested in our success. It was understandable. They'd been abandoned in a galaxy where humans were far from the top of the food chain and any parity with the powerful Abasi was important to them.

With that additional burden, I did some quick math and answered, "I bet the stands are full. We have forty Abasi dignitaries and over a hundred workers on Petersburg right now. Ortel and Priloe's biggest court holds thirty spectators."

"You better sack up then, Hoffen," Tabby replied, smacking her hands together like a boxer. "This is one match we're not losing."

Ortel Licht smiled as we approached the entry to the court. He'd thickened since we'd last met. When he'd joined us at seventeen stans, he'd been rail thin, as most spacers are. Over the last twenty ten-days, however, he'd put on mass, which was also common for asteroid miners. "Liam, Tabby – I gotta say, this is very exciting," he said with a confidence I hadn't seen in him before. "Come on in. We'll get you introduced. Majida and Duma are already inside and they're really getting the crowd whipped up."

"Where's Priloe?" I asked, looking for the orphan Mom had taken in. He and Ortel, even with their substantial age difference, had discovered in each other a kindred spirit and were rarely seen apart.

Ortel leaned in and whispered low. "Don't tell your mom. He's got a book going right now. I don't have to tell you there's a lot riding on this match."

"He's taking bets?" I asked, surprised and annoyed.

"You can take the boy out of the slum... " Tabby said, putting her hand on my back and pushing me toward the door. "Get focused, Hoffen. You're wasting time."

"We're going to talk, Ortel," I said over my shoulder as I stepped through the hatch.

A wave of nostalgia passed over me as I entered the court and looked up into the stands. Growing up, Nick's brother Jack, Tabby, and I had been one of the top teams at our home, Colony-40. With Nick as our sideline strategist, Jack as our defensive man, and Tabby as shooter, I ended up owning the middle ground, both defending and attacking. Life had changed since those days, and Tabby's confidence had done nothing but grow, not to mention her aggressive approach to all things resembling combat. She would be the attacker and my job would be to feed her the ball and defend our goal.

On its surface, the game of pod-ball was simple. Playing natural – as it was commonly called – was by far the best game. At each end of a symmetric court, there are goals. A point is scored by placing the ball into the goal by any means. Part of the fun of pod-ball is that the home team is allowed to place obstacles onto the court, modify gravity, change lighting and so on. The only requirement is that the visiting team be provided a full layout in advance and that the court's layout is symmetric. Players are not allowed to carry anything, their suits cannot interfere with the actions of others, and there is no use of arc-jets or really anything that would provide a boost. Of course, every rule was allowed modification if both teams agreed, but we hadn't.

There are numerous rules about contact, some of which are so nuanced that you need to be a player to even understand them. Majida, by rejecting these contact rules, basically called for a free-for-all, and I hoped she would at least respect the spirit of the game. Otherwise, it could devolve into two-on-two combat, something I worried Majida might actually want.

Looking into the stands, I found Mom standing between Mshindi Prime and Zakia, Mshindi Second. I couldn't help but wave at her as I'd always done when playing at home. I felt a flutter of sadness as I recognized that Dad would normally have been next to her. Fortunately, the energy of the crowd wasn't about to allow for those types of reflections and I waved in recognition of the many that stood and cheered behind the armor glass.

Together, Tabby and I approached the center where Majida, Mshindi Tertiary, stood next to a tall, sinewy, feral-looking Felio female. The two wore identical, simple garb: a six-centimeter-wide strap around their chest and low, tight shorts around their nethers. Beyond that, they wore no boots or gloves.

"Mshindi Tertiary," I nodded as we approached. I held my forearm in front of my body at forty-five degrees.

"Hoffen Liam, Masters Tabitha. Pleased to introduce my childhood partner, Duma," Majida said, lightly bumping my arm with her own. I moved across to Duma and bumped her arm. Her lips split in a grimace as her fangs slid into view.

"Ladies and Gentlemen, honored Abasi guests." Ortel's amplified voice filled the room as he strutted into the middle of the court. "Today we have the first recorded pod-ball match between Felio and humans. Representing House Mshindi we have the fierce, the lithe, the always ready for a fight – Majida! At her side, the highly decorated and powerful Duma!"

He waited as cheers from both human and Felio echoed through the court, transmitted between the armor glass panels by electronic means.

"Representing the underdogs of Dwingeloo, the scrappy species that never says die, the one, the only, Liam Hoffen and his ass-kicking partner, Tabby Masters!" As Ortel spoke, his voice rose and trailed off like an old-fashioned circus barker from ancient vids. I had to hand it to him, he was getting the crowd riled up.

"House Mshindi – are you ready?" Ortel turned dramatically to Majida.

"Get on with it, mouse," she replied, unimpressed.

"I'll take that as affirmative," he replied and turned to Tabby and me. "Loose Nuts – are you ready?"

Tabby nodded to me and I walked three meters toward the goal we would defend and placed the back of my foot against one of several obstacles. She would stay next to where the ball would drop from the ceiling a fraction of a second before gravity was nullified and things like floors and ceilings became irrelevant.

"Let's go, Ortel," Tabby said, twisting her neck, loosening up.

"The match ends after three ten-minute periods or five goals, whichever comes first," Ortel said. "By agreement of both teams, personal fouls are lifted. Broken bones and deep cuts will be assessed by AI and the offending player will be ejected from game. Take your positions, match starts in fifteen seconds."

Ortel turned and jogged off court. The lights dimmed, steam began pouring in from vents in the walls and rays of light, resembling blaster fire, danced around the room. If I survived, I'd be paying Ortel back for the spectacle. I hated strobes while playing, as they were just a distraction.

I watched nervously as the time clicked down. Neither Majida nor Duma backed away from center court and I considered that I might have made a tactical error in not joining what was sure to be a furball. I wasn't about to change up just yet, though, as I had no doubt Tabby could hold her own.

A second before the ball dropped, Duma launched herself into Tabby's midsection, catching her off guard and launching the two just as gravity switched to zero-g. It was a good move and I was a little surprised Tabby had been caught by it.

"Stop her," Tabby ordered as Majida leapt and easily grabbed the free ball, her inertia sending her toward what had become the ceiling.

Patiently I waited, knowing she would redirect toward the goal once she contacted the lightly carpeted surface. Of the things you get good at in pod-ball, anticipating where someone will go based on a push-off is number one. Majida's new vector had her headed toward our goal and on a direct line with the obstacle that blocked any direct shot. Once she reached that obstacle, she would redirect and either shoot at or head toward the goal for a stuff.

I grabbed the obstacle I had backed into and swung myself toward our goal. She had a ricochet shot available and I gambled she'd ignore it, especially since she had one-on-one odds with me, something I was sure she enjoyed.

"I'm coming for you, Hoffen," Majida said as she streaked toward the obstacle. I didn't respond. I'd never been a talker while playing.

As expected, I arrived moments before she did, and positioned myself adjacent to the goal, allowing my feet to land behind it. I absorbed my inertia with bent legs, waiting for her to contact the obstacle. It was a trick I'd developed over years of playing. For a few moments, I could store inertia by continuing to bend with impact. At some point, I'd either bounce away from the bulkhead or ideally, release the energy by pushing and springing away.

When Majida reached the obstacle, she grabbed the edge with the claws of her feet fully extended. She brilliantly used the edge to swing her around and I launched forward in anticipation of her throw. At the last moment, however, she twisted and instead of releasing the ball, held it and carried forward. It wasn't as if I didn't know her move was a possibility, there were always a dozen possible moves any player could make. I stretched out and prepared for contact as we sailed at each other at a good clip.

Following the ball's motion, I was surprised by the feeling of claws digging into my back and I arched defensively. Majida, expecting the move, pulled hind legs beneath her and pushed into my stomach, just as she fired the ball successfully into the goal. A moment later, Tabby slammed into the rear bulkhead, missing the action by a fraction.

I swiped my hand across my back where Majida had raked me and brought it around to inspect. I was bleeding, but it wasn't that deep.

Tabby floated up next to me, grabbed my hand, and then spun me around. "What the frak, Majida? What part of no blood don't you get?" she spat.

"It is my error, Masters," Majida said, her tail twitching. "I did not realize human flesh was so soft. It is like a newborn."

"I'm fine," I said. "Just surprised."

"That's crap," Tabby said. "We'll take a minute and put a patch on. Are you sure you want to keep going?"

"I said I'm fine," I wasn't about to give Majida the satisfaction.

"Bad plan drawing first blood, Majida," Tabby said. "Let's hope you don't bleed so easily."

The four of us floated back to the center and I blinked acceptance at Tabby's tactical request. She wanted to pull me from defense and put us both on attack. I chinned through a menu and let her know I intended to take Majida again. I believed that the Felio would expect Tabby to be on tilt. Her slow response to my suggestion told me she didn't love the idea, but accepted it just the same.

This time when the ball was released, Duma backpedaled in defense of their goal. They wanted to show us a different look, which was interesting, but I keyed on Majida and streamed toward her as she and Tabby jumped for the ball. I overshot a little and ended up grabbing her tail, close to its base, eliciting a yowl and an instant spin so that she oriented on me. Tabby, ignoring the kerfuffle, grabbed the ball and turned toward the goal.

An open-clawed paw smacked the side of my face and the tips of Majida's nails bit into my cheek. I brought a knee up, landing it in her stomach as I cartwheeled away from her.

"So you want to play rough, soft man," Majida growled, completely ignoring the ball and Tabby. I held to the side as I waited for her to make her move. She pushed off and sailed directly at me with speed I found surprising. I jumped away, only to be impacted a moment later as she plowed into me. I felt a paw between my legs and the possibility of the worst sort of injury entered my mind for the first time I could remember. The only thing I could think to do was a head butt, which I did. Turns out, there's a saying I've often heard that is completely accurate: no one wins in a head butt. It had the intended effect, however, of removing Majida's paw from my sensitive areas. She yowled and kicked away. I saw stars at the same moment I heard the sound of Tabby making a goal at the opposite end.

For twenty-five grueling minutes, the four of us, having felt each other out (more literally than I'd have liked), fell into the most brutal style of pod-ball play I'd ever been part of. I have never felt quite so physically out-matched as I did with the Felio and it took every gram of tenaciousness I had to keep up. Tabby was clearly superior, but she lacked the physical grace of the Felio. If it had been a fight to the death, she'd have won hands (or paws) down. As it was, she followed the rules as much as possible, while I did my best to hang with them.

In the end, time simply ran out, the score four goals apiece.

"Masters, you are a worthy opponent," Majida summed up as we waved to the crowd that hadn't thinned. "And Hoffen Liam, you are not nearly so soft. I would not have believed you would stand when we desisted. For this I recognize you."

"You're an asshat," I said through gritted teeth, smiling as I waved to the crowds.

Majida and Duma exchanged looks, and snorts of surprise were shortly followed by peals of throaty, growling laughter as their AIs translated my phrase.

Tabby dropped an arm over my shoulder protectively as I limped for the hatch. "You held your own, babe. Don't let 'em get to you."

I sighed – Dwingeloo Galaxy was a tough place to be a man.

Chapter 7

REMNANT

"I will tend your arm," Sklisk said, pulling Jaelisk away from the short wall atop the ruins of their ancestor's home. The Kroerak running in the streets below had not seen them, but seemed to be searching for something.

"I failed you, mate," Jaelisk said. "My injury is my shame. I bring death to you if we travel together. You would be better to leave me here."

Sklisk considered his life-mate. Flicking his tongue, he tasted her misery and shame. "We will be together always. When you are injured, I am injured."

For a full five minutes, Jaelisk stared back at him as they locked eyes. Sklisk had been raised in a non-traditional nest that did not believe in reversion, but growing up, she'd been taught a strong mate was the difference between life and death for her nest. She had no doubt that both her mother and father would advise Sklisk to find a new mate when they saw her injury.

"Why?" she finally found the strength to ask, a small ray of hope burning low within her chest.

"We are not mates solely to grow our nest," Sklisk said. "I have wanted to be with you since the first moment we swam within the grotto of the Iskstar. It was not because of your pleasing shape and warmth. It is more than that. We are joined, Jaelisk. I know you understand this. You would have mated with Foelerd if you did not."

"Foelerd's mind is as thick as a rock and his tongue found my breasts more than once when others looked away. I would never mate with one such as that."

"Foelerd is stronger than I, he runs faster, and has a preferred nest. He has already started to revert and there are many would follow him to a new nesting ground, your parents included," he said.

"I want to be with you, Sklisk. Foelerd is all those things and I do not want them."

"Then do not settle for a future of skittering from sight and accepting the death of our once great people. I would die before I gave up on my people. I will die before I give up on you," he said. "Will you now allow me to look at your wound?"

Jaelisk held out her hastily bandaged arm. "I will fight beside you until we have no breath, and I will no longer settle for only living beneath the ground."

Sklisk closed his eyes and rubbed the side of his face against Jaelisk's, momentarily ignoring her proffered arm. A few moments later they separated and he unwrapped her bandages. For the Piscivoru, tongues and tails would regrow, but hands would not. Fortunately, the under-skin had already closed and a light layer of dense outer-skin was forming.

"It heals well," he said. "You should be able to place weight on it by second moon's rest if we are able to find water."

"There is water below," Jaelisk said. "Can you not taste it?"

Sklisk parted his mouth, pulling his already thin lips to narrow lines, flicked the end of his tongue out just as he closed his left inner eyelid and opened all three lids on his right. It was a comical look that Jaelisk had often chided him on.

"You are such a broodling," she said, using a common insult given to those who bit the ends of their long tongues off. "The pink nub is starting to grow. Hopefully you can keep it from between your teeth today."

Sklisk dropped to his belly and walked to the large hole that punched through the ruined building's roof. At the edge, he flicked his tongue and tasted the familiar smells of molds and a plethora of plant life he did not recognize. The smells of bug warriors was thick, but they were carried on the winds and were not from below.

"Will the star fire return after the moons' cycle as Engirisk taught?" Jaelisk asked as she followed Sklisk over the broken roof and into the center of the building. Her movement was slowed as she only had three claws with which to grip the building, but it was something all Piscivoru were used to when carrying bundles.

"Of course," Sklisk answered, hanging momentarily by his back legs and falling to the floor below. "That is why they call it moons' cycle. As the star disappears from the sky, the moons rise."

Dropping was a little more difficult with a missing hand, but Jaelisk had determined she would not complain, even though pain from her nub caused white lights to cloud her vision as she landed next to him.

Sklisk dropped again, landing on an unstable outcropping of broken floor. He adjusted as the floor crumbled and dropped heavy chunks of stone-like material beneath him. Together, they repeated the cycle, unaware of the attention the falling concrete had gained from a bug patrol moving past the building.

"Look here," Sklisk said, jumping across to a tree that grew in the middle of the building. Something shiny had caught his eye and he leapt to it. So far, he'd not found a single piece of evidence of his ancestor's life. And while he hadn't expected anything, given the vast amount of time that had passed, he remained hopeful.

He picked up a strange-looking, flat piece of metal. Strange in that it was silver color and was almost glossy. The only metal he was aware of was the bronze of the weapons he and Jaelisk carried. Turning it over, Sklisk was further interested in the pocked, transparent material over its surface. It looked identical to the surface on Engirisk's damaged machine. A fleeting image flashed across the object – that of a Piscivoru female covered in very odd clothing. Just as quickly as it appeared, the image disappeared.

"Do not waste time with that," Jaelisk urged.

He blinked his middle eyelids, communicating for Jaelisk to follow. Together they jumped back to the thickening tree trunk and skittered to the ground. Sklisk dipped his mouth into the water. The leafy detritus gave it a taste he didn't care for, but it was safe enough and he drank deeply.

Sated, still holding the strange item, he turned it over, trying to discern its purpose.

"What is it you have?" Jaelisk asked.

Sklisk gave her the object and for a few moments it remained dark. As he adjusted his hand, the image of a young Piscivoru female dressed in bright clothing and walking through a field of flowers appeared through the cracks. Her head tipped to the side as she looked straight at Jaelisk and spoke, although the pad provided no sound. The sentiment expressed, however, was clear. The female was very much in love with whomever she was talking to.

"She is so happy," Jaelisk whispered, leaning heavily on Sklisk. "I have never seen so many flowers in a single place. They are beautiful. Our people must see this. We have lost so much."

"We will show them," Sklisk said, resting his cheek against hers as they watched the female slowly fade and then reappear several times.

"How will we reach Engirisk's building?" Jaelisk whispered. "There are many more warriors than we could hope to fight."

"Engirisk teaches that the warriors cannot climb and that they have poor eyesight for distance. Like us, they have a good sense of smell. We will leap from one building to the next and avoid their detection," Sklisk answered. "Do you think you can do this?"

"You have never leapt further than I," she answered. "This will not change – even if I have not my hand."

Through the mud, they both felt the vibrations of the warriors Jaelisk had warned about, much closer than before.

"Warriors are about. They have felt us within this great nest," Jaelisk warned unnecessarily.

Thirty hands above their heads, a loud crash outside of the building alerted them to the scouting party's presence. Instinctively, they oriented on the noise and froze in place. What the Kroerak had in abundance was strength. From the vibrations, Sklisk believed the bugs would enter the building in short order.

"*We are discovered,*" Jaelisk communicated, vibrating her tongue, but producing no sound.

"*Steady,*" Sklisk answered. He understood that all predators shared the same proclivity to chase movement. The trick to evading was to move when out of the line of sight when there was distraction.

A great crashing resounded as the bugs battered through the exterior wall swirling up a cloud of dust and debris. The Piscivoru needed no further prompting and leapt from their position by the muddy pool of water, slipping onto the back of the tree. Their gait up the heavy trunk was jerky, each spurt of movement perfectly timed by the movement of the scouting party until they were nearly to the top of the building.

"We should have killed them," Jaelisk said.

"Others would smell their death," Sklisk argued.

"They will smell our presence in the mud."

"Do not fret. Before this moon cycle ends, we will have dipped the Iskstar into many Kroo Ack," Sklisk promised.

Without warning the top of the building exploded. Sklisk could feel the flight of long, narrow objects as they passed through the floor above them, loosening great chunks of the building's side. Together, Sklisk and Jaelisk jumped clear of the debris.

"*Follow!*" Sklisk trilled with his tongue.

Even as the building disintegrated around them, he leapt through an opening in the wall, narrowly avoiding falling material. Sklisk twisted in mid-air as he fell and slapped into the adjacent building. Next to him Jaelisk landed, skidding down the building's side, unable to slow as easily. For a moment, Sklisk observed her descent, worried she might not be able to stop. Two dozen hand spans later, she slowed.

An excited chitter from ground level was the only warning Sklisk received before he felt the impact of more ranged weapons. He did not require further prompting to move out of their way and together, they skittered across the face of the building and around the side.

A short burst of panic from Jaelisk warned him of trouble. She had grabbed loose material and momentarily lost her grip. Sklisk ran toward his mate, but she had already managed to find solid material again and reclaim the distance lost. Further chittering from the growing horde of bug warriors meant they were still being stalked. Sure enough, seconds later, long narrow spikes hit the building behind them. Instinctively dropping and running, they avoided the impacts as well as raining debris.

"*Inside,*" Sklisk urged. He slipped through a section of broken wall and held fast to the ceiling, leading Jaelisk to the opposite side of the room.

"We are discovered," she whispered.

"We are yet free," Sklisk answered with a traditional Piscivoru response. He wedged through a hole in the ceiling and climbed along an inner wall. The building they were in was heavily damaged and moonlight shone through the roof. Working upward, he kept them in shadow even as more bug weapons struck the building.

Daring a quick glimpse, he stuck his head out and looked to the adjacent building. It was a much longer jump and while he was confident he could make it, he felt fearful that Jaelisk would not.

Sensing his hesitance, Jaelisk pushed him. "Go, I will follow."

Fearing the bug weapons might crumble the building around them, Sklisk leapt across the open space with all his strength. He slid against the building's face and slowed, turning to make sure Jaelisk also made it. He'd always enjoyed watching her jump and could tell she would succeed as she sailed toward him. Time stood still as Sklisk realized incoming projectiles would strike the building above him just as Jaelisk would land. He had no choice but to move to the side to be out of their path.

Jaelisk clawed at the crumbling building, trying to arrest her horizontal movement. It was critical to grasp something when jumping for risk of simply bouncing off. The crumbling rubble, however, had given her nothing to catch and she flew away from the building.

Knowing she had little choice, Jaelisk pushed against the debris to separate herself from the falling rock but was unable to angle back to grab hold of either building. Flattening out, she accepted the fall and landed hard on the ground.

Sklisk looked at the street filling with bug warriors tracking their location. He could not understand how the bugs pursued so easily. His mind fixated on the picture device he'd found. Ripping it from his pouch, he threw it as far as he could. He had no idea if it could cause them problems, but reasoned that if Engirisk's machine was detectable, the pad might be as well.

Sklisk frantically searched for a solution as bug warriors raced toward Jaelisk from all angles. She'd been wounded further, but was alert enough to understand the danger as she sluggishly pulled her Iskstar weapon from her back and prepared to meet the onslaught. Sklisk's eyes lit on a round disk embedded in the once-flat, but now crumbling roadway. The disk was made of iron and while he wasn't sure of its purpose, he knew two things: it was Piscivoru made and if opened, would provide more cover than standing in the open where Jaelisk was currently trapped.

Sklisk skittered downward and timed his leap from the building to meet the first of the bug warriors. The warrior's face held no expression as he plunged the end of his Iskstar into its open proboscis. Sklisk slid to the ground, drawing the blade through the bug's breast plate. He spun to meet the second bug but saw, with some satisfaction that Jaelisk had already drawn deep furrows into its underside and would finish it.

"Leave me," Jaelisk demanded.

Three more bugs skidded to a halt and rose to attack, as the sounds of many sharp pincers clacking against the stony surface rang out. Sklisk was pushed forward as a claw struck his back. He rolled with the strike, his scaled back deflecting the claw to the side. Wincing at the pain from the forceful attack, he instinctively reacted. With a swift swing of the Iskstar pole, Sklisk cut off the bug's pincered hand. Without pause, he spun the weapon through the bug's carapace, killing it.

Understanding slowly sank in and he understood how their deaths would come. An individual strike from any bug would do a small amount of damage and that bug would pay with its life. The bugs, however, had no concern for their lives and would not stop coming, regardless of the price paid. He and Jaelisk were fighting a microcosm of the battle his ancestors had been fighting since the Kroo Ack arrived on Picis.

He turned again and searched the ground for the iron disk. He'd been pushed away from it, as had Jaelisk. A great horde of the bugs flowed over the rubble like water, coming for them even though piles of dead bugs grew around them.

"To me!" Sklisk sang out and dropped to his stomach, running for the iron disk's position. A weak strike on his back was followed by a second. Sklisk had been told that the bugs had difficulty striking at the low target of a Piscivoru on the ground, but to experience it while in combat was a lesson well learned. Two of his adversaries collided above them as he and Jaelisk arrived near the disk at roughly the same moment. Swinging around, he dropped one of the bugs, unfortunately it fell directly atop the disk.

"I have always loved you," Jaelisk said, her strength flagging.

"Do not give up," Sklisk ordered, pushing his shoulder into the bug that blocked the disk. He was unable to move it.

"What are you doing?" Jaelisk asked.

"Help me move this," he demanded, not explaining.

Jaelisk pushed with him, but the bug's weight made it difficult. Sklisk jumped back to a defensive posture, slicing into another warrior that had clambered over rubble to attack. Turning back, he sliced into the husk of the bug at their feet and ripped away at its body.

"Have you gone feral? They come for us!" Jaelisk exclaimed, fighting off another.

Sklisk didn't answer but dug through the pieces of the warrior's body, his blade finally hitting the iron of the disk. Rushing, he clawed frantically, pushing the remains away until he found what he was looking for. Just then, a warrior crashed into him from behind, rolling him and several of the body pieces away from the disk. Jaelisk, while not understanding the objective, recognized the danger he was in and jumped atop the pile, slicing her blade across the attacker's chest.

"The disk on the ground!" Sklisk yelled as he freed himself from the viscera. "It is a tunnel."

Jaelisk turned and discovered the target of Sklisk's interest. Without hesitation she jammed the end of her Iskstar staff into a hole at one edge of the disk in an attempt to pry it up. Nothing happened and the disk appeared so impossible to move that she straightened, intending to remove the staff and try something else. Before she could finish the thought, Sklisk's feet landed on one end of the staff, driving it from her hands. The staff bent precariously under his weight and yet miraculously, the iron lid flipped up onto the ground, exposing a darkened hole.

"Go!" Sklisk said, urging Jaelisk through.

"My weapon," Jaelisk cried back as she slid into the darkness below.

Sklisk looked for the staff, but it had been flung many body lengths away. For a few moments he considered going after it, but quickly decided against the thought. A warrior had grabbed the weapon in its maw, turned from the fight, and raced off. Shocked, but with nothing else to lose, Sklisk turned and dove into the hole behind Jaelisk.

Bouncing against smooth walls, he allowed gravity to pull him downward. Tentatively, he reached out with his feet, seeing if he could grip the sides. He was gratified to discover he was able to hold on just enough to control his fall. Blinking, he pulled back his inner eyelids and peered around the tunnel. Before Sklisk could see much, he collided with Jaelisk, who had come to rest at the bottom.

Still concerned about the bugs, he looked up, calculating the distance that separated them from the surface. He estimated they had gone three seconds in free fall and no bug warrior would ever fit within the hole they'd dropped through.

"We're safe for now," he said, turning to where Jaelisk still sat. He could feel that something was off as she began moving; her actions seemed slow and distracted. "Are you hurt?"

It was at that moment his eyes fell on a scene he would never forget. For as far as he could see, mummified remains of Piscivoru lay haphazardly against the rounded walls of the long tunnel.

Chapter 8

BORN TO BE WILD

I sat on the corner of the bed, staring at the floor with my throbbing head in my hands. I was waiting for the med-patch nanobots to finally decide that my headache was a priority. My body had taken quite a pounding during the pod-ball match, mostly from the claws of Mshindi Tertiary.

"You going to be okay?" Tabby asked as she stepped from the shower room. She leaned over to wrap her hair into a turban with the luxurious towels that were standard in the station's new VIP suite.

I'll admit it; I'm a very visual person. Even with my entire body aching, the sight of my beautiful warrior queen caused me to think of other things. She'd faced away from me at a slight angle and my eyes traced up her angular legs to her bottom and along her six-pack abs. She finally stood back up and turned toward me.

"Um ..." was all I could manage.

She smiled that smile she reserved only for me, then walked confidently over to place a cool hand on my forehead. Pushing hair away from one of my numerous injuries, she sank to my level to place a kiss on it.

"Why, Mr. Hoffen, I do believe your answer, while terse, communicates all that is necessary," she said, pushing me gently back onto the bed, straddling me.

There is very little a man is not capable of doing when his very beautiful – might I add, naked – woman whom he loves, brings herself into such proximity. A distant and almost closed-off part of my brain registered complaints from my body as injuries were exacerbated in the activities that followed.

Twenty minutes later, worse for wear but happier because of it, I gratefully allowed Tabby to reapply med patches to the numerous injuries across my body. "Oh, Liam, you should have stopped me," Tabby said, removing a patch that had soaked through with blood from my back. "Are you sure you shouldn't be in the tank? My AI is showing damage to your kidneys. Majida did this?"

"You can't expect to parade naked in front of me without consequences," I said, not wanting to give Mshindi Tertiary any further credit. The pod-ball match had turned into a bare-handed brawl, which was entirely to the benefit of Felio, who have claws at the end of their hands. Call it hubris if you need, but give me a decent weapon and I'd rematch Majida any time, any place. Of course, that could just be my bruised ego talking.

"You're ignoring my question. I can't believe she caused this kind of damage," Tabby said, inspecting the wound. "We need to say something. This isn't okay."

She was sitting on my legs with her knees on either side of my body, her warmth causing a certain drain of my cognitive abilities – again. "Just put a new patch on," I said, trying to fight the battle I would lose if she continued to sit atop me. "Med advisor says I'll be fine. I don't want her getting wind of the fact that she did enough damage to warrant the tank."

Tabby sighed and wiped a disposable towel across the wound, immediately clotting the sections that had opened. "I don't know what her problem is with you." She lifted her leg off and pushed me onto my back, her focus on my other wounds, most of which were smaller and had been closed already. Of course, the move exposed the fact that my mind had wandered during the conversation. She leaned down and looked into my face with an unraised eyebrow. "No. Not until your back wound is fully closed."

I shrugged innocently.

"You're such a bad man," she said, leaping off the bed as I lunged for her. My hand slid from her bottom as she easily escaped me. "Get in the shower. We'll talk about things tonight."

"We'll be sailing for Abeline by tonight," I complained, looking for an angle that was not in my body's best interest. "I'm not even sure what the sleeping arrangements will be."

"Are you saying *Gaylon Brighton* has no dual-bunked quarters?" Tabby asked, pulling a freshly-folded suit liner from where it sat next to the suit freshener. "I believe the captain should have considered this before deciding to take her on such a long journey to the Central Planets."

Recognizing I was fighting a losing battle, I rolled from the bed and gingerly stood, walking stiffly to the shower. With warm water washing over me, I pushed pain from consideration and switched from thinking about play time to that of our mission. Jonathan had a thin lead regarding the information he'd gleaned from the Kroerak noble about the Piscivoru. According to what Jonathan had come up with in his research, they needed to talk to an information broker who worked out of a bar on the planet Abeline.

The mission was straightforward – sail to Abeline, some fourteen wormhole jumps and three ten-days away if we sailed at maximum speed on our fastest ship. In reality, we'd end up taking our second fastest ship. *Fleet Afoot* was faster by six or seven percent than *Gaylon Brighton*, but she lacked the state-of-the-art Mars Protectorate sloop armor, weaponry, and somewhat limited stealth capacity. I would be lying if I said I wasn't looking forward to taking command of the little marvel. The sloop was hardly in the right weight class for taking on Kroerak, but then that wasn't the mission this time around – at least that's what I believed at the moment.

"You're like a light switch," Tabby said, when I got out of the shower and dried off. "Might give a girl whiplash."

I grinned, looking up at her. She'd already braided her long coppery hair and was in her tight fitting grav-suit. I could have pointed out that it was her actions that had redirected me, but I'd learned she didn't have quite the same capability to compartmentalize. I looked into her eyes as I approached, rested my fingers beneath her chin, and kissed her lightly. "I happen to know the captain's quarters has a queen-sized bed configuration. I've already sent instructions."

"Who all is going?" Tabby asked.

She'd been in on the initial conversations, but we hadn't made any decisions, wanting to give people time to talk about the trip and respond. In my mind, the ideal complement was my original crew: Marny, Nick, Ada, Tabby, and me. The fact was, however, that Nick had a business to run, Marny had reservations about allowing Munay free reign, and Ada wasn't about to abandon her baby, *Intrepid,* while it was being worked on.

"So far it's Sendrei, Jonathan, you and me," I said.

"Extras? What about Semper, Robie, and Jester Ripples?"

"We need them working on *Hornblower*, we can't afford to lose their productivity, especially Jester Ripples and Semper," I said.

"Semper?" Tabby asked.

"Seriously. She and Jester Ripples have worked out a quirky style of communication where she's almost an extension of him. He's taken to sleeping in her quarters and everything," I said.

"I wondered where the little guy had gotten off to," she said. "That's going to leave us running pretty short-handed for a thirty-day journey."

"Nick's got a line on a couple of rookies we could bring along. One's a Petty Officer from Mars. She was part of *Gaylon Brighton's* original crew – Larkin Bray, and a man Nick hired from York – Todd Hunter. Believe it or not, Nick had him working on the plant's gray water processing system."

Tabby smiled at the inside joke. I always complained about being put into the position of fixing our septic systems, but I really only minded the smell. "Let's hope *Gaylon Brighton* doesn't need any of that."

NOT THE TYPE TO overpack or make long goodbyes, Tabby and I gave final hugs to friends and family who would remain behind and stepped onto the catwalk that led onto the thirty-meter long *Gaylon Brighton*. As far as ship designs went, she was something of a mix between our first and second ships; *Sterra's Gift* and *Hotspur*. With the light-and-signal-absorptive armor, top and bottom turrets, and twin missile tubes, *Gaylon Brighton* was stealthy and had nearly as much punch as *Hotspur*. Not as focused on cargo, however, she boasted only a single deck and carried ten very comfortably. In a pinch, passenger capacity could be doubled with no stress on the triple-redundant biological systems.

Turning aft, I nodded to the two new crew members, Bray and Hunter, who looked up from where they were stowing supplies in the galley. They both sported Ada's newly-designed two-tone crew vac-suits; the top was a deep blood-red and the attached leggings were matte black. The boots and gloves had small, built-in arc-jets that looked to be handy in a pinch, but I worried they wouldn't be much in an extended EVA situation.

"Welcome aboard, Sir," the blonde-haired Petty Officer Larkin Bray quickly added, stiffening to a semblance of attention. Todd Hunter, from York on the planet's surface, nodded back. He didn't have any military background, but seemed comfortable enough with the formality.

"Are we good to go?" I asked.

"Aye, Sir. Absolutely," Bray answered immediately, her eager Petty Officer attitude still intact.

"We'll be underway in a few minutes," I said. "I'll be looking for a ready check shortly."

"Aye, aye!" Bray answered yet again, earning her a bemused look from Hunter.

Turning forward, we walked past closed hatches en route to the bridge. I nodded to myself, it was good practice to keep hatches shut, especially when near other ships. Damage from a hull breach, while not likely next to Petersburg station, was easily dealt with if a compartment was closed.

"She's beautiful," Tabby said, running her hand along the glossy, bright two-tone white and gray bulkhead.

"Not quite the Belirand fit and finish," I said. "More than I'd have expected from Mars Protectorate, though."

I placed my palm on the bridge door and heard the familiar whistle announcing my arrival as the hatch disappeared to the portside.

"Captain on the bridge," Sendrei's deep baritone announced.

"Your timing is good, Captain," Jonathan said. "Nicholas has deposited the prototype machines we are to deliver to a distributor on Abeline. We have sufficient supplies and fuel for a direct trip. I believe there is no reason for further delay."

"Sendrei, are we good for missiles?" I asked. In studying the ship's design, I'd learned the turrets had the capacity for both energy-based blasters and projectiles. My AI showed we had three missiles aboard. We had capacity for six, but we would have to make an additional stop if we were to take on further ordnance.

"Like you, I'd rather have a full load," he said. "I don't believe our mission parameters justify a stop only for this purpose, though."

As with most ships I'd sailed, *Gaylon Brighton* had two adjustable pilot's chairs at the extreme forward of the bridge. New to me, however, was the fact that all chairs within the bridge were configurable for any purpose. According to what I'd read, the chairs could be stowed in the deck out of the way, turned to face center, lined up in a row, or pushed to any of the stations that lined the aft and interior bulkheads.

"All hands, this is the captain. Please prepare for immediate departure," I said, comfortable that the ship's AI would route communications appropriately. Before boarding, I'd assigned responsibility for each of the ship's critical systems to different crew members. It would be their responsibility to run the checklists against their systems and report back with a simple go/no-go when given the preparation order. I immediately received 'go' from all stations.

"Petersburg, this is *Gaylon Brighton* requesting exit vector. We're ready for departure," I said.

"*Gaylon Brighton*, your navigation is approved. Safe travels and happy hunting," Katherine LeGrande's bust appeared on a crystal-clear holo projection centered forward of the pilot's chairs. Accompanying her projection, a navigation path was also transmitted. Ultimately, Katherine wanted us to stay clear of the activity around *Hornblower*, but otherwise we had open space.

"One last thing, Petersburg. Please patch me into station public address," I said.

"What? Oh." Katherine chuckled. "You're live, *Gaylon Brighton*."

"Cue Steppenwolf – *Born to be Wild*," I instructed.

Tabby shook her head as electric guitars from ages long past played on both the station's and *Gaylon Brighton's* sound systems.

Get your motor runnin'
Head out on the highway
Lookin' for adventure
And whatever comes our way

With theme music in place, I rolled the acceleration stick forward and twisted slightly on the directional stick. "All hands, prepare for hard burn." Giving it a moment, I pushed the stick forward until we reached a Class B, hard-burn acceleration. I forced my breathing to slow as I was pushed back into the pilot's seat while inertial and gravity systems negotiated. The actual acceleration of hard-burn was generally the point where the two systems resulted in a constant 1.25g to 1.5g downward force. Given that we'd be sailing for an extended period, the preference was to keep it at the lower end of the range for comfort.

"Classic," Tabby said and I beamed at her acknowledgement of the music.

"Pretty great, right?" I said.

"Ship feels good, although she's no *Intrepid*." Tabby said what I was also thinking. Our actual acceleration was considerably more than was possible on *Intrepid* and unlike *Sterra's Gift*, the transition to hard burn was graceful to the point where it was hardly noticeable.

"Everything is so tidy," I said, looking at the clean lines of the forward bulkhead that sat just beneath the broad armored glass looking out to the stars. "Sendrei, you mind taking the helm while Tabbs and I take a look around? This is our first time on a Hermes class sloop."

"I've taken the liberty of proposing a watch schedule, Captain," Sendrei said. "If acceptable, first watch falls to Jonathan."

"Tentatively, I accept," I agreed. "I'll look at it in further detail while we're underway."

"Aye, Captain."

"Captain, have you anything to report?" Jonathan asked, recognizing our long-standing helm turn-over procedures.

"Negative. All systems are functioning within norms and we've nothing but wide-open space between us and the Tamu wormhole," I answered Jonathan's formal start to helm change procedure.

"Captain, I offer my relief."

"I stand relieved."

"I'll show you around," Sendrei said, standing with Tabby and me. "Mars might have added a bit of sizzle to the old girl, but their Hermes sloop isn't anything too new."

"Says every nanker sailor ever born," Tabby needled as the three of us headed aft. Her term 'nanker' was a derisive term used by Mars Protectorate sailors when describing the North Americans. "Just because it has engines, atmo, navigation and a bilge doesn't mean the North Americans invented it."

Sendrei chuckled. "Ah yes, I had forgotten your service. It truly is a delightful ship. I am pleased to give credit to the Mars engineers for their modifications to the sloop design. Truly there are only so many changes possible when improving upon something so tried and tested."

I smiled, knowing that the war of words between Tabby and Sendrei was just heating up. I pushed open the first hatch we came across on the port side. Within I found good-sized quarters I knew to be the captain's. Thoughtfully, someone had already dropped the bags we'd left in the aft passage.

"Seems roomy," Tabby said, leaning over my back, resting her chin on my shoulder. While I agreed, I found the statement ironic. The VIP room on Petersburg Station was easily five times the size of the room where we now stood. The fact was, however, there was a bed, desk, storage for clothing, and a table that could accommodate four if you were willing to sit on the corner of the bed.

"No private head," Sendrei said. "North Americans would never put up with that, but these ships were made for deep-space exploration and essentials took priority. Saving space, however, has allowed for some amenities we'll all appreciate."

"Like what?"

"There are two heads, identical in shape and function," Sendrei said, crossing the hallway and pushing open the hatch opposite the captain's quarters. "There are two private shower stalls and three zero-gravity commodes. Nothing fancy, but if this ship were at capacity, you'd appreciate it. There are two single officer bunks and two shared junior officer quarters next in line. I put Jonathan directly aft of your quarters and I will occupy the other single. This leaves crewmen Hunter and Bray using the junior officer bunks. Nick wanted as much storage as possible and we've flexed the normal crew quarters to cargo. Even so, we're only sailing at fifty percent capacity."

"So, bunks and toilets," Tabby said, raising an eyebrow. "I'm not sure I'd consider those to be add-ons. Impress me already."

"How about a fully stocked armory, recreation room for watching vids, playing cards and general relaxation materials, and a two-cell brig? The ship has a Class-B mil-spec replicator capable of making small-arms ammunition and most ship parts, given enough time," he responded. "She's truly designed for long range missions. I haven't even mentioned the best part, since I really want to see it for myself first."

"I'd prefer *Intrepid*, but it's hard to argue against the design. Any thoughts on assigning crew duties while underway?" I asked. Marny had told me that she'd talked to Sendrei about running the crew, but I wanted to make sure he was up for it.

"We'll run eight-hour work shifts each twenty-four unless you're on bridge duty where we'll be running a standard four-hour watch. There is no shortage of tasks to keep the crew busy," he said. "Petty Officer Bray is familiar with standard bridge watches and we'll have her and Hunter man one watch every thirty-six. I've sent you the details in a briefing. Let me know if you'd like changes."

"You can take the man out of the Navy ..." Tabby quipped as we continued down the passageway.

"Organization frees the mind from mundane tasks," Sendrei replied.

"What's next?" I asked, nodding at Hunter and Bray who were up to their elbows in packages they were stowing inside the galley cabinetry.

"Coffee, Captain?" Hunter asked, closing a door and locking it with a standard magneto slide hasp.

"Not about to turn that down, thanks," I said. "Todd, isn't it?"

"That's right, Captain," he said, handing me a cup of muddy-looking liquid. He waited while I tasted it, watching while I took a quick sip.

"Something wrong?" he asked when I grimaced.

"Have you ever had coffee?" I asked.

"Negative. We received a briefing from Ada Chen. She said it was your favorite and we decided to try making it. The instructions seemed simple; I'm not sure how we messed it up," he said.

"Petty Officer Bray?" I asked. "Surely North Americans drink coffee."

"Copy that, Captain," she answered brightly. "This coffee is one-hundred percent certified genuine North American. I would go so far as to say that a finer cup has never been served aboard this vessel."

I grinned at her enthusiasm. "Now that I might believe," I said. "But then, I've never been partial to military-baked coffee. I'm going to ask for a favor. Now, this is not an order – as much as it is a plea."

"What's on your mind, Captain?" Hunter asked.

"I've just sent instructions to the replicator for a specialized cleaning solution that I'd like to have run through the coffee unit. After the solution has been run through no less than three times, we'll need to soak a specially-made squeegee in that same solution and push it through the supply and delivery tubes. Only when that squeegee exits the delivery tube without brown on it, are we done. This might take a few tries, but believe me, it's worth it. After that, it's critical we have the exact measure of ground coffee beans to water and that those beans are only ground moments before delivery. I assume the coffee unit will bring the water to correct temperature?" I asked hopefully.

"That's quite a lot of work," Hunter said. "Are you sure you wouldn't rather have juice or water?"

"Oh, my good man, no," I said.

"Sacrilege," Bray agreed.

I turned to her. "So you agree, good coffee is worth the effort?"

"Totally," she answered. "I just don't believe coffee gets better than this." She saluted with a cup she picked from the counter and smiled as she happily drank from it.

"Give me seventy-two hours and I'll ruin you for life," I said.

"Challenge accepted," she answered.

"Is this all storage?" Tabby asked, looking down the hallway, apparently losing interest in the coffee conversation.

"Crew quarters are on the port side," Sendrei said, pointing at one of three hatches in the aft hallway. "Engine and electronics access are through the panel in the deck. The 'tween deck provides one-hundred fifty centimeters headroom and runs the length of the ship. Starboard side, however, is a gem you'll no doubt appreciate."

"What's that?" I asked, curiosity getting the better of me as I followed him to the hatch.

"North Americans had an initiative to deal with the negative mental health effects of long-term space flights. You'll never believe the gym they put together."

"Really?" I asked. "I thought we had it pretty good on *Hotspur*, with a full boxing ring, weight equipment, running tracks and the like."

He pushed the hatch open. "Check this out."

Stepping into the room felt like entering another world entirely. While I recognized much of the equipment, it was the setting that was so different. The bulkheads were covered in vid-screen material that projected a bright blue sky overhead. As I looked around, it appeared as if we were in a forest. A light breeze smelling of pine wafted across, adding to the illusion. Along the outer wall a 125cm wide stream ran the length of the room, fully integrated with the scenery.

"A river?" I asked.

"That's backup drinking water, so don't go peeing in it," Sendrei said.

"Ewww," Tabby wrinkled her nose comically.

"The water feature can be programmed for soaking, laps or just as scenery. There are eighty different location settings, a lot of which are recordings from Earth and Mars."

"There's no dueling ring," Tabby complained.

"Machines can retract and there's a full-size dojo sparring config-uration," he said. "They really spared no expense."

"We're going to want one of these on *Intrepid*."

My comm chimed and Jonathan's voice broke in. "Captain, our apologies. There is a matter that requires your attention on the bridge."

"Copy that, Jonathan, I'm headed forward. What's the issue?" I answered, nodding at Tabby to follow.

"We believe there is a craft that follows," he answered. "It is blocking transponder signal output and is heavily armed."

"Frak," I said, accelerating to a run.

Chapter 9

DIGITUS IMPUDICUS

The whistle announced my return to the bridge, Tabby and Sendrei sprinting in right behind me. A holo projection, centered in the eight-meter-round space of the bridge, showed another sloop-sized ship menacingly close, just aft of our position. Its heading was in a direct line to the Tamu gate and exactly matched *Gaylon Brighton's*.

"Any communications?" I asked.

"Negative, Captain," Jonathan answered. "We've identified the ship as Kasumi."

"Kasumi?"

"Yes. Kasumi are distant relatives of the Felio from the opposite side of the Aeratroas region," Jonathan said, replacing the image of the ship with a male and a female Kasumi. The species did indeed resemble Felio if you didn't look too closely. Unlike Felio however, their fur was much shorter. Upon further inspection, it dawned on me that they also had hair like human or Pogona and their hands were long digits instead of paws. In the right light, it would not be difficult to mistake a Kasumi for human.

"They're pretty far from home. What do you suppose they're doing?"

"We do not believe the timing of the Kasumi ship is coincidence," Jonathan said. "As you know, the odds of a chance encounter while sailing are remote. This is mitigated somewhat in that we are sailing on a direct line between Petersburg Station and the Tamu wormhole. According to the station's records, however, the Kasumi ship did not dock for services. In short, we surmise this ship has specific interest in *Gaylon Brighton*."

"Sendrei, talk to me about their offensive capacity," I said.

"Sloop class, just as *Gaylon Brighton*." He poked his large hand into the center of the holo image, dismissed the Kasumi form, and centered a rendering of a slowly rotating ship. "Armor appears to be kinetic repulser, with shielding against nuclear and electromagnetic. It is difficult to know for sure, but what we're seeing is consistent with other high-grade ships in Dwingeloo. There are four forward mounted blasters and a single missile port. It is reasonable to expect there are also aft-mounted blasters not currently visible."

"That's aggressive," I observed. "Do their guns look big to you?" Where technology was concerned, size didn't always matter but my AI showed the turrets were forty percent larger than our own.

"Yes," he answered simply.

"You should not draw conclusions from common ancestry of Kasumi and Felio," Jonathan interjected. "The Kasumi did not rise to dominance on their home planet. Instead they share a planet with two other sentient species, one of which you interacted with – Golenti. The history of these three species vying for their home planet's resources is violent and replete with long running wars."

Flashing to a memory of the violent gangster, Goboble, I frowned. "Just keeps getting better."

"How did we become aware of this ship?" I asked.

"The ship appeared from the opposite side of Zuri," Jonathan said. "and has matched our acceleration to within half a percent, keeping a twenty-thousand-kilometer set-back."

"Show delta-v on holo."

One of the ship's many AIs accepted my command and traced a short red line in front of the Kasumi ship. At twenty thousand kilometers of separation, I wasn't concerned about immediate conflict. We were on a long journey, however, and the troubling fact was that they were gaining on us, albeit slowly.

"Project separation to when we reach Tamu wormhole," Tabby ordered, instinctively understanding my focus. The field being projected grew to show our two ships with a point of light in the distance, obviously the Tamu gate. Running at twenty-times speed, we watched as the Kasumi ship closed to within ten thousand kilometers by the time we reached the gate.

"It would not be difficult for the Kasumi to change their deceleration as they approach the gate," Sendrei observed. "Even a small delay would allow them to overtake our position."

"They'd only get a single strike at us if they did," I said, resetting the holo simulation and demonstrating the fact that coming from so far behind would cause them to rocket past the gate at high speed.

"It is an approach the ship is well built for," he said. "If I were intent on taking this ship, I would target the engines, desiring to knock out your worm-hole drive before you could transition. I would do it at this point." He grabbed the two ships in the simulation and pulled them back along their flight vectors.

"We could peel off and let them pass," I said.

"And have them wait for us at the wormhole?" Tabby asked. "That's not a good solution."

"No, don't peel off now," I said. "Let's assume Sendrei's theory is right. We peel off once we're within a few thousand kilometers of the wormhole. The big idea is we don't let them know we're concerned until it's critical. Maybe they just have issues with personal space."

"We recommend a reconsideration if they cross twelve thousand kilometers," Jonathan said.

"Sendrei, could you make that a standing order?" I asked.

"Copy that, Captain," Sendrei answered. "I will also set the ship's AI to monitor and alert all crew if the ship breaches twelve thousand kilometers."

"Thank you," I said. "I think I'll go back and help the crew unpack our supplies."

"Hold on there, flyboy," Tabby said. "Marny left word with me that I was to get you back into your exercise regimen. Why don't you give me thirty minutes on the running track, first?"

"Seriously?" I might have whined a little. "I'm wounded from pod-ball."

"I seem to recall you were quite vigorous this morning," she said.

Sendrei raised an eyebrow as he looked from Tabby to me. "North Americans believe that pain is simply the weakness leaving your body. If, with proper motivation, you can – well – do things, certainly a few minutes on a running track would not end you. A top-notch crew needs a fit captain."

"Really? You too?" I asked, returning Sendrei's broad grin. I could always tell when he was working me over, because his speech turned more formal. It was like he was adopting his previous persona as a Lieutenant in the North American Navy.

"I'll go with you," he said. "I desperately need to stretch my legs."

"I really want to be you when I grow up," I said, hanging my head as I followed him aft.

THREE DAYS LATER, we were on final approach to the wormhole and the distance between us and the Kasumi craft had dwindled to eleven thousand kilometers. I'd made the strategic decision not to react when they crossed twelve thousand kilometers, as I'd wanted to maintain the illusion of not caring. The fact was, we had no idea if our ship was faster or nimbler. I'd also hoped to see other traffic through the wormhole, possibly using it as a diversion in case things headed toward the bilge, as they so often did. In my mind, however, I'd given up on their proximity as anything but provocative.

"Delta-v is elevating," Jonathan announced. The difference between our acceleration vectors (or in this case deceleration vectors) was generally referred to as delta-v.

"Bringing weapons online," Sendrei said. "I recommend active restraints."

"All hands, let's get strapped in," I said. "We're on approach to the wormhole and if anything is going to happen, it'll be here."

Over the last three days, I'd gotten to know both Hunter and Petty Officer Bray better. Through the course of a few card games, we'd discussed the potential danger the pursuing ship signified. Bray, a veteran of several conflicts, had grimly accepted the news, understanding it was just part of the job. Hunter, on the other hand, understandably had a number of concerns. As a result, I'd been careful not to overstate the danger.

"We're secure, Captain," Bray answered a moment later.

"Copy that, Bray," I answered.

I adjusted the trim on our engines by a fraction. The move, while slight, would have us miss the wormhole by ten kilometers, a distance we could make up in a few seconds with *Gaylon Brighton's* powerful engines.

"They're matching," Tabby warned, telling me something I'd already seen.

"Copy," I answered and adjusted a bit more, pushing our eventual destination even further away. The Kasumi ship matched our changes one-for-one and in response, I continued to adjust away from the wormhole at the same time I started bleeding off our deceleration, which initially caused the distance between our ships to increase. My end game was simple; I needed to increase the distance between the two ships such that we could also zero-out delta-v with the wormhole once out of their weapon's range.

"I think they're on to you," Tabby said as I continued to flare out, away from the ideal deceleration vector with the wormhole. The Kasumi captain had changed their approach and was lining up more directly with the wormhole. Without heroic measures, they would not be able to zero-out with the wormhole any better than we could, not to mention they would not get a pass with their weapons.

"Doesn't matter. I got what I wanted." I activated the pre-programmed deceleration plan. "All hands, prepare for combat burn and brace for possible enemy fire."

"They're going to get a shot on us," Tabby said, watching a prediction path play out.

I was going to burn more fuel than I wanted and we'd have to take some on later in our journey, but I felt like I'd given us our best shot at avoiding combat with a more heavily-armed ship.

"Only if their engines and inertial systems are as good as *Gaylon Brighton's*."

I hate to admit that I mostly held my breath as we slowed to a crawl, pinned to our chairs under the heavy hand of a combat burn.

"Enemy weapons are charging," Sendrei said.

The distance that separated us was more than I'd planned for when executing the maneuver. The Kasumi ship had strong engines, but they gave up at least ten percent to *Gaylon Brighton*.

"We're out of weapon's range." I spoke with more hope than knowledge, unable to pull my eyes from the navigation path we were on. We had mere seconds before I could transition *Gaylon Brighton* through the wormhole into Tamu and I willed the ship closer.

"They're firing," Sendrei said, his voice tense but professional. "Return fire?"

"Negative," I said, knowing the Kasumi were beyond our range.

Blaster bolts fly as fast as you'd think. *Gaylon Brighton* shuddered as twin bolts impacted her aft quarter, five meters forward of the engine compartments. A familiar bang of rapid decompression vibrated through the ship no more than half a second before I engaged the wormhole drives.

My heart fluttered with worry for roughly a second and a half, the time it took to transition.

"Jonathan, status!" I demanded, even while the universe turned inside out. Jonathan would come out of the momentary stupor caused by transition more quickly than the rest of us.

"Engines are fully operational," Jonathan's firm voice announced as the light of Tamu's star began to register. "There are no ships in the immediate vicinity."

"Engage combat burn on primary navigation plan," I ordered.

"I think they holed us," Tabby said a few moments later when it became clear we were beyond immediate danger.

"Bray, Hunter, check in," I said, concerned they were close to where the powerful blaster bolts had impacted.

"We're both up, Captain," Bray answered after a few moments, her voice tight with exertion. "There's a breach forward of engine two's superstructure. Hunter and I are working through the tween with a patch. Any chance we could stay clear of rocks for a while?"

I smiled at her casual reference to rockets. It seemed that Naval officers, even NCOs, enjoyed understated swagger in the face of fire.

"Copy that, Bray," I answered. "Enemy is off the scope, but we're going to bust hump for the next sixty beats and clear the wormhole. Might be best if you hold position until we drop back from hard burn."

As much as I wanted to, under max combat burn there would be no way to see when the Kasumi ship exited the wormhole. I'd considered dropping engines and relying on our stealth armor, but we had a speed advantage. While I would take crap from Tabby for not standing our ground, a fight avoided was worth more than one in the win column.

For two minutes we sat pinned to our chairs as *Gaylon Brighton* showed the universe exactly what she was designed to do – run. "All hands, dropping burn for ten seconds to gather data and we'll resume hard burn for the Phreish wormhole."

As WE SAILED from one wormhole to the next, two things became abundantly clear. First, the Kasumi ship was either no longer pursuing us or they were doing a much better job of hiding. Second, there were a lot of sentients in the Aeratroas region of the Dwingeloo galaxy, most of whom seemed to be either heading to or coming from Abeline.

The damage we'd taken on *Gaylon Brighton* turned out to be easily fixed. Once we cut from combat burn, Hunter and Bray vented a small section of the hull, applied a temporary patch and then installed a temporary bulkhead just in case the patch failed. The latter was a step I hadn't previously considered and would be something I'd add to future emergency fixes.

"We are eighteenth in queue," Sendrei announced as I joined him on the bridge for the start of my watch. The structure was something I hadn't expected, but so many ships moved through the wormholes in the central core of planets that the wormholes were actively managed. At eighteen deep, the queue for the gate from Kneble to Mandhan (the system where our destination, Abeline, was located) wasn't even the longest we'd run into in the last few jumps. Although, according to local news feeds, we'd hit a particularly busy time due to a bi-annual, religious pilgrimage by a sect of peaceful, armadillo-faced aliens.

"That's not horrible," I said, looking at the lineup Sendrei showed on the holo projector. Upon inspection, I realized we were eighteenth in line with another forty behind us and he'd probably spent the better part of the last half of his shift in line.

"At least we're finally getting there," he said. "That exercise room is nice, but three ten-days aboard makes a man look forward to just about any port."

"How are we doing for fuel?" I asked, mostly to prompt my AI, which projected current levels onto my HUD.

"Down to a quarter," he said. "Good thing we're just about there. I don't know if you noticed, but our Kasumi friends have rejoined the party."

"Frak, seriously?" I asked, studying the line of ships queuing to pop through to the Abeline system. Sure enough, the Kasumi ship was fifteen ships behind us. They had stowed turrets close-in to the hull.

"I don't believe they'll be a problem," he said. "I've been reading about how the central core deals with unprovoked aggression in high traffic areas. It's not pretty. Basically, no matter the grudge, they don't want to stop the flow of commerce. Whoever shoots first or otherwise acts out can be declared a FFAT."

"FFAT?"

"Free-for-all target. You can thank me for the acronym," Sendrei said. "FFATs are like someone dropping a bucket of cinnamon rolls in a pen full of pigs."

I struggled for a moment to work through the analogy. "The rolls get dirty?"

Sendrei tipped his head back and laughed deeply. It was one of the things I really enjoyed about his personality. When he laughed, the world seemed to smile. "I'm guessing you haven't spent a lot of time around hogs."

"And you have?" I asked.

"Wasn't always a Navy man or a prisoner," he said. "I grew up on a hog confinement. My dad owned the place, but he wanted to make sure us kids understood the value of a credit. Hogs, by and large, are smart animals and they've a keen sense of smell. You'd be mauled just trying to walk a bucket of cinnamon rolls into the middle of a pen, much less get a chance to drop them onto the ground."

"You're saying they like cinnamon," I said, chuckling.

"Yup. That and everything else that's remotely edible. They also don't mind running over whatever is in their path to get it," he said. "You following me?"

"Free-for-all is bad for people. Pigs like 'em," I answered.

"Yeah, don't be the bucket of cinnamon rolls," he said, then blinked at me while furrowing his brow. "Are you intentionally trying to make this hard?"

"Farm animal analogies don't make much sense to me," I said. "I didn't have real meat until I was seventeen stans old. I didn't see a farm animal until we visited Freedom Station and even then, I wasn't extra impressed with how it worked out. They're messy."

"Here we go," he said as the line suddenly started moving again. The queue allowed twenty ships to pass through in one direction before reversing and allowing ships from the opposite side to traverse the passage.

"Frak, that Kasumi ship is making a move," I said, watching the ship jump out of position. "Switch with me. I'm taking helm, you take fire control."

"Copy," Sendrei agreed. "Helm is yours."

"All hands, strap in. Kasumi sloop is on scope and potentially making a move. We could be jumping to combat burn." I watched Sendrei unlimber the turrets and orient them in the Kasumi's general direction.

"Abasi ship, *Gaylon Brighton,* you are warned, provocative actions are strictly barred in the Central Core controlled space," an alien that resembled Pogona appeared on my forward screen. "Please respond acknowledging your understanding of Code-12 violations."

"Central Core, this is *Gaylon Brighton,*" I answered. "We acknowledge Central Core authority regarding Code-12."

"The Kasumi is closing on us," Sendrei said.

"You will lock down your turrets or risk being found in violation of Code-12," the alien said. It almost appeared that we were boring him or her, I wasn't sure which.

I made up my mind. "Lock it down, Sendrei."

"Copy that, Captain," Sendrei replied, spinning the turrets back and allowing the stubby barrels to rest in recessed cradles.

"What in Jupiter is going on?" Tabby asked, flying through the bridge hatch, jumping into a bridge station chair and wrestling with the restraints.

"Kasumi ship," I pointed at the ship on the holo that had jumped out of position and was slowly sailing over the line of queued ships.

"What is it doing?"

"I'd say getting a look at us," I said, pressing my middle finger into the armored glass above me as they sailed over the top of us. It was an immature gesture, likely lost on an alien species, but it was truly the only thing I had left.

"Yeah, nice," Tabby said. "That showed 'em."

"It's not as off-topic as you might expect," Sendrei said. "They will now need to worry about your capacity to fire arrows at them."

I looked at him, confused. "Is this another farm analogy?" I asked.

"Older," he chuckled.

Chapter 10

ABELINE

We watched as the Kasumi ship sailed slowly over the top of us. It was a ballsy move that begged us to take action. Someone either didn't want us making it to Abeline or wanted to take us out of the action altogether. Unfortunately, the list of those who might want to do us harm wasn't short. That said, the expense had to be substantial to hire someone to hunt us down over such a long trip.

"You were wise in not engaging, Captain," Jonathan said. "We believed there was a thirty-eight percent chance that you would. Do you care to explain why you decided against taking action? Was it simply a matter of the Central Core authority's threat?"

"That part was hard to ignore," I answered, sluggishly moving *Gaylon Brighton* forward as one-by-one the ships ahead of us disappeared through the wormhole. "The fact that the Kasumi had their weapons stowed tipped me off that they were trying to get us to flinch."

"It provided valuable insight," Jonathan said.

"How's that?" Tabby asked.

"Your enemy is intent on your destruction. There was no desire for conversation," he answered. "Did you know that almost all sentient species have a desire for what you refer to as closure?"

"As in if they're going to kill you, they want to see it happen?" I asked.

"Precisely, in this case," he replied. "We believe this limits the likely perpetrators."

"You don't think Genteresk sent them, then?" I asked. Up until now, I'd believed Belvakuski, the Pogona pirate we'd defeated, was somehow behind the threatening actions. Of course, the fact she'd been recently executed made that unlikely.

"No. Pogona tribes value strength," he answered. "Sending another to eliminate competition would show weakness. For Genteresk to regain prominence, they will need to defeat Loose Nuts most publicly."

"Not sure how this helps," I said and then announced. "All hands, prepare for transition to the Mandhan system."

"It helps tremendously," Jonathan said. "Is it true you find it difficult to know what is behind the Kasumi attack on *Gaylon Brighton*?"

"Yes," I answered, only paying half attention as I engaged the wormhole drive.

For a moment, the universe blinked from existence before reappearing. I focused on the heavy traffic surrounding the wormhole leading back to the Kneble system. A flashing 'imminent collision' warning caught my attention, and I tossed the flight stick to the side and accelerated away from the path of a ship transiting the wormhole.

The visual confusion of near-space was almost overwhelming. Small ships flitted about, racing between massive structures which had been constructed near the wormhole. Closely packed and numerous, the ships formed wide traffic lanes between the two areas. Ship-sized advertising billboards hung next to each structure, showing vids of aliens doing all sort of different things including consuming beverages and playing sports. I blinked, trying to make sense of some of the other screens, their images completely alien. Once again, my display showed the potential of collision and I responded, peeling off to starboard, and toward the steel city. These emergencies continued every few minutes and I tried diligently to keep us from crashing into the smaller ships that were jetting everywhere.

"Jonathan, is there a traffic lane or something available for navigation assistance?"

"Affirmative, Captain," he answered.

Traffic lane overlays showed on my HUD. Somehow, I'd drifted into a lane painted red. Big, fluffy arrows chugged toward us in the wrong direction. The arrows, however, weren't the only thing coming our way. I dropped the stick, barely avoiding an ugly rectangular ship that had few lights on it and did not seem to mind the prospect of collision.

"Port," Tabby offered. "Declination twenty degrees."

I searched the lanes and saw what she had, a slow-moving lane with blue arrows moving in the direction we were headed. I rolled *Gaylon Brighton* port and downward catching my breath once we were safe.

"As we were saying," Jonathan continued and I struggled to remember what the conversation had even been about. "Eliminating Belvakuski leaves those sympathetic to Goboble. It is our opinion that his syndicate was not sufficiently funded to pay for a bounty hunter."

"Who said anything about a bounty hunter?" I asked.

"Piss off any Kasumi lately?" Tabby asked. "No way would a pirate chase us all the way from Santaloo system. We're just not that easy of targets. I just don't see who else would be gunning for us like this."

"You are forgetting something," Sendrei said, nodding at Jonathan.

"What?" I asked, understanding starting to permeate my consciousness. "Seriously?"

"We should be surprised it has not happened sooner," Sendrei said.

"Who? What hasn't happened?" Tabby asked, not appreciating being left to wonder.

"Kroerak," I said. "They think Kroerak hired a Kasumi bounty hunter to take us out."

"It is the most logical answer. You have been present at too many

Kroerak encounters. To Kroerak, one defeat such as on Cradle could be a coincidence." He was referring to a much earlier action when we'd discovered tens of thousands of humans being bred in captivity by Kroerak as an exotic food source. With Mars Protectorate's help, we'd not only rescued the people, but also handed the Kroerak a significant defeat. "But in fact, Loose Nuts was instrumental in the Kroerak defeat at Earth, as well as the capture of a long-buried Kroerak cruiser that was the source of much intelligence and research."

"I can't imagine someone taking money from Kroerak," I said. "That's suicidal."

"Bounty hunters and assassins are not particularly well known for their strategic view of things," Sendrei said.

"It is possible the noble that Sendrei defeated was able to communicate our knowledge of the Piscivoru," Jonathan said. "The Kroerak's irrational fear of a nearly extinct species and the ability of Loose Nuts to successfully complete otherwise low-percentage-odds missions could explain the presence of a persistent hunter."

"Neat," I said. "Set in a course for Abeline."

A path appeared on my HUD, but with all the traffic around the city, it would take an hour to break free. Fortunately, it was only another thirty-hour burn from that point.

"Why do you suppose that wormhole is so busy?" Tabby asked as I accelerated to the max velocity allowed in the traffic lane.

"There are seven wormholes in the Mandhan system, all of which *Gaylon Brighton* could reach within twenty-four hours," Jonathan explained. "The city we find ourselves in is called Mandhan City for obvious reasons. Originally it was just a platform for short-term storage of trade-goods. The growth you see here has happened within the last four hundred stans."

"Business must be good," Tabby said, gawking through the armor glass at the bright lights and towering structures that surrounded us. Just like the first time we visited Mars, I had a strong sense of how insignificant we all were in this universe. It was hard to imagine the Kroerak thinking we were important enough to send a bounty hunter. However, if one thing was clear, it was that someone was chasing us and they weren't playing nice.

———————

"YOU KNOW, you'd think all this alien stuff would be more ... you know ... alien," Tabby said. "If I didn't know better, I'd say we were on approach to Puskar Stellar, not Abeline – a completely alien world in a frakking random galaxy."

"Not so crazy to me," Todd Hunter said. We'd invited him and Larkin Bray to join us on the bridge during our approach to Abeline. Planetfall wasn't the sort of thing most people got to experience in their life and I wasn't about to deny either of them the awe-inspiring moment.

"You're the one who's crazy, Hunter," Larkin said. "Don't you wonder why humanity and all these aliens build structures, planets, hell even societies that are basically the same?"

"Do you really believe life is so different for humans and other species? Basic needs like eating and the desire for safety aren't unique to humans. Cooperation between species is its own selection mechanism. Those who cooperate are naturally more powerful than loners," Hunter argued.

"I suppose," Larkin answered. "Alcohol though? I might understand things like electricity, iron and things like that. Or the way ships are shaped. The fact that all species might want to see out the front through glass. But beer? There are a million things that are familiar, but don't necessarily seem like they would translate across species. It's just so much to take in."

I smiled, Larkin was struggling with the same questions I had.

"It's probably because we're both from Sol," I said. "But I'm with Larkin on this one, Todd. I feel like I'm justifying why it makes sense that things are familiar."

"The human psyche is fantastic in its ability to adapt to new stimulus," Jonathan said. "We've observed that humans from Earth are dismissing or assimilating changes presented to them within moments of observation."

"Example?" I asked.

"Describe the skin of a Golenti," he said.

"Not that much different than human," I said. "Dark gray, has a rough texture and covers their body, just like our skin does."

"Golenti skin resembles stone much more than it does human tissue," Jonathan said. "The *only* similarity is that it covers the host. The stone skin is a covering that develops over time."

"A better example is you, Jonathan," Larkin said.

"Fantastic, Ms. Bray," Jonathan said. "Why?"

"There are no obvious physical similarities between us," she said.

"And yet, Liam – and Loose Nuts for that matter – has accepted us into his tribe almost from the point we were discovered."

"And now we're back to Todd's point," I said. "Success from cooperation. We would not have survived without Jonathan's help. Our trust was well placed."

"The opposite is also true," Jonathan agreed. "You have come to our rescue more than once."

"Great conversation and all," Tabby interrupted. "But I'm going to need a navigation plan pretty soon."

"Bhusal," I said, pinching coordinates for a transfer station in an industrial park within the city called Bhusal. I flicked the coordinates to Tabby, knowing she could work out a nav plan. "Nick has a shipping company meeting us there. Apparently, they've been on standby for over a ten-day. They're really excited by his bot designs."

"Construction and stevedore bots?" Tabby asked. "They're hardly his designs. He filched the intellectual property from Mars Protectorate."

"And now they're ours," I said, not the least bit abashed by the direction Nick was taking. He'd negotiated fair and square for the rights to the designs. "Even better, secure docking in Bhusal is expensive, but we have use of it for twenty hours, on Nick. What do you say? Hunter, Larkin, you up for a little bar crawling?"

"What of the mission?" Larkin asked.

"Whoa, there, Bray," Hunter said. "If Captain offers a night out, don't ruin it for everyone else. Haven't you had enough of scrubbing O2 filters and checking gray water levels?"

"Maybe you've forgotten what we're up against. Do you think the Kroerak are taking a night off for beers?" Larkin asked, her voice rising. The petty officer, with her wavy blonde hair and fair skin was pretty by most standards, although I wasn't dumb enough to say that to Tabby. When she got annoyed, however, her fair complexion gave her away. Todd was clearly pushing her buttons as a blotchy red blush had already crept up her neck and onto her cheeks.

"Take it down a notch, kids," I said. "This is one of those moments when we get to have our beer and drink it too. Our contact works out of a bar called the Nexus."

"Our selection of industrial parks was not accidental," Jonathan said. "The Nexus is located two kilometers from where we'll set down. I've taken the liberty of manufacturing hooded cloaks. The weather over Bhusal is rainy, which is to our advantage. While there are many species on Abeline, humans will stand out. It is advisable that while on the street you keep your hoods raised."

"I am not comfortable leaving *Gaylon Brighton* unmanned," Sendrei said.

"We are leaving a contingent behind," Jonathan said. "*Gaylon Brighton* will be secure."

"Who's staying?" Sendrei asked.

"Twelve from our Phentera group," Jonathan said.

"I retract my objection, Captain," Sendrei said, his voice suddenly serious. Ever since he and Jonathan had spent a couple of months depending on each other for survival aboard the Kroerak ship, his respect and insight for the alien collective had done nothing but grow.

"Check out the surface of Abeline," Tabby interrupted. "Tell me if you can see any part of it that isn't covered by city."

My eyes flitted between the holographic rendering of the planet that sat just off Tabby's left side and what I could see through the armor-glass view screen ahead of us. Wherever the planet was cast in shadow, lights dotted the surface. Tabby was right, from the planet's northern pole all the way to the southern end, there didn't appear to be any open spaces, large bodies of water, or any geographical markers other than cityscape. Sure, there was variation in the density of the lights, but nothing at all biological visible from this distance.

"How in the world do they feed the population?" Hunter asked.

"Abeline imports eighty percent of food consumed by the population," Jonathan said. "Food production, however, exceeds the population's caloric consumption. Growth is limited to high value crops which are all cultivated in enclosed plants where environmental factors are strictly controlled."

"Let me guess, the property value is too high to actually grow crops," Hunter replied. "What a crazy place."

"That is a logical conclusion, Mr. Hunter," Jonathan answered. "According to public information, the amount of capital required to acquire the use of even a small amount of land places it well beyond practical limits for growing ordinary crops."

"With all that import/export business, no wonder they're interested in Nick's stevedore bots," I said. "I tell you, that guy is always one step ahead."

"You might want to take a seat," Tabby said. "Abeline has given us permission to enter Bhusal airspace and they didn't give us much of a window. I'm going to take us in by hand."

Without further warning, she banked hard to port and surged down toward the dark side of Abeline. We descended peacefully for a few minutes until flashing collision trajectories started popping onto the forward vid screen as the traffic increased. Unlike the semi-controlled lanes around Mandhan City, there appeared to be no rhyme or reason in the vehicle flow. Ships of varying sizes darted here and there, dodging each other, often with only a dozen meters to spare. I struggled with a desire to take the controls and had to remind myself that Tabby was every bit the pilot I was.

"We're gonna die," Hunter exclaimed, when a ship passed above us with a very narrow margin.

"Stow it, crewman," I said, chuckling. Tabby had a rhythm to her flying which I was in tune with. I could see her lining up moves well in advance. Most likely in response to Hunter's exclamation, Tabby twisted *Gaylon Brighton* around in a spiral as she accelerated. Flames of violently compressed atmosphere heralded our arrival and the ship bucked as Tabby fought to keep to her intended path.

Done with showboating, Tabby snapped the stick back and leveled out our flight at six thousand meters above the planet's surface. We'd formally and spectacularly entered Bhusal's airspace. Ironically, traffic lanes popped up on the vid-screens and, sure enough, Tabby had us locked in to the exact spot we'd been assigned. The cityscape below primarily consisted of low buildings, most dark, except for regularly-spaced security lights.

"Local time is 0030," Sendrei announced. "Looks like the streets are rolled up for the night."

"Industrial park," Tabby said. "We're up there." She pinched the coordinates of our destination and tossed them forward. My AI recognized the gesture and highlighted our destination in a cluster of buildings. As if in response to her action, a bright green light flashed three times and went dark.

"They're signaling us," Larkin said, obviously having seen the same thing we had.

"Copy that. Bray, Hunter, go aft and suit up with the cloaks Jonathan replicated. Also, I want you both to check out a flechette pistol. I just got a ping from Nick's contact. They're waiting at the loading bay," I said.

"Aye, aye," Larkin responded and unclipped from the seat where she'd been sitting.

"You got this, Tabbs?" I asked.

"Roger that."

I grinned around the room. "Sendrei, let's go make some money."

The two of us followed Bray and Hunter back to the armory, picking up the dark cloaks Jonathan had manufactured.

"Ever read 'The Hobbit'?" Sendrei asked, pulling the cloak around his shoulders.

"Book?" I responded, my AI showing a picture of an ancient text and a vid that had been produced roughly around the same time. I furrowed my brow as I watched a squat human with furry feet running through grass, wearing a hooded cloak.

He strapped a steel sword to his back, its scabbard well hidden by the cloak. "Never mind."

I picked a new handgun from the rack. It was replicated from a recent piece of intellectual property Munay had procured. The owner of the IP was Springfield Armory, a North American firm. During the short war with the Kroerak, they'd released their IP to be freely used by any military. Since this mission was still on point, we'd been grandfathered in. The handgun was called a 1911. I hadn't had a chance to test-fire it yet, but it felt comfortably at home in my hand. From the rifle rack, I grabbed a blaster rifle, handed it to Sendrei and picked a second one for myself.

A slight jarring transmitted through the deck, alerting us to the fact that we'd set down. Sendrei and I joined Larkin and Todd aft in the cargo area, which was over two-thirds full of crates.

"Liam, we have company," Tabby said. "I'm shutting her down."

"Copy that, Tabbs." I placed my hand against the security panel that allowed the cargo ramp to start lowering. Holding an electronic pad out to Bray, I nodded. "You know how to run a cargo transfer, Larkin?"

"Try being an Petty Officer without," she said, accepting the pad with a quick smile.

"You know, I've been meaning to ask you, what do you think of the coffee now that we're cleaning the pipes out regularly?" I asked. The difference in taste was obvious to me, but I wasn't sure if she'd notice.

"The difference is quite remarkable," she said. "All we needed to do was keep the machine cleaner? When I served in the Navy, we scrubbed those pots all the time and ran soapy water through. Not sure I understand what we did differently this time."

"Coffee has an oil that isn't easily broken down with soap and water," I said. "That solution I gave you is the perfect antidote."

"Someone should tell the North American naval brass," she said.

Our conversation was interrupted by the appearance of four humanoid figures who were behind the ship. A heavy rain poured down and I couldn't discern what species they might be, beyond the fact that they were slightly wider, shorter, and had pinched faces resembling a rat.

"Captain Hoffen, welcome to Bhusal." Over my AI's translation, I heard a high-pitched squeaking that did nothing to dispel the impression of a rat.

"Greetings," I answered, holding my hand out for a shake. I'd long since learned that translation units had the capacity to communicate common gestures. Ratman accepted my hand loosely and reciprocated the shake. "Much appreciated."

"We are most excited to receive the test units from Loose Nuts Corporation," he continued, his squeaking a bit distracting, as was the heavy rain.

"Would you like a demonstration?" I asked. "Just tell Petty Officer Bray where you'd like the crates and stand back."

"Oh, no," he answered, concerned. "The units are too precious to risk while rain falls."

"However you want to do it," I said. "We'll bring the crates to the end of the loading ramp and you can do with them what you see fit."

"Very gracious," he answered, bowing and gesturing. A crowd of similarly shaped rat-faced humanoids scurried from beneath the overhang five meters from where we'd set down.

"Petty Officer, just make sure we sign 'em all off before they're on the deck," I said.

"Roger that, Captain," she said, as three of the rat-men walked up the ramp, intent on picking up the crates.

"No, no," I said, holding my free hand up and standing in their way. "We'll bring them to you."

My movement was sufficient to make them unsure of their steps and they held up.

"Petty Officer, show 'em," I said.

"Roger," she answered and tapped on the pad she held.

Surprising the rat-men, one of the stevedore bots we had lashed to the cargo bay's bulkhead freed itself, swung over and grasped the first crate. With all the similarities we'd found between cultures, I was surprised no one here had developed something similar to our bots. The machines were nothing more than an anti-gravity unit with long bar-like arms that could either slide beneath a crate or grasp it on the sides.

With load in tow, the stevedore bot paused next to Petty Officer Bray long enough for her to bump the ident on the crate and record it in the transfer log. The rat-men stumbled backward down the ramp as the bot slowly moved toward them, beeping a warning because they were standing in the way. With a clear path, the first stevedore bot lowered the crate to the deck, released it and turned back to the hold, passing the second bot now laden with a similar crate. It didn't take long for the home team to understand the rules of the game and they moved to the growing pile, lifting the crates by hand and jogging back through the rain.

For thirty minutes, the scene repeated itself until the hold was finally empty with the exception of three larger crates, the design of which made me smile. I hadn't realized we'd packed the Popeyes (mechanized infantry suits).

"Is that everything, Petty Officer?" I asked, already knowing it was, having checked the bill of lading.

"Aye, Captain."

The original rat-faced man approached and we exchanged electronic acknowledgements of successful transfer.

"I don't know about you all," I said, when the Bhusal natives were finally gone. "But I'm starting to feel a bit thirsty."

"One moment," Jonathan said as he joined us in the cargo bay. He walked over to a man-sized crate that was held fast against the starboard bulkhead. The side of the crate swung open and I did a double take. Seemingly asleep was another figure, identical to Jonathan. Jonathan walked up to his doppelganger and a halo appeared around both of them. The projection we knew to be our Jonathan dissipated, leaving behind a floating, smooth black egg-shaped object about the size of a human head. As the floating egg and the boxed mannequin came in contact, the sleeping figure's eyes fluttered open.

"That's not weird," I said, turning back to the aft cargo hatch that had closed, locking it.

"We felt it would reduce confusion to limit our occupation to only one humanoid host at a time. We also believe a corporeal form in an unfamiliar environment is desirable." Jonathan's voice came from the figure that stepped from the crate and I struggled to rectify the fact that he'd moved residences. Well at least most of them had.

"Might have been easier if we'd been drinking," I said, chuckling.

Chapter 11

INFORMATION DROP

We'd landed in a terminal at the edge of an industrial park. The loading dock was at ground level and surrounded by soaring stacks of private hangars. The opening Tabby had dropped into was more than wide enough for three *Gaylon Brightons*. Upon off-loading Nick's cargo and verifying receipt of payment, we'd received instructions regarding which of the myriad hangars had been reserved for us.

"Hang on, folks," I said as I lifted *Gaylon Brighton* from the dock and spun slowly to orient her tail to the mostly-full honey-comb of hangar bays. As much as I loved my older ships, *Hotspur* and *Sterra's Gift*, I had to admit that *Gaylon Brighton* was as smooth as silk when it came to tight maneuvering. With excellent visibility provided by the ship's sensor packages and an assist from the AI, I backed in. The landing struts flexed as we settled and I found it difficult to tell we'd actually come to a rest.

"You're getting better at that," Tabby quipped.

I smirked. We'd always competed when it came to sailing, and backing into a berth had occasionally been a place where I'd, let's say, marked up a few bulkheads.

"Backward is stupid," I said. "Everyone ready?" I pulled the cape's hood over my head and whisked past the milling crew.

"Flechettes still okay?" Hunter asked.

"Weapons are acceptable within Bhusal as long as they are within plain sight," Sendrei said. "It is also allowed to cover them by coat while transiting a public walkway."

Once we exited the airlock, I turned back, placing my hand on the security pad. Inadvertently, I looked through the glass. Jonathan's hovering, egg-shaped twin seemed to be staring back out at us.

"Are your Phentera boys going to be okay, Jonathan?" I asked. "They look lonely."

"I assure you. They are satisfied with their role," he said. "It is unusual for our collective to experience physical separation. They are, as you might say, seeing us off."

"Aww," Tabby said, wrapping an arm around Jonathan's shoulders. "That's kind of cute, if you think about it."

I chuckled as a range of emotions crossed Jonathan's face until he finally resumed his usual, passive gaze. The collective could quickly process and understand new situations, but some of the subtleties of human expression still caused them confusion.

At the back of the ship's berth we found a locked door which opened after a security challenge. We crossed through into a rounded hallway that encircled the entire docking terminal, giving access to the individual bays. Regular openings on the outside wall provided a view of the city, and misty rain gusted in, pelting us.

"This way," I said, following the light blue arrows that seemed to be painted on the walkway, but were actually projected onto my eye. It was getting late and I was concerned we might miss our opportunity to meet Jonathan's contact.

"I recommend against the lift system," Jonathan said as we approached metal doors. "The use of gravity technology is limited within Aeratroas region and this building utilizes a mechanical lift."

An alternative path displayed and without hesitation, I redirected to a second set of doors which placed us on a wide set of stairs.

"What's in the pack?" I asked.

He lightly tapped the bag beneath his cloak. "We have provided trade goods."

"I won't even ask."

We finally reached the bottom of the stairs and exited onto a darkened street. The bar was less than a couple of kilometers, so I picked up the pace. Having fallen in next to Sendrei, I continued the conversation. "What do you make of the supposed bounty hunter we ran into?"

"We have not seen the last of them," he said. He turned and allowed a small barrel to show from under his cloak.

"Pfft." The sound of propellent warned me of something being fired.

Sendrei smiled as he saw my questioning look. "One can never have too many sensors deployed in enemy territory," he said with a shrug.

"Paranoid much?" I asked.

"Yes," he answered sincerely.

With access to a sensor at ten meters elevation, my HUD filled in details I was missing. Instead of being alone on the darkened, rainy street, I discovered two souls hunkered down, cleverly hidden in the shadow and obscured by a blanket. I gave the mystery guests my full attention as we passed, keeping at least five meters away from their location. They were obviously aware of our presence, but grew still, not wanting our attention.

We continued along the darkened street and I wondered just what was inside the buildings we passed. It was hard to imagine a planet covered entirely by manmade structures. The miner in me was boggled by the raw materials required for such a venture. The buildings we walked past weren't in great shape. The tang of rust was in the air, as was the odd smell I'd come to associate with a city, which always seemed worse with precipitation.

Tabby drew up next to me. "We're being followed."

"Not seeing it," I said, inspecting my HUD, expecting my AI to highlight her concern.

"No. It's something I'm hearing," she said. "Soft footfalls, scrapes against metal. Stay alert."

I unbuckled the strap holding my 1911 slug thrower firmly in its holster. "Gotcha. We're not far from our destination."

We rounded the final corner in our trek to the Nexus bar. At the end of the street, about two hundred meters ahead, was a conical building illuminated with dim purple and green lights. Above a pair of black double doors, blinking orange script alternated with the picture of a bubbly drink in a narrow glass. My AI promptly translated the alien text to read 'Nexus.'

A blinking warning on my HUD alerted me to the presence of someone on the roof of an adjacent building. By the time I turned, the figure had disappeared. Sendrei's sensors, however, had captured a picture and froze it in place. It was the angular face of a woman covered by light-colored fur. Atop her head were cat ears. I didn't need Jonathan's pronouncement to know that she was Kasumi and concluded she was likely the same Kasumi who had followed us from the Santaloo system.

I withdrew my pistol from its holster and held it beneath my cloak as I pushed the group into a jog. Covering the last two hundred meters seemed to take a lifetime and I was relieved to finally reach the bar. Pushing my back against the building, I pulled open the door as I scanned the tops of the buildings around us. The Kasumi must have known we'd seen her, as the sensor didn't detect her or any other movement. Our group entered the building.

"I'll hang out here for a few," Tabby said, not following the rest of the team as they moved deeper into the sparsely populated room. Instead, she stepped to a table close to the entry where she could size up the bar's occupants as well as any new arrivals.

"Copy," I agreed. Being separated from the group put Tabby at some risk, but she would be able to intercept trouble if it followed us through the door.

Nexus bar was both foreign and familiar. Just about every humanoid sentient we'd ever met seemed to share three things relevant to a bar: the enjoyment of an intoxicating beverage, a desire to sit and relax while enjoying said drink, and a desire for communication or entertainment while doing so. In short, most bars – even alien bars – followed a familiar pattern.

"This look okay?" Sendrei asked, gesturing to two tables along the wall.

"That should work," I agreed.

"I'm going to get something to drink," Hunter said. "You with me, Bray?"

"Of course. A sailor needs to drink. Suppose they have vodka?" she asked, following behind him.

He waited for her to catch up. "They have to have something like that."

"Think they'll be okay?" I asked, my mind flitting back to a crew member we'd lost once before in a bar.

"We're right here," Sendrei said. "It should be fine."

I sat in a chair with my back to the wall and looked out over the room. A multi-armed robotic bartender stood behind the counter of a circular bar. Bottles filled the clear shelves all around the central hub behind him. The bartender had moved to stand in front of where Hunter and Bray had pulled up stools and was filling glasses as they spoke.

Movement across the room caught my attention as a circular, meter-and-a-half-diameter platform lowered from the ceiling. Through the center of the platform was a pole and currently wrapped around this pole were shapely, albeit furry legs. As the platform continued to lower, I found it difficult to pull my eyes away from the scantily dressed Kasumi female who danced slowly to the background music.

"Frak, is that her?" I asked, resting my hand on Sendrei's arm and leaning over to him.

"It is the female from atop the building," he answered, quietly. "We do not know that it is she who hunts us."

"Better than fair chance," Tabby said, pulling a chair next to mine.

"Our contact is the bartender," Jonathan said. "His name is Zeke Steele and he prefers to be simply referred to as Zeke."

"Are you in contact with him?" I asked.

"He knows why we are here," Jonathan said. "He does not trust electronic communication and prefers to meet in close physical proximity."

"He's a robot," I said. "Isn't that the definition of electronic communication?"

"The translation of biological or analog signals to discrete electronic signals creates a unique challenge when attempting hostile, networked penetration. It is a reasonable precaution on his part," Jonathan said.

I tried to untangle what he'd just said. "You're saying he doesn't trust you?"

"That is correct. Zeke Steele does not trust our sentient collective," he answered. "We mean him no harm, but he has wisely constructed defenses against us."

"Can you guys keep things friendly out here?" I asked, looking from Tabby to Sendrei.

"Get me a drink before you go," Tabby said, kicking back so her chair leaned against the wall.

"Sendrei?"

He removed the pack Jonathan had given him. "Nothing for me."

Taking the pack, I followed Jonathan to the bar and slid in next to Hunter. "Find something you like?" I asked.

"The man's got a crazy long list," he said, lifting a glass of dark brown liquid in Zeke Steele's direction. "And he can make literally anything. This is an ale from Zuri. I'd swear he imports it, because I can't tell the difference. Doesn't make sense how he'd have it all the way out here, though."

"Two words," Bray said, finishing off a narrow glass of a clear drink that had a splash of purple color in it. "Gift. Horse." As Larkin set the finished drink on the counter, she gestured to Zeke, pointing at her glass.

"What?" Hunter asked. "And you might want to slow down. That's your third one already."

"You never look a gift horse in the mouth," she said, her words not exactly slurring, but she was starting to lose some function. "And, hells bells, my man, everyone knows it takes four to get a good buzz. Don't be such a killjoy."

I smiled. Petty Officer Bray was a consummate professional on the ship. This was an entirely new side of her. I reached into my pocket, pulled out two med-patches, and placed them on the bar. They would clear up intoxication within minutes. "Knock yourselves out, kids," I said. "Life is definitely too short." It was a comment I'd remember later, but at the time it seemed the right thing to say.

"A drink, Liam Hoffen?" Zeke Steele's voice had a slightly mechanical edge to it.

When we first entered the bar, I'd assumed Zeke to be no more than a robotic bartender. That is, I didn't know he was sentient. His slightly stiff movements and speech intonations certainly supported my assumption, but I wasn't about to underestimate him.

"Maybe you have a suggestion? I like a little lighter taste than what Mr. Hunter is drinking," I said. "And how about whatever Bray there is drinking for my fiancée."

"Very well," He pulled two glasses from beneath the counter with two of his four arms, filling them with spouts held by the other two arms and extending them to me. "We will allow credit to accumulate to fifty credits. Do you agree?"

I looked at the bubbling blue liquid in the first glass and then to the clear drink in a narrow glass that resembled the one Bray was drinking from. Clearly the blue liquid was for me.

"What's this?" I asked.

"Marfon ale," he answered, still with the mechanical edge to his voice. "The coloring suggests a sweet flavor, but I assure you, you will find it to be most delightful. Do you accept the terms as I have outlined them?"

"Oh, right. Sure," I agreed. He released both glasses and I walked the drink back to Tabby, leaving my pack behind on the chair.

"That's quite a drink you have there," Tabby needled after I handed her drink over and kept the blue concoction for myself.

I shrugged. "When in Rome." I lifted the drink to smell it and was surprised to discover hops. Without further hesitation I took a drink. Surprisingly, it had a nice, light taste and wasn't a bit sweet – as Zeke had promised. I set the glass on the table and turned back to the bar. "Back in a few."

"You want to talk?" Zeke Steele asked. I was shocked at the lack of pretense.

"Sure. You want to do it here?"

"Follow me," he said and glided to the far end of the bar.

Jonathan and I followed. I could feel the eyes of the Kasumi dancer on us as we passed in front of her elevated stage and I fought to not look up, trusting that Tabby would be watching.

A warning chimed in my ear as we entered a plain room behind Steele. The room was heavily shielded from EM and once the door was shut, we'd be cut off from the outside world. I suppose I shouldn't have been surprised by the precaution.

"You have placed Zeke Steele in grave danger by requesting the information," Steele started.

He turned to face us, rotating at his narrow, circular waist. He wasn't much to look at – a narrow, shiny steel torso that raised and lowered on a thick piston and was connected to tripod legs with large, rubberized wheels. His arms were bulky with one more segment than most humanoids had, and each hand had five fingers, complete with opposable thumbs.

"The information was transmitted with highest level encryption," Jonathan said.

"The void chatters that Kroerak seek the destruction of Loose Nuts. A contract of high value has been offered for your destruction. You are at great risk in Bhusal. My employee, Miko, followed you from the docking terminal. There is a team of hunters on your trail. They will take you when you leave Nexus this morning."

"They might try," I growled.

"Kasumi hunters are very good," he answered. "Survival is estimated at forty percent."

"Feels like a discount on information is in order in that case," I said. "In that we won't be around to use it and all."

Gears whirred as Steele rose and turned so that his eyes were on level with my own. "Humor is not detectable. Do you value your lives so little as to ignore the danger you have found yourself within?"

"We've faced down Kroerak hordes on more than a couple occasions," I said. "A handful of angry cat-people aren't exactly at the top of our enemy list. We're here to learn of the Piscivoru. Did we come to the right place or are we wasting our time?" I stared into the mechanical face that still considered me, looking for any sort of tell. Steele's expression was unchanged as I mentioned the species he was thought to have information regarding.

"I know of the Piscivoru, but the information has value," he said. "What have you to trade for it?"

"Anything in the bag," I said, setting it on the table.

"What is in this bag?"

"A regular trove of treasures," I bluffed as I opened it slightly so I could figure out what Sendrei had packed. I smiled and nodded my head as I recognized the contents. "Ever have coffee?"

"I have not. What is it?"

"A drink that's consumed by better than half the entire adult population of humanity," I said.

"That is a market not currently available to me," he answered.

"Surely you've noticed we're all basically the same. Human, Pogona, Felio. You name a humanoid and I'll tell you, they're a fresh market just waiting to be converted."

"I would sample this product," he said.

"What, so you can do your chemical analysis and reproduce it?" I asked. "Doesn't work. Humans have been trying to synthesize coffee for millennia. A connoisseur can tell. No, you have to grow coffee from beans, then roast and grind them if you want a truly exceptional cup."

"My information is worth more than a beverage," he said. "My current rate for a new recipe is fifty free as long as you buy them within Nexus."

I pulled the tube that contained two coffee bean plants from the backpack and set it on the table. Next to the plants, I placed a sealed carafe that contained Hunter's last brew. "I'm offering seedling plants and information on how to grow and care for them. You're looking at a billion-credit industry, just waiting for your careful grooming. Or perhaps you have a partner who would trade for it."

"It is still not enough," he said.

"Kroerak have destroyed trillions. They've decimated entire species. And they aren't done with the Aeratroas region of Dwingeloo. They're coming back. I guarantee it, because I know something you don't."

"What?"

"Information has value, Zeke Steele. Once I tell you, it will cease to have trading value," I said.

"Tell me what it is," Steele said. "I'll assess its value."

"Doesn't work that way," I said. "I assure you, what I know is real and it's a game changer."

For a solid minute Steele stood still, not moving even a little. "Does it have to do with the ship that Loose Nuts uncovered on Zuri?"

"It has to do with the noble we captured and killed on the ship that we uncovered on Zuri," I said.

"So, there *was* a noble that was killed," Steele said. "You should not have given that piece of information for free."

"That's nothing. I'll go even further. She had two attendants and you'll never guess what happened to them," I said. "What I have is juicier. Way bigger."

Steele fidgeted, his metal face shivering slightly. My best guess was that he was excited. "What were these attendants? What happened to them?" he asked, his speech pattern rushed as if he were struggling to get the words out faster than physically possible.

"Nah. Enough freebies. We trade information on the Piscivoru for information about the increased Kroerak threat," I said.

"The coffee plant and liquid are to be part of this deal," he said.

"You can have the carafe," I said. "I'll keep the seedlings. Maybe you can synthesize a brew that's just as good."

"Acceptable," he said, opening the carafe and dipping a finger into the steaming hot liquid. "What is this information you have about Kroerak?"

"I'm afraid it's your turn," I said. "Since you've already consummated the deal, that is."

"There is a Piscivoru that lives atop a mountain in the great desert of Jarwain," he said. "She should have the information you seek."

"That's crap," I said. "Piscivoru were killed off five hundred stans ago. There isn't even a reference to them in available histories."

"There was a colony of Piscivoru that lived on Jarwain," he said. "They traded with a Jarwain village for use of land and supplies. I have transmitted the location of this village."

"That's it?" I asked. "Just the location of a village? Not even the whereabouts of this living Piscivoru?"

"It is much more than you had. Such is the nature of this type of trade," Steele answered. "Now the information you promised."

"The Kroerak noble from Zuri was able to breed warriors that were resistant to selich root," I said. "She communicated that information to others before she was killed. It is only a matter of time before the Kroerak return to those that were protected by selich."

"You can prove this?"

"We have the information," Jonathan piped up. "You simply need to make yourself open to the receipt."

"No. Not me." Steele pulled what looked like a tiny glass straw from a previously closed hatch in the side of his torso. "Place the information on the memory device."

"As you wish," Jonathan answered. "But you will instruct your employee, Miko, to accompany us back to our ship."

"The trade is fairly executed," Steele answered, accepting the data storage back from Jonathan.

"You have no reason to fear us," Jonathan said. "We will not attempt to draw you into our collective. We are independent of those that would bring harm to you."

"So say you," Steele answered. "My caution has allowed for long life."

"A solitary life does not suit our people," Jonathan said. "We would have community with you."

"I have gained too much to share with any," Steele answered and wheeled past us, opening the door and zooming through, not looking back.

I caught Tabby's eye as Jonathan and I followed, exiting the small room. I thumbed my ring. The stone inside the band was a twin to the one in Tabby's ring. Two slivers of a left-over quantum crystal, they were too small to be used for intergalactic communication, but could transmit a pulse when touched. With the bump, I communicated that everything was good. She returned the bump telling me the status in the bar was the same as when we'd left.

"Miko will join you in ten minutes," Steele said. "It would be best if you left immediately. I prefer to leave violence outside of my establishment."

"How about another Marfon Blue for the road?" I asked, noticing Tabby had finished the beer I'd left on the table.

"That is acceptable," Steele answered, pulling out a glass and pouring into it as he spoke.

Chapter 12

HUNTED

"There are too many of you," Miko complained. "There is no way to hide such a group."

"What about three?" I asked.

We'd gathered in a small room behind the bar. Bray and Hunter were currently nursing hangovers as the impairment med-patches pushed nano-bots through their systems to remove the alcohol. "You wouldn't dare," Bray said, through clenched teeth.

"Dare what? Leave you guys behind?" I asked, exasperated. "You're right, I wouldn't. I'm sending you, Hunter, and Jonathan back with Miko. Sendrei, Tabby and I will draw the Kasumi hunters off."

"That is a bad plan," Miko said. "Five Kasumi have given chase. You will not survive."

"Can you take these three?" I asked, pointing at Jonathan and the two crew members.

"The bounty is on the heads of Sendrei Buhari, Liam Hoffen, Marny Bertrand, and Tabitha Masters. It is you they will pursue."

"We need to warn Marny," I said.

"I am sending a warning," Jonathan nodded. "We implore you to be careful, Liam."

"It's definitely high on my list of priorities," I said. "Give us a couple of minutes to make sure they're on our trail. Then you guys get moving."

"Then go," Miko said. "I have another set in thirty minutes."

I handed my 1911 pistol to Bray. "No hesitation," I said. "There's a lot riding on our entire crew."

She handed back the pistol. "No way am I taking that. The heat's coming after you. We'll be fine."

I refused to accept the pistol. "I always carry an extra weapon," I said, looking over to the door where Sendrei and Tabby had moved so they could keep an eye on anyone entering the bar. "And besides, it's not like either of them are going to let me take a shot."

"See you aboard, Captain," she said, pushing the pistol into the band of her vac-suit.

"Copy that," I said and hustled back to join Sendrei and Tabby.

"Let's go," Tabby said, leaning her shoulder against the swinging exit door and throwing the cloak she'd been wearing on the floor beside her. In one hand she held a laser pistol and in the other I saw the tip of a nano-blade.

"You should not go out ..." Steele said, his voice trailing off as we walked through the first set of vestibule doors.

"Go!" Sendrei shouted and Tabby hit the front door in a dive, tucking and rolling as she exited. The sound of gunfire rang out and the door swung backward. Together, Sendrei and I raced through after Tabby.

The three of us had trained as a quartet, most often with Marny running the show. The fact was, we'd also drilled on three-man teams and knew what was expected. My job was relatively simple. I was to keep from getting hit and mark targets. In combat, it's impossible to hit someone you can't see.

The gunfire had come from atop one of the buildings and instead of returning fire, Tabby sprinted to the end of the street, willing us to catch up as she would not take the corner unless we were close enough to support her.

Close-in blasts rang out as Sendrei laid down covering fire at the position I had marked as the shooter, then together we sprinted to Tabby's position.

"I don't have any targets," I said, exasperated as we got close.

"They're using the buildings," Tabby said. As a unit, we flowed around the corner of the building and cleared our assigned fire lanes. "That's what Miko did when she tracked us."

"Let's do it," I answered, grabbing Sendrei's arm. Tabby, immediately understanding my objective, grabbed his other side and together we used our grav-suits to lift him to the top of the two-story building flanking the street. Not unexpectedly, gunfire rang out as our prey tracked us.

"I'm hit," Tabby said as we dropped Sendrei heavily onto the rain-slicked roof.

"How bad?" I asked as the three of us hunkered down for a moment.

"Slug. Not sure if it exited. Their ammo can pierce our armor," she said, slapping a med patch over the tiny hole. "I'm good. Let's move."

Once we'd cleared the side of the building, my AI picked up three threats. It had been tracking one in particular who was in our line of sight. I hastily marked its position and almost immediately, both Tabby and Sendrei fired, eliciting a yelp.

"Move," I said, unnecessarily as they both took off.

The sound of a bullet as it passes your ear and cuts through the atmosphere is one of the most intensely disturbing sounds a person can hear. I'd taken to gliding along behind Tabby and Sendrei, searching the night for our pursuers, when the first bullet zipped past. The second caught me straight in the shoulder and spun me around. At first I felt no pain, but I knew that was only the initial shock.

My AI traced back along the trajectory of the bullet, illuminating my attacker. In a single fluid movement, Tabby spun and fired a twelve-shot spray into the darkness, directed precisely at the location highlighted.

"Can you move?" she asked to the sound of answering automatic gunfire. Strangely enough, the bullets weren't coming our way, but were lighting up the rooftop across the street where Tabby had sent her last volley. We watched as a dark figure spun out of control on his way down to the street, finger apparently seizing on the trigger as he fell.

"Go," I said. "I'll be fine."

Grateful to be able to glide, I trailed behind Sendrei and Tabby as I struggled to pull out a med patch with my left hand. I was surprised when a heavy body hit me from the side and pushed me down onto the graveled rooftop. My suit hardened as a blade slashed across my chest. With my only working arm, I grappled with my assailant, rolling over and kicking my legs into the female Kasumi's midsection. I saw what looked to be annoyance at her blade's failure to find pay dirt.

She rolled away and back onto her feet, only to be tackled by Tabby, who landed with a knee straight to the Kasumi's side. The sound of steel-on-steel caused me to spin as I fumbled left-handed, trying to draw my backup flechette from an ankle holster. Silhouetted against the distant purple lights of the Nexus bar, Sendrei blocked the blade of one attacker with his sword, kicking away from a second. Shots rang out as one of the Kasumi decided to upgrade the fight from knives to guns.

Steadying my left hand, I fired. Intentional in my desire to miss Sendrei, I over-compensated and my darts flew wide. I dropped the weapon, knowing I was just as likely to hit Sendrei as I was his attackers. I grabbed my nano blade and rushed toward the melee.

The sound of high-pitched sirens interrupted the fight, and Sendrei's attackers broke away to flee over the side of the building. Turning to Tabby, I watched as she violently wrenched the female Kasumi's arm backward at an impossible angle until I heard the sound of breaking cartilage and bone. The howl from the Kasumi left no doubt as to the pain she suffered.

Blinking red lights preceded a bright white wash of light that illuminated the building's roof. Demands for the immediate cessation of hostilities were pumped over loud speakers and the three of us dropped to our knees, pushing weapons to the side and placing our hands behind our heads – well at least, I was able to place my left hand behind my head. The pain of my wound nearly caused me to black out as we waited to see what happened next.

Unexpectedly, the female Kasumi stood from where Tabby had dropped her, her arm dangling at an impossible angle. She attempted to run from the roof, only to be cut down by a short burst of gunfire from one of the law enforcement vehicles that had arrived.

———

"WHAT WERE you doing atop the warehouse building?" a rat-faced humanoid in a uniform asked me for the tenth time. I'd learned this species was an Abelineian native and more importantly, their medical technology wasn't nearly as good as what we had on *Gaylon Brighton*. While they'd stopped the bleeding, my wound felt like it was on fire.

"Our suits have limited gravity lift," I said. "We were running from the Kasumi. We just wanted to get back to our ship."

"Why are you in Bhusal?" he asked, for the tenth time.

"Trade," I said. "We dropped a load of experimental bots off with a local corporation. I have the bill of lading if you'd let me get it."

A knock on the door got our attention and my interrogator's whiskers flicked. No doubt he wasn't getting what he wanted.

"Their story checks out, Jeggs," a second Abelineian said. "We ran down their contact with the Bessock company. These three just unloaded cargo from a ship half a kilometer from the Nexus bar no more than five hours ago. Their ship came through the Kneble wormhole three days ago. I think they're on the up and up."

"Then why'd they get jumped by Kasumi? Traders don't get hunted by Kasumi. They're up to something, I can feel it," my interrogator spat.

"Captain says we gotta let 'em go. Bessock is threatening a lawsuit if we hold 'em. Apparently, they got some tech Bessock is real excited about."

"Yeah, I'll bet," Jeggs replied, turning away in frustration from the junior officer. Jeggs waited in silence until the underling left, then slammed the door. "It's always the same thing with these corporate types. So, why don't you tell me what you are *really* doing here?"

"You gonna let us go?" I asked.

"Don't have much of a choice," he answered.

"Look, I get it, you're just doing your job, " I said. "I appreciate that you showed up. We were taking a pretty good beating."

"Nah, you weren't," he said. "That was a full Kasumi pride after you. You know how much that costs?"

"No idea," I answered.

"A million credits. Minimum," he said. "Thing that itches my ass is that the three of you are still alive and walking around. There's more going on here than you're saying. I can smell it." The end of his nose twitched, emphasizing the last thing he said. "Nobody crosses Kasumi and lives to talk about it."

"I guess you guys showed up just in time," I said.

"Yeah. Whatever you say, bub."

Chapter 13

TRADING UP

Happy to be underway, I sat back into *Gaylon Brighton's* medical tank and waited for the fluid to fill. Even though the tank's medical gel was heated to exact body temperature and was a neutral PH, it always felt a little creepy as it covered my skin. While med patches put out the fire in my shoulder, the bullet had shattered several bones and the Abelineian medical techs hadn't managed to even set it correctly.

I'd been given a choice between sleeping through the surgery or staying awake and I'd chosen to stay awake. If you were claustrophobic, the sensation of the medical gel covering your face and the confined space within the glass and metal enclosure were about as bad as it gets. It was something Tabby disliked a great deal. Since I'd been old enough to light my arc-jets, Big Pete (my dad) had sent me into holes in asteroids to set charges and made me slither into broken mining machines. That kind of claustrophobia wasn't my issue. Put me in a room with a hundred people and no way out, now that was a problem.

Tabby, who I made sure had time in the tank before me, had been gut shot. For a normal person, this would have been fatal. Many of her lower organs had been replaced, though, when she'd lost her legs in the pirate attack on our childhood home, Colony-40. The bullet had done quite a bit of damage, but her synthetic intestines had the capacity to simply shut down and seal off in the case of traumatic injury. In fact, the Abelineian officer hadn't even realized she'd been shot, given that her suit had sealed around the bullet's entry point.

After ninety minutes and some very odd-feeling snaps, tugs, tears and jolts, the tank's AI finally announced that I was good to go. In fact, I was even slightly better off than I had been before the fight. Apparently, I'd sustained injury to my rotator cuff from repeated use and impact while playing pod-ball growing up. The shoulder hadn't caused me much trouble, but under the right circumstances, I could hear it click when I moved it around.

"Any sign of the Kasumi ship?" I asked, joining Jonathan and Tabby on the bridge. We'd been underway for four days and hadn't seen any sign of the mercenaries.

"Nothing has changed in the last hour," Tabby said, peevishly.

"What's eating you?" I asked.

"If those cops hadn't shown up, we'd have put those Kasumi down," she said. "And we'd know why they were hunting us."

"The cop who was talking to me said a group of Kasumi that size would get at least a million credits," I said. "I can think of exactly two of our enemies who could afford that: Strix or Kroerak."

"How the frak would Kroerak hire mercs?"

"It is not as outrageous as you suggest," Jonathan said. "We saw the Kroerak successfully negotiate with Belirand Corporation. The Kasumi are well known mercenaries, easily as well-known in some circles as Belirand."

"Give us an over/under," I said. "Strix vs. Kroerak."

"A poll of the collective shows eighty-two percent believe Kroerak are behind the attack, eight percent identify Strix and the remaining members abstain, believing we have not gathered sufficient information," he answered.

"I received a message from Marny this morning," I said, changing subjects. "She says everything is quiet and they haven't had any central core traffic through Petersburg. She has increased their security posture, whatever that means. Also, Abasi have come through with their promise to supply armaments. She says we won't recognize *Hornblower* when we get back. They've added five thousand tonnes of armor to her and cut down on her profile a little."

"Munay still causing Marny trouble?" Tabby asked.

I chuckled. "That I'd like to see. She has a short fuse for insubordination. I also told her we'd be out for another five or six ten-days at a minimum."

"Shouldn't we reach Jarwain in three ten-days?" Tabby asked.

"Right. Still got to get home, though," I said. "And that's if we come up dry in Jarwain." I didn't realize at the time just how ironic that statement would end up being.

THE CONTRAST between the unnamed sector we'd been sailing through for the last two ten-days and Aeratroas's central core couldn't have been more dramatic. Instead of ships stacked in every corner, we hadn't seen evidence of a single ship for over one hundred twenty hours. Time was marked by shift changes, worm-hole transitions, card-games and getting my head pounded by Tabby or Sendrei. After our run-in with the Kasumi, both had decided I needed to brush up on my martial skills. Best I could tell, the only skill I was brushing up on was how to take a beating.

No one was happier than me when the unrelenting boredom was interrupted by our arrival in the Arkanis system. The system boasted two features of interest: a huge, dying yellow star and the sand-planet, Jarwain. The population on the surface was listed as 50,000 Jarwainians. We hoped for 49,999 Jarwainians and one helpful Piscivoru.

"That's a big planet on which to find one little alien," Tabby said, pulling the virtual beige ball that was Jarwain onto the forward holo projector. "Tell me we aren't searching the entire thing for one Piscivoru, especially when we don't even know what they look like."

"No. Zeke Steele said there was a single colony of Piscivoru," I said. "The Jarwain village he is sending us to is small. I'm betting someone down there has an idea where that colony is located."

"Right – because Steele wouldn't send us on a wild goose chase," Tabby said. It had been an annoyingly long seventy-hour approach from the wormhole and I shared Tabby's impatience to get on with the search.

"It is not to his benefit to deceive," Jonathan said. "As an information broker who provides bad information, he would lose credibility."

"There isn't a single ship in orbit," Sendrei said as we slowed and adjusted the ship's attitude to high orbit.

"Think they'll have fuel?" Tabby asked, a wry expression on her face.

"Doesn't look hopeful," I said. "All hands, prepare for atmospheric entry."

"I am unable to find a central authority for the planet's sole township," Jonathan said as we burned through the atmosphere.

"They might not need it," I said.

I leveled our flight out at eight thousand meters, staying above a dust storm that was blowing across and obscuring the town. We'd come in at the tail end of what looked like an intense storm and I held our elevation until it had passed before setting *Gaylon Brighton* down at the town's edge.

"Not much of a town," Tabby observed, looking out the armor glass screen. She was right; the buildings were nothing more than low rounded brick buildings, haphazardly collected over a hundred-meter area. "How many natives are we looking at?"

"Our scans show we are only seeing the topmost portion of the structures. Habitation is primarily underground. We estimate sixty villagers," Jonathan said. " Outside temperature is ten degrees and the position of the planet within its orbit around the star suggests we have arrived at the beginning of the summer period."

"Ten degrees for summer? That's only a bit above freezing," I said. "You'd think a desert planet like this would be hot."

"The star produces minimally-viable energy for inhabitation," Jonathan answered. "This society is likely subsistence based."

"Not following," I said.

"The star's low energy production combined with minimal available water, makes it likely the Jarwain people spend most of their daily efforts in producing food and maintaining shelter. Such a society is likely to be unwelcoming to strangers, as the impact of more bodies requiring sustenance will cause shortages," he continued.

"They don't look that unfriendly," Tabby said, waving at someone outside the ship.

I followed her gaze and discovered that several dozen people, all dressed in robes of varying shades of beige, stood outside and were waving at us.

"Caution should be taken, Captain," Jonathan warned. "There is no authority here and this ship alone represents more wealth than is held by the entire population of the planet."

"Sendrei, Tabby, you're with me," I said. "Jonathan, I'd like you and the crew to remain behind and monitor, just in case things get out of control."

"Captain," Bray's voice came over the comms. "They're banging on the ship. I think they're trying to get in."

"How hard?" I asked.

"Not that hard. They're mostly just using hands," she said.

"Let me know if it escalates," I answered. "Jonathan, protect the ship, but I'd rather you dust off than cause damage to any of the natives."

"An admirable stance, Captain," he answered. "We will generate a 0.5g repulse field around the ship. It will not prevent the curious from approaching, but it will require effort to maintain contact."

"Perfect," I said.

"Sendrei, Tabby, let's go," I said, exiting the bridge.

"Wooden staves are a better option than pistols," Sendrei said as I turned the corner to the airlock.

I stopped in mid step. "Staves?"

"Did you see those people?" Sendrei asked. "They are overly thin. A blaster weapon would likely cause fatality. A bo staff will allow you to keep distance without causing serious injury if it comes to that. Your skill has increased with staves."

I pulled my 1911 slug thrower from my waist holster and handed it to Sendrei. It was an impractical weapon compared to the hidden particle blaster I kept in my boot. Limited in number of rounds, the 1911 had one thing I really appreciated: intimidation. Slug throwers were all explosion and flame and there was nothing better when you wanted to garner the right kind of attention.

"Good call, Sendrei," Tabby agreed as he handed back the light-weight, but extremely durable sticks we used when we trained bo staff.

"The faces of Jarwain remind me of the people of Cradle," he said. "There is much desperation outside this ship."

I nodded. There was little to be learned from standing around, so I moved into the airlock with Tabby, and Sendrei close behind and cycled us through.

Jonathan's repulser field lessened at the stairs which extended from the airlock and rested in the sand. The bony, four-fingered hand that grasped the railing was the dark brown of stained wood. I looked up into the face of a Jarwainian male. The whites of his eyes were yellowed, but otherwise familiar, with deep brown irises. Angular, from what I imagined to be malnutrition, his face was far more pinched than could be explained by a lack of food alone. The cheeks and jaw structure narrowed almost to points and where the nose should be, just two slits were visible.

The first words from his mouth were completely unintelligible, as Jonathan had warned us to expect. Jarwain speech was not part of the Confederation of Planets' interpretation library.

"Liam Hoffen," I said, placing a hand over my heart. "And these are my friends Sendrei Buhari and Tabitha Masters." I gestured, hoping the eavesdropping AI was picking up enough conversation from the milling crowd of at least forty to start providing translation.

"Return ... water ..." The man who had greeted us turned his face to indicate the crowd that continued to press toward the ship, only to be pushed back by the repulse field.

"Jonathan, are you getting this?" I asked.

"Yes. We believe the one who greets you is trying to instruct the remainder to return the water gathered from the ice that formed on the ship in the upper atmosphere," Jonathan answered. "It is a precious commodity, I believe he wishes to show they are not stealing from you."

"That doesn't make sense. There's thirty-five percent humidity. There's plenty of moisture to extract it directly from the air with a condenser," I said.

"Big Galtawain," the man said, placing his narrow hand over the middle of his chest. I nodded. "Come."

"We are working to provide translation," I said. I was impressed that my suit's external speakers were using considerably more phonemes in the translation.

"Working, it is. Follow, please," he said. "We will share our water."

Sendrei, Tabby and I were finally able to step off the stairs and into the soft sand. It was hard walking as we followed the man toward the low buildings a hundred meters from our position. Most of the group followed along, although unlike me, they seemed to almost float over the sand. Not wanting to be outdone, I raised slightly with my grav-suit so I walked along the top of the sand instead of sinking in.

He led us to a round-topped shed no more than five meters across. Sand had drifted against one side, the drift almost reaching the roof. We walked around to the opposite end where there was less sand and an opening wide enough for two at a time. Inside, we discovered that Jonathan had been right. We walked down a dusty stone stairway and into an underground room that looked like it could seat twenty comfortably. The Jarwain who'd done all of the talking so far pushed back the hood of his cloak, exposing the same brown skin and lighter-colored scales that resembled a snake's over his skull.

"The Jarwain welcome traders," he said. The AI translator had apparently received enough dialog to decode the Jarwainian language, as the translations were now immediate and smooth. "We are a humble people and have always shared what is ours. What brings such a space vehicle to our hearth stone?"

As he spoke, the beige-robed crowd filtered into the room, quietly observing, standing very close to one another so more could enter.

"Offer them rest, Galtawain," a female said, turning abruptly from where she was grinding something on a wide flat stone. "They must have come a great distance."

"Yes, Peris," he answered, gesturing to a long, cloth-covered bench. "My mate offers rest at our hearth. We offer the meager bounty of what is ours."

"Yes, they understand we have little, Galtawain," Peris snapped. "If they have arrived by vehicle from the stars, this is abundant within their eyes."

"There is no cause for harsh words. I only wish to make our visitors comfortable."

"And see to it they are uncomfortable sharing a meal with us," she said again peevishly, pulling her hood back. Her skin, while a lighter shade, had much the same hue as Galtawain's and her scales, while perhaps the same shade, seemed darker. Overall, the species was sufficiently symmetrical that they were pleasant enough looking.

"If it's all the same," I said, breaking into the middle of what I suspected might be a never-ending argument, "Tabitha, Sendrei, and I haven't come to find food. Although to the extent it's customary, we would be honored to share a meal with you."

"Smooth," Tabby said unhelpfully under her breath.

I shot her a glance and continued. "We've come in search of a person and would be very grateful to trade for information that helps us find who we seek."

"You seek a Jarwain?" Peris asked, setting down the stone she was using to grind what appeared to be a plant.

"A Piscivoru," I said. "Our information says there was a colony on Jarwain a long time ago."

"I know of ..." Galtawain started, just before Peris backhanded him, shutting him up.

"You know nothing," Peris said. "What is it that you would trade for this information, if we were to have it?"

I shifted in my seat under the gaze of at least thirty sets of eyes. The Jarwain had squeezed more into the room than I'd thought possible, while still maintaining a non-threatening space between us. If Jonathan's estimates were correct, over half of the village had crowded into this single home.

"We would make a fair trade," I said. "It is difficult for us to know what has value on Jarwain. We have food stores and water. Also, we have precious minerals. We can manufacture material or radios. Really, I just need a little help."

"It is true that food would fill our bellies for several days and we would feel satisfaction. Water would slake the ever-present thirst," she said. "These indeed have value, but that value is fleeting. Minerals have little value to us and we are quite capable of making our own garments."

"He talked of our broken condenser," Galtawain said.

"They could not know of our condenser," she answered. "It is hidden within the shop of Biertwain."

"Is that true?" I asked. "Do you have a moisture condenser that is broken? I'm sure we could fix it. We're pretty handy."

Peris held my gaze for a moment and her narrow lips tugged upward at the sides. "Do you truly believe that? We would trade information for repair to our moisture condenser."

"If you can lead us to the Piscivoru, I'll do better than that," I said. "We'll manufacture two brand new units."

"And repair our machine?" She looked skeptical. "We will provide information when water gathers to the depth of my arm."

"Captain, we have preemptively started manufacture of the units you have promised," Jonathan said over the comm channel. "Depending on reservoir, it might take as many as twenty hours to gather the water she identifies."

"No. We will provide two units and repair your machine. When your machine has produced a liter of water, you will provide the information you have on the Piscivoru. In exchange for this consideration, we offer an additional five hundred liters of water from the store we carry aboard the ship."

I could hear a gasp within the room, but it was quickly stifled as Peris glared out over the gathered Jarwainians.

"You would trade five hundred liters for this information?"

"And we'll fix your machine and provide two additional," I said. "There is no reason for Jarwain to suffer without water. It is abundant within the galaxy if not on the surface of Jarwain."

"Your offer is accepted," Peris said.

"Where would you receive the water?" I asked. "We should be able to deliver in two hours."

"You would bring the water here?" she asked. Even though she was alien, I could tell she wondered what she was missing in the conversation.

"What about food?" Tabby asked, pulling a meal bar from a pouch under her belt. "You can't just trade for water. That's crap."

"And you are Sendrei or Tabby?" she asked.

"Tabby," Tabby answered, standing up and handing the meal bar to Peris.

"You feel the trade is not lucrative enough? Do you need food?" Peris asked, confused. "We would trade food for the water you've offered."

"No. We have a lot of water," she said. "We also have food. I'm saying we need to give you some of our food to make the deal more fair to you."

Peris looked from Tabby and back to me. "The deal is struck. There is no reason to change it."

"We could offer four crates of meal bars," I said, looking back to Tabby for approval. It was enough calories to last two people for standard year. Tabby nodded her acceptance.

"Your negotiation is unusual," Peris said. "We accept the offer unless the quiet man must further modify the agreement."

"Not me," Sendrei said.

"Then we will share a meal as is our custom when greeting friends," she said.

As bowls were filled with a pasty gruel she was preparing, the crowd was thinned out by Galtawain until there were just eight of us. Instead of sitting around a table, some sat on the long bench and others on a thin rug on the floor.

"CAPTAIN, the water containers, meal bars, and condensers are ready to be transported," Bray informed me over comms about an hour later.

"Have them brought to my current location," I answered.

"How many remain on your ship?" Peris asked, witnessing my exchange.

"Not many," I said. We'd had a good talk, but I wasn't about to give away tactical details. "The supplies we've discussed are in transit. Are you sure you want it all in here?"

"This will be fine," she answered.

"We should look at your broken machine," I said, standing. The gruel wasn't without taste, but its consistency was a bit too slimy for me.

"Galtawain will escort your companions," she said. "Perhaps you could remain until the water arrives?" The woman was generally very stoic and I couldn't tell if her demeanor was a species thing or just her personality. Perhaps involuntarily, she also had the same reaction every time water was mentioned: she would lick her thin lips, hungrily.

"That's fine," I said. "Tabby, Sendrei, you want to take a look at the condenser? I suspect Jonathan will have some ideas on a repair."

"Sure. But just so we're clear," she said, standing and point at me. "That one is my mate. No harm comes to him."

Peris stood, faced Tabby and nodded, closing her browless eyes as she did. "We are peaceful, Tabitha. No harm will come to your mate."

"Good, because I'm only peaceful to a point."

"Your mate is a warrior?" Peris asked as Tabby and Sendrei followed Galtawain out.

I nodded, smiling. "Yes, she's all that and jealous too."

My response brought a smile to Peris's face, showing bright white teeth as she did. "I respect that. I think our people would become good friends after a time."

"I'd like to think that too," I agreed.

A moment later the first stevedore bot arrived with a palette of newly manufactured, fifty-liter water containers. I pointed to a spot against the wall where there was room enough for the entire load. The second bot arrived a moment later, depositing the remaining water containers and food crates.

"One more trip," I said. "Our condensers are ready. Do you have someone we can show how to operate them? If the Piscivoru are close by, we could leave two of our crew behind to help get them set up."

"Your offer is accepted. Cerith, fetch Bertwain," she said to a smaller female I'd assumed was her daughter. "Jarwain will once again give its water to us and we will thrive."

"Now it's your turn," I said.

She nodded slightly. "The Piscivoru live in the mountains to the north in a cave that is only visible from the south. The cave is on a high rock face that is not accessible by ordinary means. The last we heard of this colony was of the birth of their final offspring, Tskir, a female."

"Final? How could you know that? You said the last time Piscivoru visited was before your parents."

"The father of this child was discovered in the sands when I was still small," she said. "He passed shortly after conveying this information. Our elders would have sent help, but their village is not accessible to Jarwainians."

"Do you know if this Tskir or her mother are still alive?"

"It is not known."

Chapter 14

HIDDEN

"Can you imagine living like that?" Tabby asked as the three of us cycled through *Gaylon Brighton's* airlock.

"It doesn't look that much different from asteroid mining," I pointed out.

"No way," she said. "Nobody is going to die of thirst as a miner."

"No, but you can run out of food and O2," I said. "Not Colony-40 as much, but I heard plenty of stories about other colonies where people died on their claims for lack of those things."

"I suppose. Just can't see why you'd stay here if you had any choice."

I palmed my way onto the bridge. "It's their home. Maybe they don't want to live somewhere else."

"All three moisture condensers are operating at peak efficiency," Jonathan reported as we entered. "We have observed movement of water to larger capacity buildings."

"Just a single replicator would change everything for them," Tabby said, not able to let it go.

I turned and reached for her hand. Externally, Tabby rarely showed empathy. I'd learned, however, the idea that kindness was a weakness had been drilled into her by her father. Emotion was also something she distrusted about her own reaction to people. The desire to help the Jarwain people had to have been difficult for her to admit and her face bore the look of someone expecting to be chastised.

"That and a small power generator to go along with it," I said. "You could remove the Class-A replicator from the main passageway if you wanted. It's not as efficient for small things, but the Class-C in the engineering bay is more than enough for us."

"You don't think it's a stupid idea?" she asked.

"A willingness to sacrifice for the good of others is a true measure of enlightened existence," Jonathan said. "It is what separates cooperative species from the Kroerak."

"My dad would say I'm being childish," she explained, looking to Jonathan.

"In all successful societies there is a balance between charity, barter, and individual productivity. The Jarwain people have asked for nothing, but it is clear the addition of replicator technology would provide considerable benefit. We find no weakness in such a gesture."

Tabby squeezed my hand. "You'd be okay leaving the Class-A behind?"

"How about this," I answered, "Work on removing it from the bulkhead while we go to the Piscivoru settlement. We'll swing back here on the way out and set it up for them. Will that work?"

"You're the best," Tabby said, hugging me suddenly.

Directions to the Piscivoru settlement were simple. We were to sail three hundred kilometers north to a mountainous region. The Piscivoru had purchased the right to use a large cave system atop one of the mountains from the Jarwainians almost half a millennium ago. According to Peris's ancestors, groups of Piscivoru showed up in the warm season to trade, though they hadn't visited at any point in her lifetime or that of her parents. It was widely believed they were deceased. We'd come a long way and I feared we'd find nothing but bad news.

"Captain, we're seeing evidence of civilization. There is indeed a large cavern opening that has been closed in by modern construction," Jonathan said.

"That is well-hidden," Sendrei said, grasping the holo image of the mountain range still twenty-five kilometers away. A broad-mouthed cave entrance was set into the sheer cliff face of the mountain. Set back ten meters into the cave was an ancient, rusty wall of iron that looked as if it hadn't been maintained for decades.

"It looks abandoned," I said, unable to find any sign of life outside the wall. "Hopefully, there's something or someone behind that wall that gives us a clue to where the Piscivoru's home planet is."

"Captain, an observation?" Jonathan offered.

"Please."

"As you are aware, virtually nothing is known of the Piscivoru. This alone suggests some sort of conspiracy – although that is not particularly relevant at the moment. Our measurements of the iron gate's few obvious portals suggest a species that is considerably smaller than most humanoids."

"How much smaller?" I asked.

"Perhaps smaller than Norigan. Also, the lack of walking paths surrounding the entrance suggests there is either an alternative entrance or that this species has a different mode of movement. There are few species that would be natively capable of scaling the vertical face of that mountain. In all cases, it would present such great risk that it would make for a very poor choice."

"Maybe that's why they constructed the big iron wall," I said. "So they don't accidently fall off."

"Perhaps. And we appreciate the value presented in your simplistic analysis," he said.

I chuckled. "Sendrei, I believe the Jonathan collective has voted me a simpleton."

"It was bound to happen," Sendrei said. "We should form a voting collective of our own."

"Perhaps our choice of words was indelicate," Jonathan said, his eyebrows raised as if to communicate surprise. "The analysis is simple. We do not consider humanity a simple species and have utmost respect for your capacity for complex analysis."

I grinned. "Sorry, Jonathan. I'm just giving you a hard time. I suppose I'm impatient to get on with this mission so I'm making trouble."

Jonathan looked at Sendrei and then back to me. I relished the confused look on his face. It had become more and more difficult to confuse the collective and I perversely enjoyed the challenge. "As we were saying ... if the Piscivoru were concerned with falling from the cliffs, a multitude of other caves are more approachable. It is our analysis that they chose the least approachable cave within range of our sensors."

"Is the apron in front of the wall wide enough for us to land?" I asked. Since the first time we'd seen her, *Gaylon Brighton* had been modified with broad wings that held extended-mission supplies.

"It is not," Jonathan replied, immediately. "We recommend landing on the foothills below and utilizing gravity technology to aid in approach." He highlighted a landing site within a bowl on the side of the mountain. Their choice was interesting in that it would shield *Gaylon Brighton* from long range sensors in most directions except directly overhead.

"Expecting trouble?" I asked.

"That was my doing," Sendrei said. "I don't believe we're done with Kasumi hunters. Hopefully I'm just being paranoid."

Flying in low, but not so low as to stir up dust from the surface, I set *Gaylon Brighton* gently on the ground.

"I vote for blaster rifles," I said, standing up and walking to the bridge exit. "Jonathan, I assume you'd like to come along. Sendrei, too?"

"Someone should stay behind, Liam," Sendrei said. "I am willing."

"I think Tabby wants to finish her project." I found Tabby with a toolbox open and the Class-A replicator almost fully removed from its bulkhead. "Tabbs, you mind watching the ship while we look around?"

She pulled on a thin translucent cable that stretched back into the bulkhead. "Copy that. Be safe."

"The Phentera group offers to stay behind and assist in monitoring the ship," Jonathan said.

"Sounds like we have a plan," I said. It was the second time a part of Jonathan's collective had willingly split off and I wondered how often it might occur in the future. According to Jonathan, the Phentera group enjoyed tactical analysis of ship-based security, including space-based and atmospheric-based combat. It was a schism that caused me concern, but I trusted the collective we knew as Jonathan and hoped they'd bring forward an issue if it was needed.

Passing me in the hallway, Sendrei reached the armory first and handed me my newest favorite slug thrower and a heavy blaster rifle.

"You should bring a cutting torch," Tabby called over the comms. "That gate is probably frozen shut."

"Good point," I said and headed aft to the engineering bay.

A few minutes later, Jonathan, Sendrei and I cycled through the airlock. The air at our elevation was less humid and cooler than it had been down in the Jarwain village.

"Kind of miss having Hunter and Bray aboard. They've turned into good crew," I said, switching to a private channel as we started up the mountain, Jonathan and Sendrei using arc-jets and me with the grav-suit.

"It is not as surprising with Petty Officer Bray," Sendrei said. "Her experience in Mars Protectorate and having been chosen for such a dangerous mission suggests she was on the fast-track. Mr. Hunter, while less refined in ship etiquette, is a hard worker and learns fast. I would be pleased to work with either of them in the future." I switched back to general comms as we crested the lip of the cave entrance.

Sendrei swiped his foot across a layer of undisturbed sand that drifted across the ground. "There is no evidence of recent activity."

"This wall is ancient." I peeled a rusted flake of steel the size of my hand from a post that had been driven into the stone floor and ceiling of the opening. The degradation of the posts along the wall was significant and the integrity of the wall had to have been severely compromised.

"We believe this to be an entrance," Jonathan said, pointing at a waist-high panel, inset within the wall. Looking further down, there were two more such panels, evenly spaced along the length of the opening.

"You said smaller," I acknowledged, joining him. I pushed on the panel and it gave a little, appearing to do so only because the metal was weak from age. I found a small hole that I suspected was some sort of keyed entrance, but it had long since rusted over.

"Either this entrance is not primary or the occupants are indeed long deceased as the Jarwain suggested," Sendrei said.

I stepped back and kicked at the door. A hollow bong echoed behind the wall. Rust dislodged and rained down, but the door didn't budge.

"Plan B." I set down my blaster rifle and detached the plasma torch from my waist.

"Copy that," Sendrei answered, swinging the butt of his blaster rifle into the door with no more effect than I'd had with my boot. I'd heard that the blaster rifles were nigh unto indestructible, but it still bothered me to see it used as a battering ram.

"Door looks rotten, but there's plenty of steel left in there," he said. "It's all yours."

With cutter in hand, I traced a molten line around the opening. The plasma stream took only a few minutes to work and the door fell inward. A plume of dust billowed out of the opening, pushed by a draft of humid air coming from inside the cave.

"I think we'll need a bigger door," I said, crouching down and sticking my head through the hole, careful not to touch the slag left behind by the torch.

"What do you see?" Sendrei asked.

"Too dark," I answered, lifting the faceplate of my helmet for an unobstructed view.

Just as I motioned for the helmet lamps to turn on, the end of a wooden stick crashed into the bridge of my nose. Instinctively, I lifted up, banging my head into the hot edge of the doorway. Realizing the danger of touching the cooling steel, I ducked out backward, falling to the ground while brushing frantically at the top of my helmet to dislodge any slag that might have stuck.

"Liam!" Sendrei grabbed my suit and pulled me away from the hole.

"Someone's in there," I temporarily forgot about the slag and lowered my hand to gently probe the area around my right eye, which felt like it was starting to swell shut. "How bad is it?" I asked, looking up at Sendrei.

"Broke the skin," he said. "AI doesn't see any permanent damage. What happened?"

"Something hit me with a stick."

"That is certainly good news," he said.

"Geez. How is getting a stick in my eye good news?"

"We wondered if the Piscivoru were alive. It appears the answer to this is yes. That and the weapon was a stick and not a gun," he said. Immediate relief came as he slapped a med-patch over my eye.

"I'm going to open up the hole," I closed my suit's helm again and accepted Sendrei's hand up. I wasn't about to take another stick to the eye.

It took a few more minutes to enlarge the opening and we stood back as a larger section of the wall fell away. With blaster rifle in hand and flood lamps blazing, I stepped through the entrance, Sendrei right on my six, prepared to meet whatever came at us.

Okay, prepared for what we saw next might have been an over-statement. Instead of cavern walls, we entered the edge of what looked like a toy town set beneath an artificial, albeit convincing, blue sky. Movement from the right caught my eye as a small figure darted up and thwacked my calf.

"What in Jupiter?" I asked.

My attacker was a narrow humanoid creature, wearing ragged tightly-wrapped strips from her upper torso down to her feet. The top of her head was covered in bumpy snake skin and a thick tail rested on the ground behind her. She only came up to my knee, which explained the small doors and dwelling spaces. Striking a second time, she chittered in a language my AI didn't recognize. For such a small being, her strikes were surprisingly sharp and if not for my armor, I'd have taken real damage.

"Be gentle, Captain," Jonathan warned. "I believe you are looking at the one Peris referred to as Tskir."

At the sound of the name, my small attacker dropped to all fours and ran sideways in front of us to face Jonathan. Her movements were abrupt and startlingly fast. Unwilling to accept risk to Jonathan, Sendrei stepped between them, although he stowed his blaster rifle as he did.

Unfazed, Jonathan chittered back at the little warrior. My AI translated as Jonathan attempted several different languages that all sounded the same. The Piscivoru, however, ceased her attack and stood with a curious look on her face somewhere in the middle of Jonathan's babbling. A minute later, the Piscivoru held up her hand, as if asking him to stop.

"Tskir," she said, placing her hand over her chest. Her voice had a hiss to it and instead of teeth, she had a sharp ridge of cartilage along the jawline. Now that Tskir had stopped her flurried attack, I was able to take in more detail. The first thing I noticed was the flick of her long, narrow tongue as she assessed our group. Her hands and feet were long and narrow, just like the rest of her body, and with only four digits on each.

"Liam Hoffen," I said, kneeling in front of her and placing my hand on chest.

"Fishette," she said, pointing at the med-patch over my eye.

"Yeah, you stuck a stick in my eye, if that's what you're getting on about," I said, opening my helm to remove the patch which had done about as much good as it was going to. It took a lot of restraint not to flinch as I allowed her to approach and consider my eye. She chittered as she lifted a delicate hand to my face and rested it on my cheek. The warmth of her palm reassured me for no reason I could understand. There was obvious intelligence in her face and I got the sense that she was very old, even though her skin, which resembled that of a snake, was tight.

She tapped her finger on the bridge of my nose where she'd struck me and chittered again just before she stepped back. From a band along her waist, she pulled a device out and offered it to Jonathan, chittering all the while. I knew if she kept talking, the translator AI would eventually recognize the language.

"What is it?" I asked as Jonathan cradled a finger-sized device.

"Memory storage device," he said. "The encoding is not recognizable, it will take time to decipher."

"This city is remarkable," Sendrei said. "No wonder they never leave. These buildings go far back into the rock and their technology is quite advanced."

"I am the last," Tskir answered, looking up at Sendrei, the AI translator parsing her words perfectly. "A sickness killed most of my ancestors, long before my parents were born. This was to be the new home of Piscivoru, but our nests are now empty and I am the last of my broodlings."

"We have information that a remnant of Piscivoru remain on your home planet," I said.

"That is impossible," she answered. "The Kroo Ack destroyed our civilization and all those who live on our planet. They hunted Piscivoru until there were none remaining. Ours was the last of all to survive. It is too late for our people. I am a shriveled old female; my eggs are long ago dried within my body."

"We may have news of importance to you," Jonathan said. "I have communed with a Kroerak noble. This very old and powerful Kroerak had information about the continued life of a small group of your people who are protected by Iskstar. What we don't know is where your home is. We only know the Kroerak fear nothing as much as they do the Iskstar."

Tskir's lips thinned as her cheeks pulled back. "It was entrusted to me to survive. We hoped that someday we would have a chance to fill our nests with happy broods. Many sacrificed to keep me alive. I had lost hope and believed I would die on Jarwain. Tell me, are you a friend to the Kroerak? Have you come to end Tskir's life? I say to you, there is no need, but I will welcome death. I have failed my people."

"Liam," Tabby's voice caught my attention. "We might have a problem. The Phentera group is tracking a ship breaking orbit. It looks like they're headed straight for the Jarwain village we visited. Signature reads like it might be the Kasumi."

"Frak," I said, turning away from the conversation. "Any sign they know we're here?"

"No, but Hunter and Bray are defenseless," she said. "There's no telling what the Kasumi might do."

"Copy that," I answered. "Stay put and don't do anything. We'll need to cut comms, just in case they're tracking EM. We found Tskir, we just need to get the location of Piscivoru home planet and we can get going."

"We need to help the Jarwainians," Tabby insisted.

"Understood," I said, cutting comms.

"I'm sorry to be abrupt, Tskir," I said. "No. We are not friends of Kroerak. In fact, the Kroerak attempted to destroy my home planet as it did yours. We stopped them, but it was only temporary. The Kroerak discovered a cure for the weapon we used against them. We need to know the location of your home planet so we can find this Iskstar. We believe it is the only way to defeat them once and for all."

"Who is hunting you, Liam Hoffen?" she asked. "I overheard your communications. I do not trust that you are telling Tskir the truth."

"We think it is agents of the Kroerak. They are trying to stop us from finding your home," I said.

"I will not tell you where my home is," she said.

"You have to," I said. "Those who chase us will surely come here and do you harm."

"I have told you. I do not fear death. I have lived many cycles by myself," she said. "I do not wish to continue."

"Then come with us," I said. "Show us your home. Stand on the ground of your ancestors. If your people still live, you will be a treasure to them."

"You would take me home?"

"Liam!" Tabby broke in again. "Phentera group says they've received transmission from Bray. She reported the Kasumi ship, but we lost contact almost immediately after."

"Yes, Tskir, but we must go now," I said, trying not to let the anxiety I felt enter my voice. "The Kasumi are attacking the Jarwain. We must help them. If you're coming, we need to go now."

"Then let us leave," she answered.

"But the information on how to get to your home," I said. "We need it."

"Do not worry. I have it with me always," she said, fingering a small chain around her wrist.

Chapter 15

INTO DARKNESS

Within the ruined city's sewers, the weight of the desiccated corpses rested heavily on Sklisk and he sank into Jaelisk. As far as either could see within the long tunnel, lay the ancient corpses of his ancestors. While he had learned of the collapse of the once-great society and talked of the numbers of his people killed by Kroerak, it had seemed entirely academic. The reality of it all was too much. Sklisk closed his eyelids hoping to erase the images.

"There were families," Jaelisk observed. "See how the broodlings rest on the parents. I cannot bear the thought of Baelisk and Boerisk dying in my arms."

"It is too much," Sklisk said. "The Kroo Ack are too much."

A sharp intake of air alerted him that Jaelisk was annoyed. "Do you not see what they have done?" The vibration of her tongue communicated anger. "Would you not fight until your last breath to stop them?"

"How?" Sklisk asked.

"Our ancestors have shown us the way. No Kroo Ack killed them," she said. "They passed down here in the tunnels."

"The Kroo Ack might as well have murdered them. Our ancestors hid from them, only to die," he answered.

"But they had not Iskstar," she said. "The Kroo Ack might have numbers, but the bugs have also fed our people for generations. If it takes a hundred hands of moon cycles, we will find Engirisk's building and his devices. We will honor our ancestors by showing them that we yet live and yet fight."

"What are you saying?"

Jaelisk twitched her eyelids in annoyance and grasped Sklisk's shoulder. "Where do you think these tunnels go? Is it not possible they pass beneath Engirisk's building?"

Sklisk's eyelids fluttered open. "Yes," he said, surprised.

"You *should* act surprised when I am brilliant," she said. "Now which way must we go?"

"We go this way," Sklisk said, moving in the direction he was fairly certain would take them toward Engirisk's building. The host of Kroerak above would likely surround every nearby exit hole. Sklisk feared he was leading them to a fight that could not be won, but they had to complete their mission.

Carefully picking their way around the partially mummified remains, he found it disturbing when his tail inadvertently made contact. In some cases, the bodies broke apart and rolled away. Sometimes the lightest touch caused complete disintegration. In his mind, the presence of the bodies gave credence to Jaelisk's notion that his ancestors watched as they struggled to complete the mission Engirisk had given them.

With little noise, they continued until finally, Sklisk stopped. It was one thing to navigate above the surface; the building shapes were easy to pick out, even with bugs surrounding them. In the tunnels, however, it was much more difficult, especially given the frequent small tunnels that branched off in all directions.

"I am disoriented," he finally admitted. "I do not know if I bring us closer or further from our destination."

"The bugs will have settled," Jaelisk said. "Provide to me your weapon and I will go above and orient."

"We go together," Sklisk said, climbing onto the wall and into a narrow chute that led to the surface. "There is no reason to separate."

Dim light filtered through small holes in the round disk covering the top of the tunnel. Wide enough for both to fit, Sklisk and Jaelisk hung onto the cover and listened for movement. Vibrations transmitted through the ground, alerting them to the presence of Kroerak. However, it was clear that the bugs were unaware of their presence.

With the palm of his hand, Sklisk pushed on the heavy disk, attempting to dislodge it. It didn't move much, but he was elated to discover it was not frozen in place.

"Brace me," he said as quietly as he could manage.

The tunnel was narrow enough that Jaelisk could push against the wall with her back and pin Sklisk in place with her front. How she wished their intimate proximity could be under different circumstances. Would she ever get another opportunity to playfully accuse her mate of taking advantage of a situation such as this?

"Such contact is merely a pleasant coincidence," Sklisk said, picking up on her unintended communication.

With a grin on his face and Jaelisk holding him, he used both hands to push against the disc. Loose dirt fell through the narrow opening and he blinked rapidly to avoid being blinded. Unwilling to push their luck too far, Sklisk paused, waiting to see if they'd attracted attention.

"You do feel good," he communicated with vibration from his tongue.

"You are such a male," she answered.

After a few minutes, he pushed again on the disc, sliding it over just enough that a single Piscivoru body would fit through. Again, they waited until both were satisfied they'd garnered no new attention.

"Careful," Jaelisk warned as he crept upward, leading with his tongue, flicking it out through the opening.

Staying low to the ground, Sklisk crawled over the lip of the opening and into scrub brush that dotted the once pristine street. Jaelisk, recognizing Sklisk was safe, followed. Many Kroerak were within only a few dozen meters, but the two Piscivoru were careful to move only when the closest bugs turned away. Reaching a tall building, they skittered around to a side that was in shadow and cautiously climbed.

"I see Engirisk's building," Jaelisk said, having poked her head around the corner of the structure on which they climbed.

"We have gone too far, almost by twice," Sklisk said.

"Half again," Jaelisk agreed. "But our direction was true. The openings to the surface are regularly spaced. We could count them."

"Engirisk will be proud of your reasoning when the story is recounted," Sklisk said, turning to run down the side of the building.

"Slow!" Jaelisk warned, but it was too late. Sklisk's enthusiasm had caught the attention of a Kroerak warrior. "No. Race. We've been discovered."

Still ten meters from ground level, Sklisk released the building and fell the remaining distance. Jaelisk followed suit, although with only three legs to absorb the impact, the shock to her body momentarily stunned her. Unwilling to leave her behind, Sklisk waited for a few breathless moments. Then he urged her forward and they skittered back to the hole. Pushing her through in front of him, Sklisk narrowly avoided the claws of a bug as it attempted to strike. Seeing opportunity, he pulled the Iskstar from his back and swung it in a graceful arc as the second bug's claw impacted the ground next to him. A bellow of pain erupted from the Kroerak warrior as the forward half meter of its heavily armored claw detached. Deftly, Sklisk snatched the limb and pushed it into the hole in front of him, allowing it to fall.

"You need to be more careful when topside. We know the bugs orient to movement," Jaelisk chastised as they climbed down, still hearing scraping as several bugs clawed ineffectively at the entry, now twenty meters above.

"I was hungry?" Sklisk defended, weakly.

Jaelisk trilled her tongue, calling him on his ridiculousness. She relented once they started down the passage toward Engirisk's building. "It will be good to feed."

Sklisk discarded the end of the claw, as it was mostly tasteless shell, and split the remaining flesh, handing the best part to his mate.

The food provided much needed energy and they ate as they ran forward, counting the openings above.

Jaelisk stopped beneath the opening that would take them to street level outside Engirisk's building. "This is it."

"The Kroo Ack know our destination," Sklisk said. "We will not be able to sneak past them within the flattened space between the structures."

"I have been thinking," Jaelisk said. "Why would these tunnels exist and what are the small tunnels that branch off?"

"I do not know, but our destination is this way," Sklisk said, crawling up to a smaller branch tunnel. The fit was so tight he had to remove his weapon and pack and push it ahead.

"Are you sure of this?" Jaelisk asked, following him.

Sklisk didn't have an answer. Instead he pushed on, discovering that the tight-fitting tunnel angled upward sharply. He dreaded the idea that the tunnel might narrow again. Crawling backward down the long distance would be difficult at best.

"There is a blockage," he said, when he discovered he could not push his staff forward. The dim light of Iskstar crystals illuminated a grate. Beyond the grate, he could feel an open space. "A room lies beyond."

"Can you push through?"

"I will," he answered. "Be ready, I may need to retreat quickly."

"I am ready."

Sklisk jammed his staff into the grate which popped up easily and clattered onto the floor, echoing loudly in the open space. Without hesitation, he skittered in. Unlike the broken building where they had spent their first night in the city, the room was completely intact.

"How do we know if we are in the right structure?" Jaelisk asked, her voice carrying a sense of awe as she surveyed the room's contents. Ancient machinery, now dormant, suggested a civilization she had difficulty comprehending.

"It is time to try Engirisk's machine once again," he answered.

"Do you not believe it is broken beyond use?"

"It is time to discover this."

She extracted the machine and handed it to Sklisk. The translucent face was spiderwebbed with lines, but when he poked the activation, the surface lit up just as it always had.

"Quickly, what does it say?" Jaelisk pushed.

"*Proceed to sub-level 2,*" the machine spoke, startling them both.

"Won't the bugs find this machine as they did on the cliff?" Jaelisk asked.

"*Current shielding is sufficient to mask electromagnetic radiation,*" the machine answered. "*Please proceed along recommended path.*" Even though the screen was cracked, an arrow indicating the direction glowed on the pad.

The landscape of the interior was foreign, but with the machine's help, Sklisk discovered the correct operation of the door that allowed exit from the room. After climbing a few levels, a crashing sound from above made Jaelisk and Sklisk freeze, fearing their presence in the building had not gone unnoticed.

"The machine is wrong," Jaelisk hissed. "We are discovered."

"We must be close to the room," Sklisk asked. "Perhaps we can hide within."

"*You have arrived on sub-level 2,*" the machine answered. "*Your destination is at the end of the hallway.*"

"We'll be trapped," Jaelisk answered, exiting the ramp leading upward and walking into the dark hallway. "Turn off the machine. We must flee."

Sklisk turned off the machine and pushed it into his pack. "I cannot leave. Our people rely on the devices Engirisk seeks. You will go to the tunnels and flee. It is to me to continue."

"Behind!" Jaelisk said, as the crumbling building crashed into the stairwell and a Kroerak warrior fell through the opening, thrashing in its attempt to gain its feet.

Sklisk scurried over, drew his weapon and cut into the bug before it could gain equilibrium. "You must go now," Sklisk said, as he dispatched a second and third warrior. The vibrations from above indicated that dozens, if not hundreds, were pushing in behind.

"I will not leave without you," Jaelisk said.

"Then we move," Sklisk said, turning away at a momentary break in the flow of bugs. Feeling a pincer on his back, Sklisk was thrown sideways into the wall. Without hesitation he spun his weapon and cleared the bug. As he fought, it occurred to Sklisk that the bugs could not fit into the passageway. Dodging pincers, he poked the Iskstar into the closest bug's skull, leaving the creature in one piece where it fell. If he could create a blockage at this end of the passage, they would be afforded a short respite, although he might end their ability to flee afterward.

They skittered down the hallway and attempted to enter the room they had struggled so hard to reach, only to discover the latch was frozen.

"They come," Jaelisk said. Sklisk dared a glance. A warrior crept forward and he felt vibrations from above as more dug their way toward this level.

Once again, he raced to the warrior and ended its progression, only this time the bug was pulled out of the way and replaced by another. A crashing sound alerted him to a break in the ceiling behind where he stood, cutting him off from Jaelisk. He turned, unwilling to leave his mate defenseless. Sklisk felt the impact of a pincer into his back and his scales gave way to the heavy claw. The pain, unlike anything he'd felt, was blinding. He responded in the only way he knew how, swinging his weapon around and cutting randomly into the bug.

A scream from Jaelisk alerted him to the danger she faced. Sklisk pushed away the pain, turned to look over the pile of debris in the passageway, and threw his staff as one would a spear. The weapon struck home and the warrior that pursued Jaelisk bellowed in pain. Sklisk raced forward, intent on retrieving his weapon when the unthinkable happened. The warrior, instead of pursuing Jaelisk or turning to fight, pulled back and scrabbled up into the crumbling ceiling, the Iskstar staff dangling from its carapace.

Knowing the weapon would be lost without action, Sklisk skittered into the ceiling and launched himself at the bug, grasping his staff. A second bellow was accompanied by a sideways swing of its great claw, which smashed Sklisk into the wall. Stunned but not completely disabled, Sklisk arced the staff through the bug's torso, pulling it free. Shaking his head to clear the confusion, he felt the bug convulse and knew he'd completed his task.

Sklisk could feel more bugs coming and he rushed back to join Jaelisk at the door. "Open it," he said with his back to her, ready to face the onslaught of Kroo Ack.

"It will not open," she said. "There is no mechanism. You must ask the machine, Sklisk. Turn it on," she pushed.

Sklisk pulled the machine from his pouch and started it. He felt the vibrations of heavy machinery turning within the walls holding the door, and a moment later it cracked open.

Chapter 16

ANY LANDING YOU CAN
WALK AWAY FROM

"We're down there," I said, pointing down the mountain to where *Gaylon Brighton* rested.

"That is your space ship?" Tskir asked.

"Yes, and we must leave now. The Jarwain need our help."

Without hesitation and to my horror, Tskir leapt over the side of the sheer cliff and quickly fell away.

"Frak!" I exclaimed, thinking she was making good on the suicidal comments from our previous conversation.

I jumped after her and accelerated against the free fall with my grav-suit. Tskir fell dangerously close to the face of the mountain and I edged in closer, preparing to pluck her from certain death when the unexpected happened. The small alien extended her feet and impacted the stone, grabbing on with her claws. Having slowed her fall by skidding against the mountain face, she jumped across and landed on the edge of an outcropping. Her unexpected redirection caused me to shoot past and when I recovered, she'd dropped even further, skipping down the face of the mountain, in complete control.

"Everything okay out there?" Tabby asked.

"Just learning about the Piscivoru," I said, trying to get my heart rate back into a normal range. "Open up and bring the weapon systems online. We'll take off as soon as we're all in."

Once we were loaded into the ship, I accepted Sendrei's weapon so he could go forward and join Tabby. I kept Tskir with me as I stowed the weapons in the armory.

"What is amiss?" Tskir asked.

"Just what I said," I answered. "Those that hunt us are attacking the Jarwain. Two of our crew were left behind and we believe they are in danger. I need you to stay in the lounge until we get it worked out."

Tskir nodded. "I will do as you ask for now." I led her back to the crew lounge and turned the vid screen to show output from the forward vid sensors.

The ship lifted as I palmed my way onto the bridge. Jumping into the pilot's chair next to Tabby, I pulled at the holo display's projection of the Jarwain village. From this distance, the only thing visible was a plume of thick black smoke.

Tabby urged *Gaylon Brighton* forward and I scanned the skies for any sign of the Kasumi ship. "No ships on sensors. Jonathan, are you finding anything?"

"Nothing beyond Petty Officer Bray's last communication," he said. "She captured the signature of the Kasumi ship that stalked us from the Santaloo system."

"Where are they then?" I asked. "Tabby, be careful, this could be a trap."

"Missiles are loaded," Sendrei said.

I wanted to take the flight stick from Tabby, but knew it would cause more problems than I had time or energy to deal with. One-on-one her skills as a pilot were fantastic, but I was the sort to want control in tight situations. With Sendrei on weapons, I had nothing to do other than sweat out the final minutes of our flight.

Even from fifty kilometers, the ship's sensors told a story of destruction I couldn't fathom. Not a single building was left standing in the peaceful village and the sensors could find no signs of either the Kasumi ship or of life on the ground.

"Frak. Frak," Tabby cursed as we arrived to within a kilometer. "Where are those bastards?"

Smoke trails curled away in the light winds and our sensors showed a scene of complete destruction.

"Set us down," I said, my eyes searching for Peris's home where we'd shared a meal no more than two hours previous.

"They're all dead," Tabby said, tears in her eyes, setting down in the sand. Next to one of the buildings, my AI showed a splotch of red that looked like part of the vac-suit material Hunter and Bray had worn. My heart raced as I considered the implications.

"Captain, we recommend caution," Jonathan said. "If the Kasumi catch you in the open, it will be difficult to defend you."

"Tabby, with me," I said. "We'll go fast, Jonathan. Gain altitude and locate the Kasumi."

"A reasonable precaution," Jonathan agreed.

At the junction to the airlock, Tskir stopped us, holding up her small hand. "Why have we landed?" she asked.

"We are at the Jarwain village," I said. "They have been attacked. I believe it is the same enemy who was attempting to keep us from finding you."

"Why would you endanger yourselves in this way?"

"We can talk when I get back, but if there are any Jarwain alive, we have to help them. We brought this danger to them. It's our responsibility to help. Please go back to the room you were in. It is safe there."

Tabby, who'd stopped at the armory, handed a blaster rifle to me. Impatient to be out the door, Tabby turned, jogged down the passageway to the airlock and opened it. I joined her and we cycled through.

"We're clear, Sendrei," I said.

"Copy that, Liam," he answered.

"Liam. Here," Tabby said. My heart sank as I looked down at a shock of blonde hair that rustled in the breeze. Blaster fire had ripped through Larkin Bray's back, cutting her down in mid-flight. Rolling her over, Tabby discovered the frail body of a dead juvenile Jarwainian Larkin had obviously been shielding in her last act.

I pulled Larkin's arms onto her chest, crossing them so that she looked peaceful. Somewhere along the line, I'd lost the capacity for tears, but it didn't stop the hollow feeling of loss from tearing at me.

"What was the point?" I asked, no one in particular "Why kill them?"

"The destruction is consistent with a Kroerak benefactor," Jonathan said. "It is a Kroerak belief that knowledge of Piscivoru must be eradicated for their survival."

"We brought this," I said. "It was not the fault of the Jarwain that the Piscivoru came here. Their blood is on my hands."

My confession quieted the comm channels as Tabby and I worked our way into the ruined building. Dead Jarwain lay everywhere and my throat constricted as Tabby laid the juvenile she'd picked up next to its family. We went from building to building. Everywhere we looked there were dead Jarwainians and our sensors showed no signs of life, although we'd yet to find Hunter.

In the home of Galtawain and Peris, my eyes found the couple lying against the hearth. Their skin was abraded, and blood stained their clothing, evidence of a violent interrogation. In the end, however, a single clean shot to the head showed how they both had perished.

"They were tortured," Tabby said, taking in the scene. "Frak. Hunter." She pointed to a corner where our other crewman lay against the wall. In one hand he had a cup of coffee, the liquid splashed on the ground in front of him.

"Didn't go down without a fight," I said.

"How's that?" Tabby asked.

"Looks like he threw that coffee on someone before they got him."

"But why the torture?" Tabby asked.

"To find us. They didn't give us up and they died for it," I said woodenly. My mind was stuck in a well of guilt at my part in bringing destruction to this simple species. I leaned down and pulled at the leather cord that hung around Peris's neck. An oval stone a centimeter in its longest dimension hung on the end. I tugged at it.

"What are you doing?" Tabby asked.

"I don't ever want to forget," I said, pushing the stone into a pouch on my waist. "Our actions, intentional or not, have consequences to those who can't protect themselves."

"We have inbound Kasumi at a thousand kilometers," Sendrei warned, breaking me from my stupor.

Turning to leave, my eyes landed on the water containers we'd delivered. Someone had shot holes in the containers spilling the contents onto the rocky floor where the water disappeared between the cracks.

"There's no one alive." I lifted Hunter's body and carried him from Peris's home.

"We need to go, Captain," Sendrei said as he brought *Gaylon Brighton* to a hover atop our position.

When a final scan showed no sign of life, Tabby picked Bray's life-less body up and turned toward the ship. Silently, we flew to the airlock and cycled through.

"What's the plan, Captain?" Sendrei asked as we carried our dead crew back to the cargo bay.

"Let's get into space," I said.

"You don't want to take down those Kasumi?" Tabby asked, her words less of a challenge than I'd have expected.

"You bet I do," I answered, exiting the armory and heading aft instead of to the bridge. "But if they take us out, this will all have been for nothing. Take the helm, I need to have a conversation."

"Liam?" Tabby asked.

"Just do it. I'm going to talk to Tskir," I said darkly, palming my way into the crew lounge where Tskir sat.

"Why did you take that woman's jewelry? Do you seek trophies from the dead?" Tskir asked defiantly as I entered.

I pulled the simple leather cord from my waist pouch, tied it around my neck, and pushed it beneath my grav-suit's collar. My cheeks burned at her suggestion and I fought back my first, angry response.

"The hunters who killed the Jarwain are coming for us. Their ship is more powerful than ours and it is likely we will not survive direct combat," I said, my voice still carrying hostility. "What I don't need is your approval. All I need from you is the location of your home planet. I don't know if there's some magical super weapon that will help us. I am, however, willing to sacrifice everyone on this ship to find out why the Kroerak are so afraid of your people. Now what's it going to be? Are you with us or against us?"

The ship shook as we transitioned from the atmosphere to space and accelerated, most likely in the wrong direction. For several minutes, Tskir and I stared at each other. I was not in a position to back down from my statement. I was too angry and grieved at the toll my actions had already taken on so many.

"Your mind is clouded with darkness," Tskir finally said. "It is a darkness I have often felt."

"What do you know of darkness?" I growled. "Do people die simply because of entering your presence? Are you a plague on all the good around you? I might as well be a frakking virus for the good I do to those around me."

"You speak as someone who has lost much," she said. "I have lost only one, but it was the only person I've ever known. I did not know my father. Can you fathom living your entire live in seclusion? Can you imagine waking every day and wishing you were dead?"

"Nobody wants to die, Tskir," I said.

"I do. Or at least I did," she said. "I want nothing else but to believe you are noble – that your cause is as just as you say it is. I have lived with only one goal and that is to survive long enough that this day would come. Now that it is here, I find I cannot trust."

"Do you really believe we are worse than Kroerak? Do you not understand? They pursue your people in order to wipe them from existence. You don't need to trust me, Tskir. I am the enemy of your enemy. That should be sufficient," I said. "Make your choice. Understand, I'm grateful the path we take next is not mine to decide and that the blood of others will finally be on someone else's hands. I've had too much."

The small, reptilian woman looked into my face and reached over with her tiny, clawed finger to touch my cheek. "It is hard for me to believe you are real," she said. "I choose to trust you this day, Liam Hoffen. It seems it is something you have forgotten."

"I trust that your wish to die may well be granted by choosing to travel with us. And it is a weight I do not enjoy carrying," I said, as she removed the chain around her wrist and handed it to me.

"My mother shared wisdom that you should take within," she said. "It is that we should not choose the time of our death, but the manner in which we live."

"Liam?" Tabby broke through on comms.

"Go ahead," I answered.

"Kasumi ship is giving chase," she said.

"I'm coming."

"HEY, BUDDY," I said, accepting the quantum communication handset from Tabby. We'd escaped the Kasumi pursuit and had been underway for a ten-day. Apparently, I'd stayed in bed and skipped my workouts too frequently for Tabby. She'd called in the big guns.

"Liam," Nick's voice sounded a little tinny over the quantum device. "What's going on? Tabby says you're acting funny."

I smiled mirthlessly. If you wanted to beat around the bush, Nick probably wouldn't be your go-to. "I'm okay," I said. "Losing Hunter and Bray kind of took the wind out of my sails."

"That was a good thing you were doing with the water," Nick answered.

"A lot of good it did anybody," I said.

"Cap?" Marny's voice cut in and I could just imagine her grabbing the handset away from Nick.

"Heya, Marny," I said.

"Remember when we took down that first Red Houzi hideout and were floating in the pitch black?" she asked.

"Sure. Hard to forget that. I thought we were goners," I said.

"Remember what I told you? What I always tell you?"

"Stop whining?" I asked.

"You gotta stay in the moment, Cap," she said.

"I'm getting good people killed, Marny," I said. "If we hadn't come here, those Jarwainians would still be alive and so would Hunter and Bray."

"You're probably right," she said. "Look at Sendrei. You willing to put him back on Cradle so the Kroerak can eat him?"

"Of course not."

"That's your contribution to this whole mess," she said. "Killing those Jarwainian, Bray, and Hunter is on the Kasumi. You need to get your head straight. The only way this works is if you stop looking back and start looking forward."

"I don't know if I've got that in me anymore," I said.

"You need to, Cap," she said. "We need you to. Little Pete needs you to. Who do you think the Kroerak are coming for once they figure out that selich poisoning thing?"

"I know. I just ... wait, what? Little Pete?"

"Wanted to wait until you were back. It's why I chose to stay behind. We just started our third trimester. Honestly, I was surprised you didn't notice before you left, I was starting to show a little."

I chuckled. "Seriously, you're pregnant and it's a boy? That's amazing. Congratulations."

"There he is," Marny said. "There's my boy. And, honestly, I'm a little offended that you *didn't* notice. Word on the street is you used to check me out from time to time."

"Uh, right. You're not kidding? Does anyone else know?" I asked.

"Your mom called me out a couple of ten-days ago," she said. "We asked her if it would be okay to call him Peter after your dad. We'll change if you want to use it."

"Heh, I don't think we're headed down that path anytime soon. Tabby is afraid of even getting married. I can't imagine the whole have-a-kid conversation," I said, sitting up in bed and leaning against the wall. "What's going on with Munay? You got him towing the line?"

"We've had our moments, but I think he's finally getting the bigger picture," she said. "You won't recognize *Hornblower* when you get back."

We continued to chat and slowly, the fog started to lift. Sailing without my full crew was hard on me, especially when I hadn't realized just how much I'd come to depend on them.

"Here, Nick wants to say goodbye to you," Marny finally relented.

"Way to keep a secret," I said, when I heard him pick up the handset.

"Pretty exciting, right?"

"Best news I've heard in a long time," I said. "Have you decided if you're going to share the Piscivoru home planet location with Abasi yet?"

"Not yet," he said. "I'm not sure who we can really trust outside of Mshindi and I'm not sure she'd keep it to herself."

"Take care of yourself, Nick. Good news on Little Pete and thanks for reaching out to set me straight," I said.

"No problem, Liam. Fair warning, though, you might get a call from Ada. I guess she and Tabby have been talking," he said.

"I'll take that call," I said. "I miss you guys."

THE TRIP to Picis turned out to be both eventful and not so much. We'd definitely taken the road less traveled. Each system we entered seemed even less populated than the last, until finally we were on the very edge of the Aeratroas region of the Dwingeloo galaxy.

As it turned out, Tskir was easier to get along with than originally expected. As different as she looked – and she definitely did at seventy-five centimeters in height and a torso as small around as my forearm – she was much like every other sentient I'd come to know. Isolation had given her some quirks, but she had many of the same thoughts and feelings about life that we did. She also took great delight in the varieties of foods we were able to produce. While she was not very good at it, I was able to rope her into playing in our daily card games. She didn't mind losing and I took some joy in watching her progress each day. Perhaps the most interesting discovery was that Tskir's body could be exposed to complete vacuum without any harm at all, aside from issues related to the cold.

"Tskir, would you come to the bridge?" I called as we approached the final wormhole that would take us into the system we'd simply come to call Picis, which was also the name of her home planet.

"How may I be of assistance?" she asked amiably. I'd learned Tskir had little understanding of the passage of time. Even though I'd set the expectation that we'd be arriving in her home system shortly, she'd seemed unaware of it.

"We're about to enter the Picis system," I said. "Why don't you come to the bridge so you can watch our approach to your long-lost home?"

"Yessss," she said. It wasn't uncommon for her words to have a hissing sound when she was excited.

"All hands, prepare for possible combat," I said. We hadn't seen the Kasumi, but I had no reason to believe they wouldn't be here. "Engaging wormhole transition."

A moment later we popped through into Picis. I accelerated even before I was fully aware of our surroundings.

"Local space is clear," Jonathan announced. "We have a lock on planet Picis."

"Any enemies on long range sensors?" I asked.

"Difficult to tell," he answered. "There is ship activity within the system. We have not identified its source."

"I suppose that's to be expected," I answered and turned *Gaylon Brighton* toward Picis and continued to accelerate but not so hard that Jonathan's data gathering would be impacted.

"We're four days to Picis," Tabby announced, flicking the navigation plan my way. The plan called for several mid-trip adjustments just in case someone was tracking us.

"This is my home?" Tskir asked.

"We're in the right solar system," I said, throwing a system view onto the holo projector. "We're here." I poked on the worm hole and it blinked, expanding for emphasis. "This is your home." The planet looked much like Earth, with blue and green patches visible through the clouds. I knew the visual had been created with information Jonathan had just gathered and was a computer estimation, but the planet was beautiful nonetheless.

"Thank you for coming to Jarwain." Tskir unstrapped, ran across the forward bulkhead and jumped onto my knee. I winced as her sharp claws dug into my leg as she balanced. "It was beyond my dreams to visit my home before passing."

"Might be a rough ride," I said. "Jonathan says there are visitors."

"I accept this."

"Do you have any suggestions on where we should look for your people first?" I asked. "It looks like a big planet."

"Yes. The Iskstar is found in only one mountain," she said, pulling out yet another memory device and handing it to Jonathan. "I now entrust you with the most important secret of the Piscivoru."

I raised my eyebrows. "Aren't you just full of surprises. I didn't think the Iskstar had been discovered when your people left."

"It hadn't," she agreed. "We learned of its existence only a hundred of your standard years ago and even then we did not know of its value."

THE NEWS WAS BAD, although not beyond what we'd expected. In-system was a single Kroerak frigate-class ship of a design we hadn't seen before. While distinctly Kroerak, the ship was narrower and less disk shaped than the cruiser we'd taken.

The mountain where the Iskstar was located was adjacent to an ancient city that had been ruined long ago. The city was lousy with Kroerak which seemed to confirm the existence of Piscivoru. Our goal was simply to drop into the atmosphere and get a good look at what the Kroerak were up to. We would formulate our plans from there.

"All right everyone, strap in," I said as we dropped from hard-burn. On our third pass of the planet, we came in as far from the cruiser's path as possible, giving us a two-hour buffer should it decide to come after us. We wouldn't get a better window to take a close pass at the city. "This could get kind of bumpy."

"Liam, I'm reading a second ship," Tabby said as we hit our cruising altitude. I'd been drawn in by the rugged beauty of the planet. Five hundred stans had done much to erase the previous civilization's mark on the surface. Now, only the ruined husks of a few dozen of the largest buildings remained beneath a brilliant blue sky.

Tabby's warning came just before blaster fire pierced *Gaylon Brighton's* left wing. I banked hard away from the surprise attack and accelerated toward the city.

"It's that Kasumi ship," Sendrei announced. "Going hot on missiles. Give me a shot, Captain."

"Copy." I tipped the nose over and accelerated hard for cover near the ancient sky scrapers.

The fire from the Kasumi ship was relentless. Their blasters were significantly hotter and fired at twice the rate of our weapons. This battle would be short if I couldn't find cover and turn to give Sendrei a shot with the missiles.

We had some speed advantage, especially while dropping toward the city, but the problem was we'd taken damage and were hemorrhaging fuel. It wasn't like we were running for home. We'd be lucky if we were able to limp back to the nearest civilization – ten wormholes back.

Blaster fire stitched through the air as I twisted around a once-proud building and spun from our pursuer. Chunks of the building exploded as the blaster finished what nature had started. In slow motion, the entire top section tilted and fell off.

"Get ready, Sendrei, coming around port," I said tightly.

"Frak, we're hit again," Tabby said.

Taking the strike was in my desperate plan to draw the Kasumi along a line I knew Sendrei would shortly have in his targeting reticle.

I swung hard starboard and just as the Kasumi blasters found us again, I performed an about-face, reversing the starboard engine as I swung around inelegantly. "Now!"

The sound of missiles leaving the ship was overshadowed by the destruction wrought by the Kasumi's gunner. He had anticipated my maneuver.

"We're hit," Tabby said again.

"Hold on, we're going to crash."

Brilliantly, the Kasumi ship exploded as *Gaylon Brighton* spun on her vertical axis and crash-landed into the base of a tall building that toppled, barely missing us. A second explosion a few clicks away rocked the ground as the Kasumi ship impacted the city with considerably more energy.

Chapter 17

KILL BOX

S klisk pushed on Jaelisk's back and the two tumbled into the darkened room. Sounds of rubble collapsing into the hallway meant the bugs had taken up the chase once again. Without hesitation he spun and pushed at the heavy door only to meet resistance. Sklisk frantically searched for the obstruction, locating several fist-sized chunks of building debris that had tumbled into the door's path.

"Close it!" Jaelisk urged, her back pushing against the door.

Sklisk attempted to clear the debris, but their pushing had pinned several pieces between the door and the frame. The scratching sounds of a bug in the hallway added to the urgency. "Stop pushing; a rock obstructs."

Jaelisk pulled back and Sklisk raked his hand across the rubble. A pincer shot through the opening and stabbed him, catching him perfectly on his already wounded side. Falling back, he watched as Jaelisk pushed at the bug's extended claw. Physically stronger by an order of magnitude, the bug would have no problem overpowering his mate. Sklisk flashed with a risky idea. He scrabbled forward and chomped on the top of the bug's claw. Piscivoru never bothered with Kroo Ack claws, as they had no meat and no nutritional value, but they were easy to bite into. Sklisk planned to furrow a line through what was the bug's wrist. No one was more surprised when Sklisk's first bite elicited a startled bellow and the immediate extraction of the claw from the doorway.

Free of obstruction, the door swung closed and Sklisk snapped his head back to avoid a serious nose pinch. Machinery, spurred into motion as the door clicked shut, vibrated beneath the palm of his hand. A muted bang at the door turned into rhythmic pounding as the bugs tried to break through.

"What manner of structure is this that Kroo Ack are unable to enter?" Jaelisk asked. They'd both seen the destructive power of the warriors.

"Look," Sklisk had turned around to find the source of the flickering light. At the back of the room were many finger-counts of large translucent panels just like the one on Engirisk's machine. While many machines flickered or had no light, several showed clear pictures of the city. "This is the building we are in."

"How is that possible?" Jaelisk asked.

"In class, Engirisk showed that his device could remember pictures of the people and display them on these panels. It is like that device we found that showed the woman in the field," he said. "It is able to remember and display."

"Are these pictures a memory?" Jaelisk asked.

"I do not think so," he replied. "The building looks just as we saw it earlier today. If it were a memory, it would appear as the picture Engirisk showed us before we started our journey. The Kroo Ack were not attacking the building in the memory he showed."

"There are so many," Jaelisk said. "How will we escape?"

"We must focus on our mission. Device – where are the items Engirisk has tasked us to find?" Sklisk said, holding Engirisk's nearly ruined machine in front of his face as he spoke.

"It is recommended that you utilize a replacement engineering pad. The screen adjacent to your location shows a suitable replacement," Engirisk's machine answered.

Sklisk glanced around, unsure as to what the machine meant. Taking a guess, he scanned the glowing video displays.

"It is there." Jaelisk figured it out more quickly and pointed at another door on the opposite side of the room. The display next to Sklisk showed that door opening, exposing long, dusty rows of shelving. About halfway down the second aisle were several stacks of machines identical to Engirisk's.

They crossed the room together, glancing nervously at the displays that showed the bugs' continued assault on the building.

"What is this place?" Jaelisk asked as Sklisk opened the door to which they'd been directed.

"*The Piscivoru Council of Twelve commissioned emergency bunkers in each of the capital cities. Within each bunker, caches of technology are stored to aid in the long-term survival of its citizenry. The engineering pad you seek has been activated.*"

A glow on the shelf drew Sklisk's attention and he plucked the intact, albeit dusty, engineering pad from its resting position. With a quick motion, he cleared the thick layer of dust from the slick surface.

"Where are the devices Engirisk sent us for?" Sklisk directed his voice at the new machine. The front surface lit, indicating another shelving unit that contained several hand-counts of canisters. Sklisk recognized the devices as identical to those that sat upon the table of the elders when he and Jaelisk had been given this mission.

Together, they followed the directions given by the engineering pad and extracted a hand-count of the items, placing them carefully into pouches, as they'd been instructed.

"What happens when these too have been exhausted?" Jaelisk asked, noting that they had taken half of the remaining stock.

Before Sklisk could answer, the entire building shook, causing dust to rain down from the shelves. Vibrations through the ground alerted them to catastrophic events above ground.

"The Kroo Ack – they have a new way to find us," Jaelisk said, fearing the worse as they ran from the supply room.

"No, there is a great fire," Sklisk said, pointing at one of the screens on the wall. A building was burning and black smoke poured from an unrecognizable mass lying at its base.

"What would cause this?"

"Data stream has been recorded, a replay is available," the new engineering pad responded. *"A significant event was recorded at time code minus forty-two. Recommend playback from this location. Is this requested?"*

Sklisk looked at Jaelisk, his eyes fluttering surprise.

"Yes," Jaelisk answered.

Jaelisk's hand found Sklisk's as the video moved forward. The voice of the machine described the fearsome battle of two warships as they exchanged fire. The entire sequence took only the time required for a few dozen beats of their hearts, but the battle was as mesmerizing as it was terrifying.

"These machines are like nothing I can imagine," Jaelisk said, unable to peel away her eyes.

"The prey has no chance, its weapons are not as numerous," Sklisk observed as *Gaylon Brighton* returned fire and attempted to squirt out from the danger it found itself in.

"It is using the buildings as cover," Jaelisk said, instinctively siding with the underdog. "It may escape."

"The damage is too great. It is falling," Sklisk said as *Gaylon Brighton* spun sloppily and launched missiles.

"It has won!" Jaelisk's exclamation was jubilant as the Kasumi ship exploded into a ball of flames and slammed into the building.

"They have both lost," Sklisk said when the camera followed the disabled *Gaylon Brighton*. The ship was under little control. Spinning on its vertical axis it clipped a building and came to rest.

"It is not overly damaged," Jaelisk said. "They might still live."

"They might," Sklisk said. "But now, they must contend with Kroo Ack." The view swung back to their building. A good quarter of the bugs that had been attacking the building had turned to stream toward the downed ship.

"ENGINES AND WEAPONS ARE OFF LINE," Jonathan reported a moment after *Gaylon Brighton* came to a complete stop.

"Is everyone up?" I asked, looking around the bridge. Tabby and Sendrei hit their ready-check and I searched for Tskir, who had not been strapped in due to her alien physiology. "Tskir?"

Tabby unclipped her belt and picked up the elder Piscivoru, who lay unmoving on the floor.

"I am well," she finally answered, pushing away from Tabby and jumping onto the forward bulkhead.

"Tell me we got 'em," I said. I'd seen an explosion, but at the time I'd been more concerned with trying to keep us from crashing directly into one of the many crumbling buildings. I hadn't had a lot of control, but I'd kept us upright and avoided a head-on collision. The armor and the skin along the top of the port wing had been peeled back – which meant we'd never hold atmosphere. Then again, we had neither engine nor weapon function, so it was mostly a moot point.

"The Kasumi ship was destroyed," Jonathan answered.

Tabby ran over and knelt next to Jonathan. "You're hurt." His leg was twisted at an impossible angle.

"We are not," Jonathan said. "It is merely our host body. We will join Phentara group within their enclosure." On cue, the egg-shaped device pushed through the bridge hatch and sailed across, coming to rest next to Jonathan's human form. "We would like to bring to your attention a new danger. Approximately eighty-two Kroerak warriors have broken from the main group and appear to be coming to inspect our downed ship. They will arrive in six minutes."

"Frak," Tabby said. "We need to get those weapons online."

"I do not believe that to be necessary," Sendrei said.

"Are you crazy? We can't stand against *three* warriors, much less the eighty-whatever Jonathan said were coming," Tabby was uncharacteristically short with Sendrei.

"Did you miss the fact that we have Popeyes in the cargo bay?" he asked, referring to the mechanized suits Marny had tucked behind the cargo we carried.

The look on Tabby's face was priceless as real distress shifted to understanding and then to delight. "You gotta be kidding me. That big, beautiful, pregnant ball of ass-kicker is pulling our butts out of the fire from two hundred light years? Frak, but I want to be Marny when I grow up."

"Hmm, that has possibilities," I quipped before I realized how much trouble it would get me into. Like lightning, Tabby's fist found my shoulder and I regretted my words.

"Remember how we've been talking about certain things that you need to keep to yourself? Like closing the door to the head when you make stinky?" she asked.

"I'll add that to the list," I said, sheepishly, jumping up to follow Sendrei off the bridge. On the way out, I grabbed the quantum comm crystal that connected us to home. "Jonathan, get Tskir clear of the ship. We'll distract the bugs."

"Would you like us to inform Nicholas and your mother as to our current plight?" he asked, establishing a comm channel.

"Negative. We've transmitted the planet location. No need to worry them at this point," I said.

"Your mom's gonna be pissed," Tabby said as we entered the mostly empty cargo hold. Without hesitation, she ripped the lids off the crates and tossed them to the floor.

I nodded but didn't reply. Crash landing on Picis was far from our plan, especially with a Kroerak frigate overhead that I expected we'd see sooner than any of us would appreciate.

The crates had been laid out on the deck next to each other and mine was in the middle, causing me to climb in from the end and kneel on the waist of the suit. I reached forward, placed my hand on the breastplate and grinned with excitement as the suit opened, recognizing my authorization. Lifting up, I spun and pushed my feet into the nano-crystalized steel legs. As soon as the bottom half of my body was positioned against the gel pads, the suit pressed in against my legs. I lay back and pushed my hands into the gloves, wiggling my fingers while I waited for the faceplate to close.

From the corner of my eye, I caught a fully-armored Tabby jump out of her crate and I followed suit. The maneuver was one that, as a rookie, I'd had difficulty executing. The arc-jets on the suit's back were so sensitive and powerful they could easily cause the operator to flip forward and land on their face.

"Show-offs." Sendrei sat up and used the arc-jets on his hands to lift to a standing position. Both Tabby and I had substantially more time in the Popeyes than Sendrei, however, during training I'd come to understand just how nicely his martial skills transferred. He was smooth and controlled in his fighting, where I tended more toward the see-a-target-smash-a-target approach.

"Conserve ammo," Tabby said. "We have no idea how many more bugs are going to pop up once we engage these suckers."

We carefully moved down the ship's cargo ramp, our suits making us taller than the bay opening. Upon exiting I checked my HUD. As you might expect, the warriors had spread out due to the city terrain.

"We need to draw them from the ship and set a choke point," I said, remembering the bug fight we'd had on Earth inside a college gymnasium. Marny, Tabby and I had taken down hundreds of Kroerak that day, but it had been primarily because we'd protected our flank.

"Copy that." Tabby bounded into the city street that had mostly returned to nature. "Follow. I've got it."

I ran after her, already anticipating her destination. Tabby leapt onto the side of a building, its jagged outer walls haphazardly sticking up into the sky. The tilting, uneven structure had been ruined long ago by the look of the vegetation that covered the crumbling walls. She clawed and climbed her way up until she reached the highest corner. With an open hand, she swept her arm across the surface, clearing a wide ledge to stand on. Tabby was now fifteen meters above the street intersection where I stood with Sendrei.

"Kill box," I said, backing into a mass of building debris and drawing my multipurpose tool from where it was strapped to my calf. "Sendrei, take the opposite side."

"Negative, Captain. This is *my* fight," Sendrei said, unstrapping his tool and holding it by the base. The great thing about the multipurpose tool was that if held on one end, it was a hammer. Held on the other end, it was both an impossible-to-break pry bar and a blunt-edged sword. "But, I'll take that." He nodded at my multipurpose tool just as the first of the Kroerak spilled around the corner.

If there was something I most appreciated about Loose Nuts, it was that we respected the tactical decisions of our peers. Sendrei recognized I was ready to go hand-to-hand with the warriors in order to draw them further into the kill-box. He also knew he was much better suited to the task. Knowing what I would do, he'd succinctly told me to adjust. I handed him my multi-tool and turned as he extended both weapons into swords.

Stepping forward, he simply said, "Go!" as he met the charge of the bugs, swinging both tools and shredding the enemy's advance guard.

I leapt in the opposite direction of where Tabby had set up, using arc-jets to guide me to a building across the street. You know that old adage about how all plans fail upon first contact with the enemy? Now, I've always considered myself to be above average when it came to planning and physical implementation under pressure. Therefore, it was humbling as I flew into the building's façade and it crumbled on contact, knocking me sideways. I battered the building with my gloves and boots in an attempt to gain some semblance of control, only managing to make things even worse as I tore the building down on top of myself.

Peripherally, I watched Sendrei mark tactical targets. I could only grit my teeth in frustration when Tabby let go with a fusillade of fire. A kill box with only one side was ineffective and I was placing my team in danger. I swore under my breath as I swam against the veritable stream of building material. The bugs would flank Sendrei. With his back exposed, he'd be significantly less effective and likely be swallowed by their advance.

"Frak, Hoffen, are you okay?" Tabby called. I heard the tension in her voice as easily as I could hear the armor-piercing rounds disgorging themselves from her weapon.

"Building was rotten. I'm hung up." I continued to claw and seemed to be making progress. "Give me a sec."

"We're just barely holding," she said, telling me what I already knew. On my HUD I watched several targets cross behind Sendrei. He dispatched them, but every time he had to turn, the Kroerak advancing from the front gained ground.

"THE BUGS ARE LEAVING," Jaelisk said, laying her hand against the door and flicking her tongue, tasting the vibrations in the air.

"They go to do battle with the mechanical people from the ruined, flying vessel," Sklisk said. "Our ancestors have provided a way for our escape."

"They are not all mechanical," Jaelisk said, pointing at one of the glowing screens. "There is Piscivoru with them and I do not know her."

"Impossible," Sklisk said, turning to where she pointed. Looking up in wonder, he saw that, indeed, exiting the broken vessel was an ancient Piscivoru wearing strange clothing. "It does not matter, we have the machine that Engirisk needs. We must return it. The strangers have provided a way for our escape."

Jaelisk walked away from the door and approached her mate, placing her hand on the side of his face. "I will take your staff and aid the strangers who fight our enemy. You will return to our nest with the devices required by Engirisk."

"You cannot," Sklisk said, looking at the second screen where the three mechanical beings ran toward the oncoming horde. "There are too many bugs. You will die."

"Can you not see? The mechanical beings have gone forth to protect the elder. I will not turn away from this," she said. "And you would not, given enough time to think on it."

Sklisk looked at the floor. So much had changed since they'd started their quest and now, at the moment when success was virtually guaranteed, Jaelisk was willing to risk it all. He fumed and looked back to the screen where the mechanical beings had taken their stand. Sklisk knew it would do him no good to argue with Jaelisk, but the fight would be on his terms.

"No. You will take the devices to Engirisk," Sklisk said, straightening. "It is to me to fight. You will swear to me that you will not stop, but will go to the mountain. If I am able, I will follow. My life is not worth that of our people. Do not lose what we have gained."

"I swear it," she said, pulling at Sklisk's pouch.

I CLAWED my way out of the rubble, only to come face-to-ass with a warrior crossing in front of me. Without a second thought, I swept my arm out – even though my legs were not quite free – and tripped the bug. It turned to face me. It had apparently slipped my mind just how much speed these creatures possessed, for I barely saw the forward movement or the claw that struck my faceplate. The armor glass held, but a deep gouge remained in the center of my vision. Given enough time, this would be a losing skirmish. I regretted the loss of my multi-purpose tool and blocked a second blow with my free hand, unfortunately causing me to slide back into the rubble.

A second claw struck the back of my suit and I felt the pressure of a bug trying to peel off my helmet. I thrashed and knocked it off, but another jumped onto my chest. I was about to call for help when a meter-tall lizard with bright blue, glowing eyes ran up my leg and swung the strangest staff I'd ever seen through the bottom of the bug. Exoskeleton and flesh simply split open and the bug fell away.

Not one to ignore good fortune, I rolled over, pushing my hands into the shifting rubble pile. As I worked to free myself, the lizard I now knew to be a Piscivoru, defended me. It took only a few seconds to extract my legs and gain a standing position.

"Guys, we have a friend," I said, "Don't hit him."

I quickly marked the unexpected Piscivoru as friendly so our suits would avoid targeting him.

"What in Jupiter?" Tabby asked.

"No idea. He's friendly though."

"Get your head back in the game, Liam," Tabby growled.

I shrugged, although she was unable to see it. Her point was right; one little lizard wasn't going to make much of a difference in this fight.

Some say that one man's trash is another man's treasure. Growing up as a poor asteroid miner, I'd had that concept drilled into me by my dad, Big Pete. True, I'd made a trash heap of the building, but the rubble was now a small mountain I could use for an elevated firing platform. I'd get my share of visiting bugs, but they'd have the disadvantage of uneven, shifting terrain to get to me.

Jumping atop the highest point I could find, I worked my legs, sliding down the loose scree until I found a stable spot. With arc-jets to help, I oriented on the fight below, then closed off the kill box, adding deadly crossfire in front of Sendrei. With the three of us operating, the Kroerak's window of opportunity closed and we slowly but surely started burning down the group.

In battle, time becomes meaningless. There's no time for terror or joy – or really anything – as you truly exist in the moment. All that exists is your enemy and your team. I barely registered that the bright sun overhead had turned to dusk and then to darkness as our munitions packs depleted.

"I'm out," I said, jumping from my position and scrabbling over the myriad Kroerak corpses lying in the battlefield between myself and Sendrei. My suit had taken numerous dents and dings and the faceplate would no longer hold against a vacuum.

A moment before impact, my HUD sounded a warning. A warrior hit me with full force. In my fatigue, I either hadn't seen it moving or had ignored it — the difference was beyond my comprehension. I rolled down a hill of dead bugs as we grappled. In hand-to-hand combat, the warriors had a slight advantage over a weaponless Popeye. My hand strength was not sufficient to crack their shells and my punches weren't powerful enough to do anything more than cause confusion.

Just before we reached the bottom of the pile, something heavy hit us from above, pinning both of us to the ground. Still under the effects of constant adrenaline, I considered what to do with this second warrior. I was formulating a plan to use one bug to block the other when my face shield cleared. The bug pressed against me was pulled back violently and I saw the hammer end of Tabby's multipurpose tool smashing into its body. Normally, she'd have to be pretty lucky to fell a warrior with the first blow, but the fierce look on Tabby's face had me betting on her. Man, did I love this woman, and I was all-in with her goal to separate me from the bugs.

"Get up, Hoffen. We're not out of this yet," she said, grabbing my glove and pulling me upright.

The warrior she'd saved me from and thrown onto the pile got up and started back toward us. I sighed, exhausted but resigned. From seemingly nowhere, Sendrei appeared with both swords raised, flying toward the bug. With impossible grace, he drove one of his swords into the warrior's neck, burying it to the hilt.

"Not technically correct; we are officially done," Sendrei said, breathing hard and extracting the multipurpose tool.

"Shite, you're a mess," I said. Sendrei's once-shiny Popeye was covered in viscera, rock chips, sand and who knew what else.

"Right," Sendrei answered. "*I'm* the mess."

Chapter 18

LIFE

Jaelisk ran through the streets toward the downed flying vessel. She'd promised to return to the people and not join Sklisk in the battle. She would not, however, do so without finding the strange Piscivoru she'd seen.

She approached the large machine that had loosed such terrifying destruction upon the city. It took every bit of courage she could muster to carefully search the area, so when she sensed movement behind her, she froze.

"Child of Picis, what has happened to your eyes?" The speaker's language, while understandable and unmistakably Piscivoru, sounded foreign to her ears. Slowly she turned, fearing she'd made an unforgivable mistake by walking into an ambush. Her twin hearts hammered in her abdomen as she took in the shrunken elder who wore strange clothing and whose eyes were flat, lacking the glow of Iskstar.

"It is you, Elder, who has strange eyes," Jaelisk answered. "You have not visited Iskstar. How is this possible? Who are you? Where have you come from?"

It was at this point Jaelisk noticed an egg-shaped object hovering nearby.

"I am Tskir of Jarwain," Tskir answered. "I have come a great distance so that I might walk on the ground of my ancestors before I pass."

"I must go," Jaelisk said. "But I wanted to speak with you before I did so. There is a great fight in the city. My mate fights so that I may return to our nest with that which will help the people hide from the Kroo Ack. You are welcome to come with me. All of our people are welcome."

"I will come. Would you allow for the being next to me also?" Tskir asked, referring to Jonathan hovering beside her.

"There is no being. There is a strange object that floats," Jaelisk said, flicking her tongue out and tasting the foreign technology in front of her.

"It has the name Jonathan," Tskir said. "It is indeed strange, but will cause no harm."

"The object is your responsibility," Jaelisk said, turning toward the mountain. "I have my own devices to carry. We must hurry, there is a great battle."

"What happened to the Piscivoru," I asked, having lost track of him.

"It is there," Sendrei pointed across the street.

I pushed back to a standing position and walked toward the Piscivoru that sat atop a pile of bugs, watching us. I'd seen him kill at least twenty, all with the blue-tipped staff he carried.

"You are Piscivoru?" I asked, using the translation we'd built from talking with Tskir.

My HUD measured the lizard at sixty centimeters, which would bring him to about mid-thigh if I weren't in a mechanized suit. His torso was about as thick as my arm. Flicking out a long tongue, he bobbed his head quickly a couple of times, staring back at me with his intelligent blue, glowing eyes.

"I am Sklisk," he said.

"Sklisk, I am Liam Hoffen and my companions are Tabitha Masters and Sendrei Buhari," I said, pointing at each one slowly. "I want to thank you for helping us with the Kroerak. You saved me on that pile of rubble."

"I thought so also," Sklisk answered. "But when I saw you fight, I realized your weapons are more powerful than anything of the people."

"This is a great conversation and I'm all about getting to know the natives," Tabby said. "But do we have any ammunition packs on *Gaylon Brighton?* The remainder of those bugs are going to be up here any minute."

Sendrei collapsed the multipurpose tool I'd given him and approached, handing it to me after shaking off some of the gore. "How many would you say you killed, Tabitha?" Sendrei asked, using an external speaker so that Sklisk could also hear.

"Who the frak knows? We need to get resupplied," she said. Her speech was fast, a sure tell that she was still jacked up and ready for a fight.

"There are no remaining Kroerak within sensor range," Sendrei said. "We dispatched 436 warriors and two batteries of lance throwers. Our only remaining danger is if the frigate we saw in orbit decides to pay us a visit."

"We killed them all?" I asked, just as surprised as Tabby.

"There are more on the mountain," Sklisk said, looking across to a rock face that was thirty kilometers away.

"How many?" Tabby asked, suddenly interested.

"Perhaps half this many," he answered.

"Frak, back to the ship," Tabby said. "We're going to need a reload."

"Copy," I agreed. "Jonathan, any update on that frigate?"

"Yes, Captain, it remains in orbit. It is consistent with a posture of containment. With *Gaylon Brighton* grounded, they will simply wait to be reinforced."

"Reinforced?" I asked. "You think there are more Kroerak coming?"

"It may take weeks, but there are assuredly more Kroerak coming," Jonathan answered. "The numbers we've seen today could not survive without regular support shipments. Unfortunately, we have no basis for estimating how quickly the Kroerak nobility will respond to news of your incursion. It is likely that the Kasumi bounty hunters transmitted intent of your destination."

"Frak. Okay, stay put, we're on our way back to the ship to resupply the Popeyes," I said. "I think we've met someone you'll want to see."

"We are no longer near *Gaylon Brighton*," Jonathan answered. "We are accompanying Tskir and a native Piscivoru who refers to herself as Jaelisk."

"Accompanying? To where?" I asked.

"Transmitting coordinates," Jonathan said. "We have traveled 1200 meters through a narrow cavern, the entrance to which is in the side of a mountain adjacent to the city. Even without the mechanized infantry suits, the human form is not compatible with our path. The Piscivoru body is considerably narrower and has a flexibility that is unusual for sentients."

"If you're in the mountain, how are you transmitting?" I asked, arriving at *Gaylon Brighton*.

"We have dropped a trail of repeaters."

"Be careful, Jonathan," I said. "We know very little of the Piscivoru."

"We appreciate your concern, Captain. As always, we will prioritize safety appropriately," he answered.

Entering a code sequence that unlocked my Popeye, I waited for the helm to lift and the chest cavity to open. I didn't mind being inside the suit, but with the damage I'd taken, my pounding headache was in dire need of a med-patch. I palmed open the cargo ramp and waited for it to lower. From the corner of my eye, I caught the quick, jerky movements of the Piscivoru who'd helped us fight the Kroerak.

"You have shed your skin?" he asked, backing up slightly. "How is it that you are smaller?"

I looked at him and then back to my Popeye. "That?" I asked. "It's a machine, not my skin." I pulled off the glove of my grav-suit so my bare hand was exposed and held it out. "And be careful; our skin is soft, not like yours, which can apparently deflect the claws of a Kroerak."

He stretched out a clawed hand and grasped one of my fingers. "You are unusual creatures," he said. "No wonder you wrap yourselves in a machine. Your digits must regrow very quickly if they are so soft."

I laughed. "They don't regrow at all," I said, directing a stevedore bot to drag the Popeye munitions, thankfully provided by Marny, out to the end of the cargo bay. "We're just really careful."

"Where does one find a flying vessel like this?" Sklisk asked. "Why did you not use it to strike the Kroo Ack?"

"It's broken," I said.

"Yes. We saw the other flying machine use fire to remove you from the sky," he said.

"Do you mind if I ask you a question about your staff?"

Sklisk stepped back warily. "Please do not make me fight with you. I do not wish to hurt an enemy of Kroo Ack."

I held my hands up defensively. "A question. I'm not trying to take it," I said. "Are the tips made of Iskstar?"

Sklisk held the weapon in front of him menacingly, but I counted it as a good sign that he didn't attempt to attack me. "What could you know of Iskstar? Are you here to steal it as the Kroo Ack?"

"So, it's true," I said. "The Kroerak want the Iskstar."

"The Kroo Ack wish to kill the people so they may take our Iskstar," he said, "but we have protected the Iskstar from the Kroerak for many generations."

"Is that what you were doing in the city? Gathering Iskstar?" I asked, taking an educated guess.

"Iskstar is not within the city," Sklisk said. "It is within the mountain, where Piscivoru live."

"I saw what your staff did to Kroerak," I said. "They cannot stand against it. It is a valuable weapon against them."

"We will not let you take our Iskstar," he said.

"We seek friendship with Piscivoru," I said. "The Kroerak have murdered many of my people just as they destroyed your ancestors.

We are joined by a common enemy that would see all Piscivoru and human dead. May I touch it? I will not try to take it; I just want to know if it's harmful."

"No, Liam," Tabby said.

"You may touch it," he said.

I stepped forward and placed my hand against the brilliant cobalt-blue crystal affixed to the end of his staff. The crystal was cool to the touch and felt like a piece of glass. I glanced at Sklisk, all thoughts of the stone forgotten, when I noticed that he had a wound in his side.

"You are hurt," I said, releasing the crystal. "It looks very painful."

"I will survive," he said. "And if I don't I have given life to my people."

"Nonsense." I pulled out a med-patch. On the trip from Jarwain, Jonathan had calibrated our medical AI so it understood Piscivoru physiology. Curing a number of Tskir's age-related ailments had been one way we'd quickly gained her trust. "This will help you. Please allow me to place it on your side."

"What will it do?" Sklisk asked.

I smiled. Aside from defending his Iskstar staff, he had little guile and seemed to trust easily. "It will heal your wound."

"Liam, we should get going," Tabby said. "I'd like to take out the warriors on the mountain before they get reinforcements.

"Just a minute, Tabbs," I said, applying a med-patch to my neck. "Sklisk is wounded."

"I will allow it," Sklisk said, flicking his long tongue.

"This whole snake thing is kind of icky," Tabby said on a private channel.

Ignoring her, I leaned in and placed the patch on Sklisk's side. The relief was obvious as his body relaxed beneath my hand. "That feel okay?" I asked.

"It must have numbing weed," he said. "I no longer feel pain."

"Give it a few minutes," I said. "I have another thing to ask. Will you take us to where the Kroerak are atop the mountain?"

"You will fight them?" he asked as we exited *Gaylon Brighton* and I climbed back into my suit.

"Absolutely," I said as I reloaded my Popeye's munitions. Unfortunately, I was only able to refill to fifty percent.

"I will show you," he said and started running toward the mountain.

"Sendrei, Tabby, go," I said. "I'll catch up."

I slid the empty crates back into the cargo hold and closed the ramp. Stepping back, I gave *Gaylon Brighton* a quick once-over. Aside from the fact that she sat half-in and half-out of a building, she wasn't in that bad of shape. Sure, she was missing some armor and one of the engines had a mouthful of building, but the damage could be fixed if only we could buy ourselves some time.

"Let's go, Hoffen" Tabby said from thirty meters away.

I turned and jogged in their direction. "I'm coming." As fast as Sklisk moved, his legs were too short to make good time. Catching them easily, I slowed and lowered my armored hand in front of him. "Jump on, Sklisk."

I wasn't sure if it was the bond we'd established in our first fight against the Kroerak or just the nature of Sklisk, but without hesitation, he jumped on and climbed until he sat on my shoulder.

"You do not blend into the surroundings very well," he observed as we exited the city at fifteen meters per second. "I have never moved so fast except when falling."

"You haven't seen the best part," I said as we bounded into the foothills. Once we were clear of crumbling buildings, we accelerated. I held my glove up, providing an air-dam to keep Sklisk from being blown off my shoulder.

"Are you capable of climbing?" he asked as we arrived at the steepest part of the mountain, which at some points was sheer cliff. "How do you know where we're going?"

"When we arrived in our ship, we saw a concentration of Kroerak atop this mountain and inside the city. I assume we're headed in the right direction," Utilizing the suit's arc-jets to provide extra lift, I leapt onto the mountainside. My AI had already mapped out a series of jumps the suit was capable of and I was mostly just responding to its instructions.

"I do not like your method of climbing." Sklisk's voice quavered as he spoke.

"You have to admit, though, it gets the job done," I said, taking a final jump onto the plateau. My HUD showed that we were only three kilometers out.

"No one should be in such a hurry," Sklisk said. "I cannot fathom how you have survived for so long."

I chuckled and slowed. We hadn't caught the Kroerak's attention and I appreciated that for once, we had a small tactical advantage. "You are not the first to feel this way, Sklisk."

"What's the plan, Sendrei?" Tabby asked, her voice carrying its annoyance at my constant chattering with Sklisk.

"There is a significant depression fifteen hundred meters ahead. It is made by the Kroerak as evidenced by the tailings. I have detected three warriors above. Surprise will be on our side for a short period, but the confined spaces of the depression will create quite a killing field. We should utilize all possible haste," he said, marking positions for each of us.

"End of the line, Sklisk," I said, gently removing him from my shoulder. "Join us when you can." I turned and raced after Sendrei and Tabby, who'd already started running at arc-jet-assisted full speed. Both were holding their multipurpose tools in hand, Tabby with a hammer and Sendrei with the sword. I found their weapon choices to be perfectly in line with their personalities. Tabby did have the capacity for elegant maneuvers, just as Sendrei could be blunt, but given a choice, they were always true to their nature.

I suppose that was the same for me, but the thought left my mind as I leapt over the hole, utilizing Tabby and Sendrei's broadcasted view of the hole to aim. Even while in midair, I loosed a volley of fire onto the disappearing primary targets. Landing on the opposite side of the indentation, I found my boots in loose soil that fell away toward the center. Several times during the fight, I had a mind to bloop a few grenades at our targets, but collapsing the ground below our feet would only make matters more difficult. We soon destroyed the aboveground defense force and the few that crawled up from below. With trepidation and more than a few flashbacks we stepped into yet another hole that would no doubt be filled with the murderous bugs.

Just as in our previous encounters, the Kroerak put up a good fight. The thing was, however, they were slow to adapt. The Kroerak we'd run into on Earth, for example, had learned to adjust to the mechanized suits, but these Kroerak seemed completely taken off guard. Later, I'd learn from Jonathan that a frigate did not possess sufficient status to warrant a noble and therefore tactical knowledge was slow to arrive.

"Keep pressing," Sendrei ordered. We had descended eight thousand meters and the tunnel system had narrowed. Only two could stand side by side in the passageway, forcing one of us to take point.

"I count forty-six," Tabby said.

I was at ten percent ammo and had switched to hammer mode, shortening the handle to a meter and a half. I tried not to jump to any conclusions about my personality based on that choice, as I genuinely had no preference between the hammer and sword. Both had their place and I felt close proximity warranted the additional PSI generated by hammer strikes.

"We've taken out more than that," I complained as I got tossed for the umpteenth time against the rocky cavern wall. The bugs had used the maneuver so often I'd developed my own counter maneuver. I would hook an arm around my attacker's appendage so it would be dragged with me into the wall. As the bug pushed, I'd tuck my weapon's blaster port beneath the soft part of its neck. The result was often a face full of bug-guts. Fact was, as long as the guts weren't mine, I considered it a success.

"Personal count. What do you have?" she asked.

I wasn't about to dignify her question with an answer, especially since I was almost ten kills behind. "Um, have you seen Sklisk?" I asked, changing subjects.

"Haven't seen him since topside – and forty-six bugs," she said, a lilt in her voice as she needled me about her higher count.

"Did you see that?" I asked.

"What is it?" Sendrei asked. "Mark it on your HUD."

My AI displayed a small view screen to my left and rewound to just before the point where I'd mentioned seeing something. In slow motion, I caught a flash of blue which was gone, just as quickly. "I think Sklisk got ahead of us."

"I'm not sure that's it," Sendrei said. "The Kroerak are turning from us. They are being attacked from behind."

"He'd do that," I said.

"No, there are multiple attackers. The Kroerak are frenzied. I have never seen such a thing," he said. I was witnessing the same thing. Kroerak warriors ordinarily had one way of doing things: attack a single target by stabbing and biting. These bugs were attacking everything in sight, including other warriors.

We pressed forward, but in almost no time at all the bugs had been torn apart and we were faced with a new problem. In front of us stood a host of Piscivoru, all armed with Iskstar staves, and they were coming hard for us.

"What's the play, Liam?" Tabby asked, unwilling to swing her hammer or fire her weapon.

"Are they hurting you?" I asked, noticing the Iskstar crystals had virtually no impact on the skin of the Popeyes.

"Um, I guess not," she said. "Kind of pissing me off, though."

"You will stop!" A Piscivoru voice was heard over the top of the constant battering on our suits. One by one our attackers relented, but only after significant urging by an unarmed Piscivoru.

"Liesh?" A male Piscivoru, who looked much like Tskir, approached. He appeared older, perhaps because of his slower movements or the fact that every lizard deferred to his command to stop attacking.

I instructed my Popeye to open and watched with some amusement as the brave Piscivoru warriors jumped back half a meter when the breastplate popped open. "I am Liam Hoffen," I said, stepping out of the suit and onto the cavern floor.

"I am Noelisk. I speak for the remnant of the Piscivoru," he said. "I have spoken to the one called Jonathan. He says you have traveled a long way to see us. We are a simple people. What is it you wish?"

Before I could answer the ground shook violently causing chunks of dirt and rock to fall from the ceiling. A moment later my grav-suit stiffened as the tunnel's air pressurized. Two Piscivoru collapsed in front of us and their leader, Noelisk, staggered, only to be held up by the guard next to him.

Chapter 19

TIGHT SQUEEZE

"You must come. This passage is not stable," Noelisk said as the ground continued to shake.

"What's your read, Sendrei?" I asked. I'd already acknowledged my AI's suggestion to follow the trail of sensor dots we'd sprinkled in the passageway behind us. "I'm showing complete blockage to twelve hundred meters."

"I have the same data," he said, opening his Popeye. "There is but one answer. The Kroerak planned to bury us and we complied by walking into their trap."

"That's crazy, they're cutting off their access to the Piscivoru," I said. A clod fell from the ceiling and ricocheted off my back.

"We must go, Liam Hoffen," Noelisk pushed again.

"Right," I said. "Tabby, let's go."

"And leave the Popeyes? Are you nuts?"

"I think it's safe to say we're free of Kroerak for the time being." I pulled a small pack from where it was stored in my Popeye's frame. "Grab your go bag."

"This is nuts," Tabby protested again, but she exited her Popeye with pack in hand.

A new round of muted explosions rattled the passageway. I looked around nervously, but nothing new broke loose. I wondered what type of weapons the Kroerak were using that they could shake us so soundly, ten kilometers beneath the mountain.

Noelisk dropped onto his arms so his body was parallel to the ground. "You must run. The passageway narrows and you are very large."

Not exactly sure what he was asking, the three of us followed him further down the tunnel which had been cleared by Kroerak. He moved quickly and we had to jog to keep up. Oddly, half the guard split off and broke into two teams, each taking a Kroerak corpse and dragging it at a much slower pace. My curiosity was quickly sated as we came to a large pile of Kroerak parts. A group of Piscivoru were tearing limbs from the corpses, discarding the claws and pincers into the pile.

Another hundred meters down, Noelisk stopped next to a rocky outcropping and turned, seeming to weigh a decision of some sort. The passage continued as far as I could see and my AI estimated there was another four hundred meters.

"I take great risk in showing this to you," he said. "If it were not for your actions in the ancient city and the appearance of our elder, Tskir, I would allow you to perish in this place."

"I don't understand," I said. "Why have you stopped?"

Noelisk grasped the rock outcropping and crawled over its face, disappearing. Even as I watched, I could not make out what I was seeing, beyond the fact that he had crawled from view.

"I think these guys have more tech than they're letting on," Tabby said.

"Hold this." I gave her my pack and allowed my grav-suit to lift me to where Noelisk had disappeared. Patting with my hands, I found what my sensors could not see, a hole not much bigger around than my head. As I touched the edges, the dimensions of the hole were highlighted by my HUD.

"That's a fricking rat hole," Tabby said. "We're not fitting in there."

I pushed my left arm forward and closed my eyes, willing my grav-suit to nudge me into the hole. Unlike the passageway behind me, this tunnel was completely lined with rock and worn from use. For a few meters, I made progress, inching my way into the tight space. A fresh bombardment from above shook the ground and panic filled me as I tried to breath. My chest was unable to move against the rock and I was in urgent need of air. My diaphragm began to spasm uncontrollably as it tried to fill my lungs.

"Liam?" Tabby said. "Your heart rate is spiking. Are you okay?"

"I can't breathe," I said, barely able to speak, my vision clouding. "It's too tight."

A tap on my helmet alerted me to Noelisk's presence. In my state, however, I didn't much care where he was and ignored him as I fought against the unyielding stone. I choked down the feeling that I might throw up and forced my face plate to retract. The stench of clay filled my nostrils and I inadvertently struck my forehead against the rock.

"You must calm yourself," Noelisk said and I felt a small but powerful hand on my forehead, cushioning it from hitting the wall again. "The passage is wider ahead. You have a small distance to pass. I will help you."

For some reason, I found his words calming. I willed my body to stop bucking and concentrated on sucking air slowly into my lungs, not expanding my chest as much. Seeing that I was listening, Noelisk backed up and grasped my outstretched arm, pulling. The small alien's strength continued to surprise me. I wriggled, pushing with my toes as he dragged me forward perhaps three centimeters, but it was enough. My chest passed the most constricted part of the tunnel and I filled my lungs.

"Hold on a second," I said as he continued to pull on me. "I just need to catch my breath."

"Liam?" Tabby asked, her voice wrought with concern. I thumbed the quantum crystal in the ring on my finger which I knew would cause a pulse in the matching ring she wore. It was our very private way of communicating with each other.

"I'm okay, Tabbs. I just had a moment there," I said.

"This way," Noelisk urged. "We must keep moving."

I chuckled. It wasn't as if I needed directions.

It turned out that Noelisk hadn't been completely truthful when he said we didn't have far to go. Possibly his perception of distance and my own were significantly different. For six hours we crept, slid, crawled and clawed our way through the tiny, rock passage. When we got stuck, the Piscivoru would pull on us and our bodies elongated more than I thought possible. My mind often went back to Sendrei, who I knew to be significantly more muscular and just generally larger. Somehow, he maintained his calm and complained only when surprised by a few particularly sharp rocks.

"We have arrived," Noelisk said, releasing my wrist as I fell down into a meter-high cavity. It felt like I'd arrived in a palace and I sat upright, with my back to the tunnel wall.

"Never again," Tabby said as she emerged from the hole with the help of one of the Piscivoru guard.

"Is this home?" A few meters ahead my HUD indicated a much larger cavern.

"Please, your lights will frighten the people. I ask that you douse them. There is mud and material if you cannot," Noelisk said.

Tabby and I turned off our lights and multiple sets of cobalt blue eyes shone in front of me. As my vision adjusted, faint, glowing outlines of the Piscivoru filled the room. "You glow," I observed.

"We are of Iskstar," Noelisk said. As he spoke, I noticed the gum cartilage in his mouth also glowed, if not quite as brightly as his eyes.

"Captain, we are pleased to learn of your arrival." Jonathan's voice filtered into my ear from the comm.

"Jonathan, we lost contact with you," I said, while watching Sendrei emerge from the tunnel. Unlike Tabby and myself, he'd stripped out of his vac-suit, and was wearing the tattered remains of a suit liner. "Where were you?"

"We have had quite a substantial journey," he answered. "We accompanied Tskir and a female named Jaelisk through an alternate entrance. We were later joined by one called Sklisk, who we understand to be Jaelisk's mate."

"What is this vibration?" Noelisk asked. In the very dim light I saw his half-meter-long tongue flick out and touch the side of my face. To his surprise, I recoiled.

"Um. Well, it's a communication device. The one called Jonathan, who arrived with Jaelisk and the elder Tskir, was talking with me," I said.

"And you speak with them?"

I pulled at the earwig, releasing it from where it was attached along my cheekbone and inside my ear. I held the device out to the curious alien. "A piece of electronics for just that purpose," I said. "Go ahead, you can touch it. It won't hurt you."

"You are just as Engirisk said you would be," he said. "You travel in the presence of machines and have them do work for you. Will you join us in our main chamber? We would speak with you."

"Of course," I responded.

We crawled slowly on hands and knees, unable to see the uneven spots in the cavern floor or the scree in our path. We entered a large room and my HUD helped map out the details, including the soaring ceiling. A wide, relatively flat surface lay ahead for twenty meters, ending in a cliff. Rays of blue light glowed from below. We had to be close to the Iskstar. The light reflected off the ceiling and made the entire chamber glow dimly. Along the walls ahead, dozens – if not hundreds – of blue eyes peered back at us as Piscivoru skittered up over the cliff edge, stopped to catch a glance of us before disappearing below the sight line of the cliff.

Finally able to stand, I stretched, pushing blood into my extremities for the first time in a number of hours. Inspecting team bios, I noticed Sendrei's medical AI was showing three cracked ribs. "Tabbs, take care of Sendrei."

"Copy," she answered, picking up one of our go bags from where the Piscivoru guard had dropped them.

"What species are you?" A Piscivoru had approached and was holding an electronic pad – unexpected, to say the least. "I do not find you within our records."

"Human. I'm Liam Hoffen," I answered. "We are not from this galaxy."

"The people call me Engirisk," he said. "How is it that you are not of this galaxy? How would one travel such a distance?"

I looked at the seventy-five-centimeter-tall alien with newfound respect. The idea of galactic distance wasn't unfamiliar to him. "We used the same technology the Kroerak used to come to my home world and invade it," I said.

"And you defeated them?" he asked, incredulous.

"Partially," I said. "There is a root grown on the planet Zuri that is poisonous to Kroerak. We filled their ships with it and they left."

"Enough, Engirisk," Noelisk said. "These are our guests and we have been reunited with our long-lost elder, Tskir. We will rest and we will eat. There will be plenty of time for conversations. But first, we will bathe in the grotto of the Iskstar."

"But the humans," Engirisk said. "What if the Iskstar harms them as it does Kroerak."

"Then we will take them from this place and have nothing more to do with them."

"That's not fair. The Iskstar is no judge of a people," Engirisk said. "We cannot allow visitors to come to harm. They fought valiantly against the Kroerak. They are powerful allies."

I exchanged glances with Tabby and Sendrei as the guards around us shifted. Engirisk was outing Noelisk's seemingly gracious agenda as something more sinister. I thought it was a better-than-fair chance we could take the small group around us, but I had no desire to start trouble in the bowels of Picis.

"The people will not accept an ally that is rejected by Iskstar," Noelisk said. "We saw how their machine skins were unaffected by Iskstar. Liam Hoffen, do you fear the Iskstar?"

"I do not know much of the Iskstar," I said. "I have only seen the crystals on the end of your guard's staves and the glow of your eyes."

"There is no mystery," an older female said, stepping from a line of older Piscivoru that had joined us, looking on quietly as Noelisk and Engirisk had talked. "Even with the dull eyes of a foreigner, you must surely be able to look upon it."

"Show me," I said.

"I have to protest," Engirisk said. "If harm comes to these humans, we may never be rid of the Kroo Ack. We will not survive another five hundred stans."

I smiled, recognizing just how good a job of translating the AI did. To me it sounded like the little alien was speaking directly to me, but in reality the AI was creating a noise cancelling wave to mute his speech and in real time projecting a realistic simulation of his voice in my language.

"It cannot hurt for them to gaze upon it," the older female pushed before Noelisk could object.

"Jonathan, where are you?" I asked.

"The Piscivoru have detained us," they answered. "Understandably, they do not trust our intentions."

"What do you know of the Iskstar?"

"We do not recognize the element," he answered. "From what we can tell, it is unique in its existence."

"Any chance it's hard on people?"

"There is insufficient data," he answered. "The fact that it has detrimental effect upon Kroerak is of substantial concern. I would proceed cautiously."

The gathering of Piscivoru in the chamber had grown and I looked out across the sea of faces that were all focused on us. "Noelisk, we seek Piscivoru help. The poison we have used to destroy Kroerak is becoming less effective. Your Iskstar is the only weapon we know of that works against this enemy. If I pass your test, will you allow us to use Iskstar to fight the Kroerak?"

"For centuries, we have fought the Kroerak," Noelisk answered. "The Iskstar is not sufficient to defeat them."

"They come for the Iskstar, just as the Kroerak," one of the elder Piscivoru said accusingly.

"And the Iskstar rejected the Kroerak," I said, unwilling to let the conversation slide away from me.

"Careful, Liam," Tabby warned. "You heard Jonathan, we don't know what it'll do to you."

"Words!" the elder Piscivoru shot back just as quickly.

Using my grav-suit, I pushed against the floor and hovered in the air. "You have failed to defeat the Kroerak because they ruined your technology and stripped the world above of your people. I have talked with Elder Tskir and she told me the history of your people. There was a time when the surface of Picis was covered with Piscivoru. You had technology that kept your people safe and you did not hide beneath a mountain, waiting for the day when the Kroerak would ferret you out."

"You know nothing of our people," the elder answered. I was in a dangerous spot. I had no idea how many people supported him and I had no capacity to read their body language. All I could see was a lot of blinking and tongue flicking.

"You speak the truth," I said. "But I *do* know the Kroerak. I have fought this enemy and will continue until I no longer draw breath. I'm not asking for something you do not want. I'm simply asking for you to join me and allow your Iskstar to fulfill its promise to your people."

"What do you know of the Iskstar?" he asked, his tongue flicking.

"I know the only thing I need – that it brings ruin to Kroerak," I said. "Noelisk, if you will promise to join us in our fight, I will take your test. To prove to you that I hide nothing. I will remove the final machine skin from my body. I say, let the Iskstar decide my fate, just as it has yours."

"Ferisk, what say you?" Noelisk asked as I lowered to the ground and started peeling off my grav-suit.

"I sense deception," the elder Ferisk said.

"Your pores reek of fear," another female elder added.

"As does this human," Ferisk answered, his tongue flicking out and touching my bare chest.

"Liam, you're moving too quickly," Tabby said. "We need to think about this."

I suppressed a laugh. "Funny coming from you. Of course I'm scared. I have no idea what this Iskstar is going to do to me."

"We agree, Liam," Jonathan added. "There are many possible dangers from this substance. The human body is quite fragile, not accepting of a wide temperature range nor swings in acidity or alkalinity. There could be many reasons this Iskstar is incompatible with human life. We should negotiate for a longer period."

I'd stripped down to my shorts, then walked to the edge of the cliff and looked over. What I saw was as terrifying as it was beautiful. Fifty meters below sat the calm, glassy surface of a clear pool. A few meters below the surface of this water, bright glowing translucent crystalline structures spread out as far as the eye could see, forming tunnels and caverns deep into the ground.

"You don't need to do this," Tabby said, stepping up next to me. "We can talk this out."

"Talk isn't going to change anything. There's no way they'll trust us if the Iskstar is harmful. Just make sure to get me out if I start boiling or something." I flashed her a smile, knowing I'd overdone it a bit with the boiling comment.

"Asshat," she said, hitting the back of my head. "And you're not jumping. It's too far. I'll take you down."

"He should have no help," Ferisk said, overhearing Tabby.

"Don't push it, snake boy," Tabby snapped as she wrapped her arms around me and lifted me off the cliff.

Descending, I noticed one side of the cliff was dotted with small holes, many of which contained one or more small sets of eyes looking out at us. "How do the kids get in there?" I asked. As if in answer to my question a tiny Piscivoru exited one of the holes and skittered out onto the vertical surface, twisting around so it could watch us pass by.

"You sure about this?" Tabby asked, stopping a few meters above the pool's surface.

"Let's do it," I said.

Tabby's hand slid down my back as I leaned over and dove toward the surface. It wasn't until I was fully submerged that I realized she'd grabbed my undershorts. I was now completely au natural. Pushing embarrassment aside, I surfaced and breast stroked until I was above a large blue crystal structure. Not used to swimming without my gravsuit, my lungs burned as I dove deeper and deeper, finally reaching the five-meter-tall crystal that was as wide as I was tall. The urgency of oxygen deprivation spurred me on and I reached out, wrapping my arms around the rock and pulling myself close to it.

On contact, I felt a small tingle of electricity, but ignored it. The moment I fully embraced the crystal, my back spasmed and I arched as what felt like a thousand volts of electricity entered my body. Losing control, my lungs bellowed out their remaining air and I tried desperately to let go. My lungs filled with water and I struggled as panic set in. The energy of the crystal no longer hurt. Maybe the electricity had burned out my pain receptors.

Strong hands wrapped around my wrist, pulling my fingers from the edge of the crystal. For the second time that day I started to black out, only this time no amount of mental self-talk could stave it off. Partially conscious, I was dimly aware of the nests along the cliff face as we sailed past. Finally, I was released onto the cold rock floor of the main chamber.

"We've got you, Liam." Sendrei's voice was confident as he worked to express the water from my lungs. I coughed up what seemed like a million liters of water and fought for the sweet taste of air. I rolled, only able to make it to my hands and knees as I leaned over to gag. After what felt like hours, but was probably only a few minutes, the wracking coughs had their intended effect and my lungs were mostly clear.

"Liam, your eyes," Tabby said, lifting my chin so I could look at her.

"You survived," Ferisk said, cautiously approaching, probably still worried about Tabby's earlier challenge.

"You knew this would happen," Tabby turned. I reached for her, hearing the dangerous undertone in her voice. "You endangered him."

"Tabby," I croaked. "No. The crystal. I'm okay."

She turned back to me, willing to ignore the pugnacious Piscivoru who clearly had a death wish. "Liam, your eyes are glowing. Just like theirs."

I smiled, recalling a favorite story. "The spice, Tabby."

"What? Don't mess with me."

"The spice must flow," I croaked, causing me to laugh, which set off a chain reaction. I now needed a lot of air, but inhaling deeply resulted in a hacking fit as I continued to expel more water.

"You're worrying me," she said. "There is no spice; we're on Picis."

"Are my eyes really blue?" I finally managed.

"Yes."

"That's fantastic!" I said, sitting back on my heels. "You really need to read your late twentieth century science fiction. *Dune* is a classic." Looking around the chamber, I was able to make out details that I hadn't seen before. It was as if someone had turned on the lights.

"Iskstar has accepted you, Liam Hoffen," Noelisk said, padding up next to me and peering into my eyes. "It is unusual for a mature adult to bond with the Iskstar and in Ferisk's defense, we had no idea how you would interact with the crystal. Your gambit was successful. There is no Piscivoru who would deny your rightful place next to the Iskstar."

"I ask that you release my friend, Jonathan," I said.

"You are our guests," he answered. "You are free to go wherever you like. We have cleared our largest nest that you might rest. Let it be known to all, that what little we have, we will share gratefully with humans and their machine friend, Jonathan."

Chapter 20

OF ISKSTAR

Turns out crawling through claustrophobic tunnels for hours and almost drowning causes a lot of stress to a human body. We were on the other side of that particular adventure, but it had left us all feeling pretty run down. Without further ceremony, we ate meal bars from the go bag. Sendrei, Tabby, and I were led to what was little more than a gash in the side of the cliff face about halfway down to the pool.

As tired as I was, I found I couldn't stop thinking about the crystals. Minutes turned into hours as I lay there thinking while Sendrei and Tabby soundly slept. Almost before I consciously knew what I was doing, I used my grav-suit to lift above the two of them. Scooting from our nest, I slowly sank toward the water. With my suit on, I couldn't feel the water's warmth, which was something I'd forgotten about until just that moment. Retracting the grav-suit's gloves, I slipped further into the water until I was directly across from the crystal that had nearly killed me only a few hours ago.

Reaching out, I placed the palm of my hand against the crystal and felt the now familiar tingle. Instead of intensifying, the pulses of energy remained at a trickle, feeling more like warm thoughts from an old friend than an electrical charge. Not quite a religious experience, the sensations were much more intense than just touching a rock in the water. There was something more here, something comfortable or in slumber. I could feel the mystery, but couldn't find the answers. Perhaps, in time, I would uncover the secret of the Iskstar.

I startled at a touch on my shoulder. Tabby had entered the water and was directly behind me. "How long have you been down here?" she asked.

"Just a couple of minutes." I raised my eyebrows as my AI displayed that I'd been submerged for more than forty minutes.

"This is reckless," she said. "Even for you. And I'm not just talking about coming down here by yourself."

"I know."

"Earlier, when you seized in the water, I thought you'd died," she said.

"I would have if you hadn't been there to pull me out," I said.

"What if I'd had the same reaction to the crystal?"

"You were in your grav-suit," I said.

"Why are you here?"

"Just a feeling," I said. "It's like this crystal is ... I don't know. It's weird."

"Jonathan wants to talk to us," she said. "The elders have prepared a meal. You need to come up."

"I will," I said. "Give me a minute."

"Only a minute," she said. "Don't make me come back down."

"I won't," I said and watched as she swam to the surface.

Motion from the corner of my eye caused me to look over at a female Piscivoru, who was missing part of her arm, swim up to me. Wordlessly she considered me for a moment and then swam off, following in Tabby's wake. Considering it my cue, I released the crystal and followed along behind her.

"Are you the one called Jaelisk?" I asked, floating up next to the rock face as she climbed.

"How would you know this?" she asked.

"Sklisk talked of you on our journey. He said you lost your arm to a Kroerak attack," I said.

"A small sacrifice for the people. With Engirisk's machine, we will easily confuse the Kroerak," she said. "They will not find our entry as it is once again well hidden."

"Not sure that matters," I said. "Kroerak bombed the tunnel shut. There's at least five hundred meters of collapsed tunnels, if not more."

"They will come again. They always do," she said. "It is more important to understand what you will do now that you have found us."

"Getting trapped put a crimp in any plans we might have had," I said. "Honestly, this is a trip based solely on faith. The Kroerak so totally fear Piscivoru, we had to find out why. Now that we're here, it seems like we've made a mess of things."

"Kroo Ack fear Iskstar, not Piscivoru," she said as we reached the upper chamber. "You are not trapped. There are many entrances they know not of."

Hearing my voice, Tabby turned. She sat cross-legged next to Sendrei in front of long flat rock slabs arranged in the center of the room. On the opposite side sat Tskir and a host of Piscivoru, many of whom I now recognized. Atop the table were chunks of what I could only imagine to be Kroerak parts.

"Breakfast?" I asked quietly as I slid down next to Tabby. My attempt at stealth was lost as all eyes, human and Piscivoru, followed my every move.

"Your mate says the Iskstar called to you," Noelisk said, breaking the silence. "Does she speak truth?"

"I don't know," I said. "I guess I just needed to see the stone – to feel it again. The desire was strange."

My answer caused a lot of hissing, tongue flicking, and blinking between the elders around the table. As this was occurring, Jonathan, in their small egg-shaped capsule slowly floated over me. It was an unnecessary move, as they could communicate easily through our comms.

"What are they saying?" I asked.

"Our best understanding is that an argument is taking place," he said. "There are those who believe you manufactured the conversation with the Iskstar crystal. The Piscivoru are at an important moment in their history. Many prefer their lives beneath the surface to that of their ancestors in homes within the cities."

"Prove to us you are of Iskstar," Ferisk finally said.

"He did," Tabby shot back immediately. "It nearly killed him. How many tests do you have? We never said we were related to your dumb rock. We just want allies to help us fight the bugs who wiped out most of your people. Is that really so frakking much to ask? Do you have a better way to fight them? Frak, everywhere we go, puissant little megalomaniacs are always the first to get in the way."

I placed my hand on Tabby's arm. Her face was bright red with anger. She was on the edge and I needed her to calm.

"Hold on, Love," I said. "What is your test, Ferisk?"

"Your companions will not eat the Kroo Ack. They say it is too hard for them to bite through. It is the same for Tskir," he said. "If you are of Iskstar, you will be able to eat of it."

"And if I do this, will you stop challenging me?" I asked.

"No, Liam," Tabby said beneath her breath. "You know we can't bite through that shell. It's like nano-crystalized steel."

Ferisk, overhearing Tabby, blinked twice in rapid succession as he stared at me. "I agree to this," he said and pushed a chunk of shell the size of my hand over to me.

"Does anyone have further challenges?" I asked, looking around the table. When none responded, I picked up the shell. My stomach lurched as I discovered a slimy covering and I shut that part of my mind off. The thing was, I felt different. Something about my contact with the crystal had changed me, but not in a bad way. I was something more and felt quite peaceful about Ferisk's challenge.

"Don't," Tabby said as I brought the shell to my mouth. "Oh, Jupiter piss, he's eating it."

I bit down and when my teeth came into contact with the shell, the thought occurred to me that I'd finally gone nuts. Something about being confined deep underground with a bunch of lizardy aliens had pushed me over the edge. Certainly, that was what Tabby was thinking.

"Spit it out, Liam," she said. "There's got to be another way."

The shell gave way and my teeth sank into it. I pulled the remainder of the shell out and held it for all to see. Although I gagged, I chewed the generous portion I'd bitten off and finally swallowed.

"Water wouldn't be the worst idea," I said, turning to her.

The look of disgust on her face told me that kissing was likely off the table for the foreseeable future. "If you hurl on me, I'm never going to forgive you," she said.

"It is too much," Ferisk said as he turned away from the table and skittered from the room.

"Is that how you feel too?" I asked Noelisk.

"Ferisk is afraid of the unknown that you represent."

"And you are not?" I asked.

"The Piscivoru have a proverb that says it is only with danger that advantage is discovered," he answered. "The assembled at this table recognize the danger humans represent. We believe it is outweighed by the promise of freedom from the Kroo Ack. On behalf of my people, I ask what it is that you seek. If it is within our capacity, we will provide it."

"Unfortunately, that's a problem. We're not sure what we need. We were hoping you'd be able to show us how to defeat the Kroerak," I said.

"Captain, if I may, we believe your statement is no longer accurate," Jonathan interjected before Noelisk could answer.

"Seriously?" I asked. "You have something already?"

"We do," he said. "Elder Noelisk, how is it the staves come to hold Iskstar crystal. Do you mine the crystal by breaking off parts from a larger crystal?"

"No," Noelisk said. It didn't take being a Piscivoru to realize the very idea made him uncomfortable. "We ask the Iskstar to provide for the weapon and after the next sleep cycle the crystal lies at the base of the pool, below where the seeker requested it."

All of a sudden, I became aware of something sharp under my belt, sticking into my waist. I felt a sense of urgency and reached to pull free a perfectly cut, glowing Iskstar crystal shard, about the length of my palm. Almost without thinking, I pulled my glove off so I could hold it against my bare hand.

"Liam?" Tabby asked. "Did you chip that off while you were in the water?"

"He could not," Noelisk said. "If the Iskstar is injured the fragment holds no life. Liam Hoffen must have asked for it."

"No idea," I said, rolling the crystal over in my hands, staring at it.

"This is quite fortuitous," Jonathan said.

"That shard is about the right size to fit in the blaster turret," Sendrei said. "Matter of fact, it is exactly the right size. I had no idea you were so knowledgeable of blaster technology, Liam."

"I'm not. What are you talking about?" I asked. I knew the energy portion of a blaster turret had to be attuned to a particular frequency and that crystals were often used for that purpose, but that's about all I knew on the subject.

Noelisk spoke before either Jonathan or Sendrei could answer. "It is not unexpected. The Iskstar has protected the people for five hundred stans. Without crystals upon our staves we would all have been killed long ago."

"Jonathan, you think putting this into *Gaylon Brighton's* blasters would do something?" I asked.

"We believe it is worth a try," they answered.

Tabby snorted derisively at Jonathan's response. "I'd like to have seen the votes on that one," she said, referring to how the collective we referred to as Jonathan often voted to formulate an answer.

"Indeed," Jonathan said. "The Iskstar presents a significant unknown, just as does Liam's interaction with it. Even as we speak, the voting fluctuates considerably as many are skeptical, believing Liam has fallen prey to a pathogen or psychotropic. Simply put, we don't see a better alternative."

"Jaelisk said there are other ways to get to the surface," I said. "Would you take us there, Noelisk?"

"It would be better for you to wait," he said. "When the bugs are upset, it takes much time before they settle. It is too dangerous for you to go now."

"How long are you thinking?" I asked.

"A standard year will yield safety," he answered, my AI translating the timeframe he provided.

"We can't wait that long," I said. "There is nothing holding the Kroerak back from attacking the Felio and twenty other species, including humanity, now that they have a cure for the selich root. We might not have a stan."

"Yup. Nope," Tabby said. "I'm not hanging out down here for a stan."

"How will you defend yourselves without your machine skins?" Sklisk asked.

"There is only one answer," Sendrei said. "Tabitha and I must encounter the Iskstar. We will become as the Piscivoru warriors."

"No," I said. "I almost died. Why do you think you'd be any different?"

"The Kroerak will slaughter us if we are caught in the open," he said. "There is no other choice."

"You can't, Tabby," I said. "We can just fly back to the ship with our grav-suits. If there are any Kroerak on the ground, we'll avoid them. We can carry Sendrei between us."

"There is another way," Noelisk said. "The Piscivoru will defend you. Many will volunteer."

"If the Kroerak find us, many Piscivoru will die," Sendrei said.

"I will go," Sklisk said.

"I will go," Jaelisk said, standing next to him.

"If it is as you hope, we will be rid of the Kroerak and bring life to Picis once again," Noelisk said.

"When can we go?" I asked, not interested in Tabby and Sendrei risking contact with the Iskstar.

Chapter 21

IN TRIPLICATE

I clawed at the debris blocking the tunnel. For ten days and nights (something impossible to distinguish below ground), we'd crawled through an ancient series of tunnels and caves. We'd spent so much time below ground that I had started to wonder if the Piscivoru intended to abandon us. This debris was different, however. It had an earthy smell that I couldn't quite place and the presence of roots gave me hope.

When my arm finally poked through and fresh air and moonlight spilled into the tunnel, I nearly wept for joy. Instead, I clawed frantically and scrabbled to the surface, flopping out onto the ground beneath the canopy of a heavily-treed forest. Tabby, right behind, crawled up next to me and pushed to her feet, stretching her arms as far as she could.

"Let's not do that again," she said, reaching down to help Sendrei out of the hole.

"I've been wondering," Sendrei said, unable to suppress the smile on his face. "Why is it we have ships if we spend so much time outside of them? I find I prefer space-faring travel."

The sound of explosions in the distance broke the light mood as we were reminded of the Kroerak's bombardment of the mountaintop entrance.

"We are thirty kilometers from our *Gaylon Brighton*," Jonathan said.

"How long will it take to get weapons back on line?" I asked.

"Before leaving the ship, we were able to affect repairs on the weapon control systems," he said. "It is a simple matter to re-engage them once we arrive. We are of the opinion that to do so will alert the Kroerak as they have shown a great capacity for sensing ship power signatures. We estimate the ships that attack the mountain will arrive within ninety seconds of initiating the power-on sequence."

"And if the crystal doesn't work?" Tabby asked.

"We recommend hiding within the city," Jonathan said. "Although we believe it unlikely the Kroerak would fail to find us."

"That's a lot of risk," I said. "It would be better if a couple of us stayed hidden while I try to power up the ship."

"For what?" Tabby asked. "So we can wait for the Kroerak to hunt us down? Or even worse, what if they don't? Sendrei and I are trapped on this stupid planet until Nick comes for us? What then? We wait it out until the Kroerak come back to Zuri? No, we do this now."

"Sendrei?" I asked.

"We are strongest as a team," he said. "We should not split up."

"We will protect you," Sklisk said, running up a tree so he could look across at me. We'd been accompanied by fifteen volunteer Piscivoru guard, each holding Iskstar-tipped staves.

I smiled. I wasn't about to dismiss the small alien. Without our Popeyes, the Piscivoru were truly our only hope against Kroerak warriors. "Let's go," I said. We had a significant journey ahead of us, but it was nothing like what we'd endured so far.

We decided to walk under the bright moon and hunker down for sleep during daylight hours. I found I had to dim my face shield to the bright light, my eyes significantly more sensitive than before. What I gave up in the daylight, however, I gained in my ability to see in the dark. Even the smallest details were visible at night, though colors had a distinctive blue wash to them.

By the end of the first evening we'd closed to ten kilometers, our pace significantly slowed by occasional sightings of small Kroerak craft. Fortunately, we didn't gain their attention and I wondered if a new ship had arrived or if the frigate we'd seen orbiting Picis was in charge of the bombing.

"You ready for tonight?" Tabby asked, lying next to me. We'd covered ourselves with the thick foliage of the forest that had long ago encroached on the dead city.

"Can't say I'm not nervous," I said.

"I wonder what Marny's up to," she said. "She could have her baby before we ever get home. I can't imagine bringing a child into this world."

"It'll be interesting to see how a baby changes her," I said.

"It already has," Tabby said. "It was her idea to stay back."

"I thought she just missed Nick."

"I don't like that we're splitting up," Tabby said. "Nick with his business, now Marny with her baby."

"Have you told anyone how you feel?" I asked.

"Not mine to decide for them," she said.

"No, but it doesn't mean they shouldn't hear what you think," I said. "They all look up to you, Tabbs."

"Okay," I could hear in her voice that she was fading off.

For me, the day seemed to drag on forever as I dozed on and off. The tension of the coming night weighed heavily on me as it often did. When the star finally hung low in the sky, I gave up any pretense of sleep.

"How's the voting going?" I asked, sitting down next to where Jonathan's glossy black vessel rested.

"Voting on a successful operation?" Jonathan asked.

"Sure," I said.

"There are many who express positive expectations."

"That bad?" I asked.

"The relationship between the Iskstar crystal and human blaster technology is too unknown," Jonathan said. "The arguments have mainly focused on how you were able to extract such a well-formed crystal in the short period of time you were in contact with the mother crystal."

"I'm telling you, I didn't do it," I said.

"And yet you cannot account for much of the time you were beneath the water," he said. "Your bio signs were reviewed. You had entered a REM sleep pattern. It is a mystery we would very much like to resolve."

"What's the leading hypothesis?"

"That a pathogen was ingested during your seizure."

"So, you're saying there was something in the water?" I summarized.

"That's correct. Do you have an alternative explanation?"

I pulled the Iskstar crystal from beneath my grav-suit. I'd found I preferred to carry it against my skin. Turning it over in my hand I looked up at Jonathan. "There's something about this crystal. It's more than just a rock."

"We feel compelled to point out that a crystal is a different structure than is a common rock, but we also believe that was not your point. Could you elaborate on why you feel the Iskstar is unusual?"

"I feel connected. Nothing I can really put words behind. I like the way it feels when I'm touching it."

"You and your feelings. They just run you," Tabby said, catching me off guard as she knelt next to me, placing her hand on my back.

Most of the camp had begun to stir. Upon hearing the conversation, the normally quiet Piscivoru gathered around us. Picis' star would fall below the horizon within the hour and it was understood we needed to get moving.

"Your broken vessel sits here," Sklisk said, drawing in the dirt with a stick. "There is a building here." He continued to draw. "If our mission becomes desperate, we will go to this building. It can be secured."

"What's in there?" I asked.

"Supplies left behind by our ancestors. There is much technology within that is foreign," he said. "The Kroo Ack were unable to enter the stronghold and it could provide safety. It is from this stronghold we watched the battle in the air between the two flying vessels."

"Watched?" I asked. "How?"

"It was shown on the wall," Jaelisk said. "We do not know how it worked."

"That sounds like a command and control bunker," I said. "If they have working sensors and video, maybe they have some old stationary weapons. This could be the key to taking back Picis."

"Sure and then the Kroerak would bomb the Piscivoru back to the stone age... again," Tabby said. "Ground-based weapons aren't going to do anyone any good. We need to focus on *Gaylon Brighton*."

"The technology level of the Kroerak is quite low when compared to most other species," Jonathan said. "We have seen no evidence of orbital bombardment capability, which is what we believe you refer to, Tabitha. We do, however, agree with your assertion that any successful plan starts with returning *Gaylon Brighton's* weapons to operational status. Perhaps we were not clear, *Gaylon Brighton* will not be capable of anything more than a short flight, presuming we're able to restore engine function."

"Sure, whatever. Let's get moving," Tabby said impatiently. Apparently, we'd reached her tolerance for strategy. Anyway, she was right — if the Iskstar crystal didn't work, no amount of planning would make this better.

Trekking through the ancient city put me in a melancholy sort of mood. Five hundred stans was a long time and most structures had been destroyed and taken over by forest undergrowth. It was a testament to the ancient Piscivoru that what I suspected was the downtown portion of the city had buildings that still stood. According to Jonathan, the materials were every bit as advanced as anything used by humanity. The knowledge did little to ease my feelings of loss as I contemplated an entire world destroyed by the single-minded bugs. I wondered how many other civilizations had been lost to them.

We'd decided to shut down our grav-suits and carry Jonathan's vessel so it could run in extreme-low-power mode.

The Kroerak could track energy or electromagnetic radiation and we felt it best if we approached with as little EM signature as possible. A tap on my shoulder from Tabby caught my attention and I followed her arm as she pointed. She'd caught sight of *Gaylon Brighton's* cockpit, sticking out of the side of the building we'd crashed into.

"Hold," Tabby whispered, sinking to her knees.

So far, we hadn't run into even a sign of Kroerak beyond the distant thunder of their continued bombing runs on the mountain.

"What is it?" I asked.

"The ship." She pointed to where the nose of *Gaylon Brighton* poked out from the building. It took me a moment to realize she couldn't see as well as I could in the dark.

"I've seen no evidence of Kroerak," I said.

"How?"

I pointed to my glowing eyes. "I've had eyes on it for the last five hundred meters."

"You should allow us to approach first," Sklisk said. While his words made sense, the idea of sending a group of lizard aliens that were barely taller than my knee to scout for Kroerak seemed almost laughable. "We will make sure no Kroerak remain."

"I agree," I said. "We'll be right behind you."

For a moment, I watched as the Piscivoru guard dropped to all fours and skittered off. Their running style resembled anything but human as they ran forward, jerkily stopping every ten meters to taste the air or abruptly turn.

"They're not exactly stealthy. We need to move," Tabby said.

"Jonathan, I think it's time to wake up," I fell in behind Tabby, who easily outpaced both Sendrei and me. I felt bad as I watched Sendrei holding his side, he'd cracked a few ribs while crawling through the tunnels and running had to be anything but pleasant.

The egg-shaped vessel that carried the collective Jonathan lifted from my grasp and sailed forward under its own power as we closed the final two hundred meters to *Gaylon Brighton*. As the debris of the crumbled building became more difficult to climb, I finally decided to reactivate my grav-suit and watched the power-up sequence impatiently, then lifted myself over the wreckage.

From the outside, *Gaylon Brighton* didn't look much like a ship that would be going anywhere, any time soon. The armored skin had been peeled back in several places and the bottom turret was buried in the rubble with its one barrel sticking up at an angle not in line with its original function. Ignoring that, however, the ship's frame was essentially straight and at least one engine was still well attached. The other engine, however, was not visible given that it was covered by several floors of the collapsed building.

"Aiyee!"

From seemingly nowhere, a Kasumi bounty hunter leapt from behind the engine cowling. In both hands were blaster pistols and they immediately erupted in fire, targeting the Piscivoru who were completely taken off guard. Horrified, I watched as the aliens were cut in half one after the other by the vicious weapon fire.

Whether unseen or ignored, the Kasumi had made a critical mistake in not targeting Tabby first. Unarmed save for a thick stick she'd picked from the forest, Tabby rushed the Kasumi who fired on the scattering Piscivoru. It wasn't until the last second that the Kasumi understood the threat. Tabby's stick caught the bounty hunter across its back, breaking on contact.

With my suit booted, I lunged forward, gaining as much acceleration as possible before I crashed into the Kasumi. Not to be fooled twice, he twisted elegantly out of my path and even managed to fire a single shot that creased my leg, burning through my grav-suit.

The reaction from the Piscivoru was nearly instantaneous as they switched from defensive to offensive. For beings with such little mass, they moved with incredible speed and had the ability to change direction almost instantly. Something within the Kasumi had a difficult time ignoring the jerky movements of the smaller prey. The Piscivoru leapt on top of the bounty hunter, striking with their Iskstar-tipped staves, which as far as I could tell did virtually nothing.

Thwarted from using blasters, the Kasumi lunged for one of her attackers, grabbing the unlucky Jaelisk as she moved just a little too slowly. I saw the lightning-fast killing blow just a fraction of a second too late. I twisted, attempting to intervene, only I was too slow by twice to stop it.

"Jupiter piss, but I'm tired of you guys," Tabby said, grabbing the Kasumi's arm at the last second. In a single fluid move, she jumped onto the Kasumi's back, wrapping her legs around its waist and riding it to the ground. The Kasumi attempted to twist its other arm around and shoot Tabby. Seeing the danger, Tabby grabbed the Kasumi's wrist and wrenched it backwards, cracking cartilage as she pulled it violently.

"Relent, Kasumi," I said. "Or you will be destroyed."

"You will all die," it hissed. "The Kroerak have been alerted and will soon turn this city to dust. I may have failed, but I have at least ensured you have also."

"You do not deserve life," Jaelisk said, standing up from where she'd fallen. And, before I could stop her, she impaled the Kasumi, driving her Iskstar staff into it.

"We need to move," Sendrei said, stumbling across the rubble. With only a tattered suit liner, he was having trouble negotiating the rocks, but it was clear he wasn't about to give up. The constantly changing scene was a lot to process, but if the Kasumi was telling the truth, we had precious few seconds before the bombers would arrive at our location.

"Tabby, get Sendrei to a combat station," I said. "Jonathan, help me get this crystal loaded. Those bombers are incoming! Sklisk, get your people to the bunker. This is about to become a very bad place to be."

I sailed up to the airlock and slapped my palm onto the security pad. It blinked red, showing that my palm print was not being recognized. "Frak. Open this!" I said, frantically.

The panel blinked green just as Jonathan arrived next to me and the door slid open. Racing forward, I ricocheted off the starboard bulkhead as I took the corner and sprinted for the engine room, where I could gain access to the top turret.

"Liam, we need power on, now!" Tabby said.

"We are booting the system," Jonathan said. "Twenty seconds."

"Frak. I can see them clearing the mountain," Tabby said. "They're almost here. There won't be enough time."

I grabbed for the tools and tried to slow my heart rate so my hand would stop jittering the tool along on the access panel. Using two hands, I steadied the tool and removed the fasteners as quickly as I could. I heard the various systems booting around me and hoped Jonathan's assessment of the blaster's condition was correct."

"Ten seconds to full power," Jonathan announced. "Liam, do you require assistance?"

"Almost there," I said, fumbling with a fastener that had become jammed. I was losing precious time as I struggled.

"Hold on!" Tabby exclaimed.

An explosion rocked the ship and I was thrown to the side. "Frak! That's too soon."

"They released too early," Tabby said, "They're lining up for a second run. Liam, we need that turret!"

I grabbed at the cutting torch, jumped up and sliced through the panel's corner, leaving a deep trail through electronics that I hoped weren't critical. Fortunately, the panel finally fell free.

"Targeting is down," Sendrei reported evenly.

"Damn, that's my bad," I said, using my grav-suit's lift to push me deeper into the blaster's electronics. As you might expect, the cradle that held the crystal was just out of reach through the tangle. "Show me non-essential components."

On my HUD several lines were highlighted and once again, I cut with the torch. I pulled the slagged electronics away and tossed them behind me as I pushed deeper into the machinery. Sitting in line with a highly polished barrel, sat the cradled yellow crystal I hadn't even known existed. It was exactly the same size and shape as the Iskstar crystal next to my skin. I'll admit I felt a sense of loss as I removed the original crystal and replaced it with the bright blue Iskstar.

"It's in," I said. "Go!"

"Get free, Liam, they're almost on us!" Tabby exclaimed.

Pulling my hands back just in time, my face shield blanked. Even through the grav-suit, I felt the heat as *Gaylon Brighton's* turret burst to life.

Working to extract myself, I slowly backed out of the space. "What's going on?" I asked.

"We can't see," Tabby said. "The building's blocking."

"Did you hit anything?"

"There were three of them, but they disappeared behind a building. Whatever you did knocked out our targeting, so we're blind," Tabby said. "Sendrei manually targeted and I think he hit at least one of them."

"My bad," I said, when a horrible idea came to mind and I leaned into my grav-suit, racing back up the hallway and out the airlock. "I'll provide your eyes."

"Liam, don't!" Tabby said. "We're already tied into the other ship sensors."

"I'm not covered by half a building."

It was mostly a moot point, I was already out the airlock and sailing skyward. The burning husk of a small ship lay in the rubble two hundred meters from our position. Two more ships were arcing and gaining elevation, keeping the building between us and them.

"They're lining up for a flyover," I said, flipping over and flying back to the airlock. "They're using the building as a shield." Being stuck on the ground wasn't going to work. If they got their bombs off before we could target them, we'd be taken out, even if we could hit them before being destroyed.

"Engine two is on line, Captain," Jonathan said. "We will not know if it is possible to receive power from the starboard engine until it is clear from the debris."

"Copy," I said, racing to the bridge where Tabby had plastered herself against the armor glass, trying to get a glimpse of the bombers. I jumped into a pilot's seat and grabbed the controls. "Hang on, everyone. The ride could get rocky." I chuckled despite our situation.

At first *Gaylon Brighton* did not want to move, but with urging, I was able to slide forward and break free of the building. It was just in time, as we were thrown forward on a blast wave of explosions behind us.

"I can't gain elevation," I complained. "Jonathan, what about that starboard engine?"

"You're carrying too much debris," Sendrei said calmly, despite our situation.

"Frak! Right," I said and rolled to the starboard. The sound of crap scraping across the ship's ruined armor as it fell away was accompanied by a jolt of power as the starboard engine came online.

"I have targeting," Sendrei announced as I scooted away from the city and flipped around.

"How is that possible? All of our systems got knocked out," I said.

"Tertiary redundant systems, Captain," Jonathan said. "Mars Protectorate had emergency systems as part of *Gaylon Brighton's* original design. We simply located and activated them."

"Three?" I asked, lining up on the two bombers that had turned away and were now fleeing.

"The ship was designed to survive without expectation of returning to Sol," Jonathan said. "Indeed, this mission demonstrates the efficacy of the design."

Catching the bombers took little effort and Sendrei dispatched them with a single, brilliant blue beam that tore easily through their armored hulls.

"The frigate," Sendrei said. "It is breaking orbit."

"Let's do this," I said, turning toward the blip he'd identified.

"Careful, Liam, they'll have lances," Tabby said.

"Show range of blasters and lances," I said, expecting my AI to pick it up.

"*Range undetermined. Unable to calibrate foreign crystal,*" the AI answered, displaying a flickering holographic image of the two ships speeding toward each other. *Gaylon Brighton's* untested blaster had an unknown range and I had no idea how many shots we would get.

"This might hurt," I warned. "Sendrei, don't take the shot until I tell you. We might only get one."

"Copy that," Sendrei answered.

"What are you doing, Liam?" Tabby asked. "Even a frigate has lance weapons, they'll tear us apart."

"Aye," I answered, straining against the controls as I rolled starboard, trying to sail under the frigate and give Sendrei a view of its heavily armored belly.

"Lance weapons away," Tabby announced.

"Frak!" I knew they were coming, but that didn't change the fact that I had no solution to keep us from being struck by the deadly wave. "Hang on!"

I reversed my pull on the yolk and when *Gaylon Brighton* didn't respond, I slammed the controls back to the starboard and pulled up. The maneuver was only partially respected by the beleaguered ship's control surfaces, but at least I would protect the turret.

"Impact!" Tabby said as the Kroerak's simple but deadly weapons impaled the port side of the ship, sheering off a portion of the wing.

I grimaced, recognizing the problem before it became a reality. I'd sacrificed most of the remaining control I had of the ship. To gain proximity, I'd given up maneuverability, something *Gaylon Brighton* didn't have in abundance. Our attitude to the frigate was perpendicular, but we would pass only fifty meters directly below the ship.

"Get ready," I said. I knew our turret wasn't aligned, but I had one final trick up my sleeve as I popped open the starboard fuel panels on the port wing and overrode the AI's dislike of the maneuver while in flight. While not pretty, nor elegant, the additional drag below the heavily damaged wing caused *Gaylon Brighton* to slowly start to roll.

"He doesn't have it!" Tabby cried as we passed beneath the ship and started separating.

"Almost there," I said, instructing the AI to dump the small amount of solid fuel stored within the wing.

"We're almost out of time," Tabby said. "The frigate will have lance weapons recharged in ten seconds."

"Target acquired," Sendrei said, his voice steady.

"Fire!" I answered, wishing I could be as cool under fire.

A moment later a blue beam stretched out from *Gaylon Brighton* and cut through the frigate as a mining laser would a bucket of grease. The pulsing beam carved off an entire third of the starboard side of the frigate. Just like that, it turned from powered ship to tumbling debris.

"Hot shite! What in the frak! Did you see that?" Tabby exclaimed, excitedly. "You just cut that thing in half! Like it wasn't even there."

"We're going down," I said, ignoring Tabby's outburst. "Buckle up, this is going to suck."

EPILOGUE

For the second time in as many ten-days, I crash landed *Gaylon Brighton* into the ancient ruins of the city. It is said that any landing you can walk away from is a successful one, however, I felt we were stretching the credible definition of success. Let's just say I was happy to be walking upright. Before exiting the ship, I made my way back to the engine room and extracted the Iskstar from the blaster weapon. It was clear we'd turned one more ship from viable to scrap, but at least we'd won the day and there was reason for hope.

"You have killed the Kroo Ack?" Sklisk and the remaining Piscivoru guard had run over to our new crash site.

"We saw it destroyed, Sklisk," Jaelisk said. "There is no question of Liam Hoffen's victory."

"It was the Iskstar," Tabby said. "The Kroerak were right to fear your people. You have a weapon they cannot defeat."

"It is more than a weapon," Jaelisk said simply. "It is a part of the people."

I nodded, fingering the crystal where it sat nestled in a pouch next to the quantum comm crystal that would connect us to Petersburg Station.

"What will you do now?" Sklisk asked.

"We have to take the fight to the Kroerak. With the Iskstar, we finally have a chance."

"In what?" Tabby asked. "One crystal isn't going to do it. Kroerak will just send a thousand ships and take us out by sheer force of numbers."

"Is not the same true for Picis?" Jaelisk asked. "When you leave, why would the Kroerak not return and destroy us."

"That is not a conversation for today," Sklisk said. "Never in our histories have the Piscivoru had success against Kroerak. We will bring news to our elders and we will celebrate the bond between Piscivoru and humanity."

"How?" Tabby asked. "It took us a ten-day to exit the mountain."

"The people do not require such large tunnels and are able to move more quickly," Jaelisk said. "Indeed, the elders have watched our victory from the cover of the forest and will arrive in only a few hours."

"Do you suppose we should let Marny know we're not dead?" Tabby asked. "We've been radio silent for quite a while."

"Oh, frak," I said. "I'll do that. Why don't you see if you can find something worth eating. I'm dying."

"Strawberry or raspberry?" Tabby quipped, with a wry grin. It was an old joke that assumed the taste of the flavored meal bars we carried could be distinguished.

"Surprise me," I answered, crawling back into the ship. I didn't bother to use the airlock as there were now several holes of sufficient size to gain entry.

Back on the ship, I entered the captain's quarters for the first time since we'd reached Picis. Even though everything was well secured for turbulence, it was a complete mess. The mattress and bedding had been dislodged and lay against the forward bulkhead. Ultimately, every item that was ordinarily held down by small gravity generators had been thrown free. A single Kroerak lance had pierced the room and was sticking through the mattress at an angle.

Compartmentalizing how I felt about a lance in my quarters, I took a moment to straighten out the desk and set the chair back in place. Sitting down, I pulled out the quantum communication crystal. Before placing it in its cradle, I considered it. The comm crystal felt like a piece of glass in my hands, much different from how I felt when holding the Iskstar. Shrugging, I set it in place.

"Petersburg Station, this is *Gaylon Brighton*, come in," I said and waited for thirty seconds before repeating it.

"Liam? Thank Jupiter you're alive," Katherine LeGrande said. "We've all been so worried."

"We had some trouble with a Kasumi bounty hunter," I said. "We got taken down in hostile territory, but we're all up. I repeat, we're all up."

"Best news. I'll relay it to Silver," she said. "Marny just arrived. She needs to talk with you."

"Thank you, Katherine," I said.

"Godspeed, Liam."

I narrowed my eyes. It was an unusual comment for her.

"Liam?" Marny asked, picking up the comms.

"Heya, Momma," I said, grinning. "How's baby Liam doing?"

"Baby Liam – that's rich," she laughed. "Little Pete is right on schedule and starting to kick a little. Is everyone okay? Katherine said everyone is up."

"That's right," I said. "We ran into some problems, but we survived. Ship is pretty toasted though and Sendrei has a few cracked ribs that are finally getting the benefit of a med-patch."

"What about the Piscivoru," she asked. "Did you find them?" Her voice was filled with urgent concern.

"We did," I said. "I'm not sure we should talk over comms about it though. What's going on, Marny?" Even though the quantum crystals were supposed to be point-to-point, we'd long suspected Belirand, the company that had originally owned the crystals, might have figured out a way to intercept the comms. If that was the case, I still didn't trust Belirand not to somehow pass information along to the Kroerak.

"No good way to say it. There have been multiple sightings of a Kroerak fleet toward the edge of Pogona-controlled space. House

Mshindi is concerned enough that they've put a fleet in orbit around Zuri," she said. "Tell me you found something good."

"Game changer, Marny, but there's bad news," I said. "Without more machinery than we have, *Gaylon Brighton* is down for the foreseeable future. We'll get to work on her, but she's in bad shape."

"Copy that, Cap," she said. "You'd be better off to concentrate on hunkering down. Can you defend your position?"

"Not currently," I said.

"Focus on that," she said. "We're coming for you."

"Are you sure? Aren't the Kroerak coming?"

"The entire Abasi fleet can't stand against the Kroerak. House Mshindi doesn't stand a chance with or without us," she answered. "Now get dug in. We're coming."

"We will, Marny. Tell everyone we miss 'em," I said.

"Copy that. Bertrand out."

I grabbed the comm crystal and pushed it into the pouch. Taking a few more minutes, I straightened up the cabin while I pondered what Marny had told me. It felt good to do something physical and I cracked off the lance, leaving a hole that would most certainly allow rain to enter. I exited the cabin, intent on grabbing the repair tools I'd need to finish sealing in our cabin. For some reason, even in the face of the perfect storm that was coming at us, I wanted some semblance of order. Plus, the idea of sleeping one more night in a cramped tunnel was too much to take.

"You get a hold of Nick or Marny?" Tabby asked, catching me as I exited the cabin.

"Marny," I said. "She thinks we might be in trouble ..."

But of course, that's another story entirely.

FURY OF THE BOLD - PREVIEW

Chapter 1 – Cowboy Up

Bright sunlight warmed my back as I stood on a hillock overlooking a lush green field. At the edge of the field, nestled against a thick forest of broad-trunked trees, stood a primitive village of animal-skin tents. Movement caught my eye and I crouched, not wanting to be discovered.

A flap of hide was thrown back as a figure exited one of the tents. I squinted, not recognizing the species. The male with his smooth hairless chest and thick brown hair along his arms and back wore nothing but tanned leather leggings and shoes. He had an impressive and powerful build. As if sensing my presence, the figure looked in my direction. I didn't move, fearing discovery. To my relief, he turned back toward the tent and spoke calmly in a language I couldn't understand, his voice carrying further than I'd have expected.

Two smaller figures exited the tent, their profiles obviously female. One was roughly the male's height, although less broad through the chest, the other a juvenile. For a moment, the three spoke. The wind was favorable, allowing me to catch snippets of their strange speech.

A loud noise from the sky startled me and as I watched, a burning object fell to the earth. On the tail of that shuttle-sized hunk of rock, hundreds, if not thousands more plummeted toward the village. Fearing for my safety, I turned to run, but my feet were frozen in place. I raised my arms protectively as the first object struck. Surprisingly, I felt nothing as the blast wave crested over my position.

A scream from the village caught my attention and I turned back. The juvenile female pointed to the sky and suddenly the village boiled to life as the tents disgorged their inhabitants. The male grabbed a long, wooden bow from where it rested against his tent. The juvenile, no doubt his daughter, wrapped her arms around his waist and cried. I didn't need a translator to understand her fear.

A great cracking sound pulled my attention back to the field where the first of many objects had landed. Through the dirt and smoke that hung in the air, fifteen Kroerak warriors pushed up between the smoldering rocks, emerging like chicks from an egg. They stood up straight on hind legs and sniffed the air. The first to emerge froze and turned toward me.

I awoke with a start.

Rolling over, my hip fell into the hole in the mattress caused by a Kroerak lance – for the millionth time it seemed. The steady drumbeat of heavy rain on the skin of *Gaylon Brighton's* hull froze me in place as I avoided waking fully. I'd successfully sealed the captain's quarters of the ruined ship from rain infiltration, but I could hear water running nearby, in places it had no business being. It was only a matter of time before the ship's salvageable systems would become unusable and I suddenly found I was unable to rest.

"Stay in bed," Tabby murmured sleepily, dragging a hand across my stomach and pulling close to me. Even with the grav-suit and suit-liner's capacities for self-cleaning, I felt grubby, having missed anything resembling a shower for the better part of two ten-days.

Only a few hours ago the elders of Piscivoru had arrived in the ruins of the ancient city of Dskirnss on their home planet of Picis. We'd been met with a mixture of emotions. As a group, they experienced a sense of awe at the scale of the once-great civilization of their ancestors. For some, that awe was soon replaced by an overwhelming feeling of loss. That sense of loss was further compounded by their one remaining technologically-savvy Piscivoru. Engirisk, who'd used an engineering pad as a sort of virtual window, showed those assembled an overlay of the city in all its previous glory.

Perhaps the Piscivoru who took the cultural disintegration the hardest was Tskir, the exile we'd rescued from the planet Jarwain. While she was thrilled to be reunited with the remnant of her species, she had lived her whole life with the technology of their ancestors and had little in common with the primitive people.

Unexpectedly, the elders had insisted on a feast to celebrate a victory over the Kroerak. Even if this freedom were to be short-lived, it was something to be rejoiced over. There had never been a time when these Piscivoru had been allowed to walk unmolested on 'the above' as they called it. As it turned out, the feast was mostly ceremonial for Sendrei, Tabby and me. We'd run out of fresh food on *Gaylon Brighton* and the small lizards considered Kroerak shell a delicacy.

But for a short period, agendas were set aside and we simply existed together, Piscivoru and human, quietly celebrating one of the few successful campaigns ever recorded against the Kroerak. The victory, while significant, was also fragile. The Iskstar-charged weapon sat atop a ruined ship, which in turn sat atop a pile of rubble. At that moment, if the Kroerak returned with any sizeable force, they would easily destroy us.

It was these thoughts that pulled me from the warm, albeit pocked mattress.

"Coffee?" Sendrei Buhari asked.

I'd wandered back to the galley, dodging the rain streaming through *Gaylon Brighton's* many holes.

I perked up. I'd thought the ship's coffee station had been among the many casualties. Gratefully, I accepted a dented cup, the cup's micro grav-generator beneath still working. Pouring some of the dark liquid into my mouth, I wasn't even disappointed by its grainy texture.

"What's in this?" The coffee also tasted slightly burned. Don't get me wrong; my taste buds recognized it and rejoiced – having been without the necessities too many times to count.

"Sorry," Sendrei Buhari answered. "We call this cowboy coffee. Brewer is broken. I had to improvise." He nodded to a blackened spot on the floor where a cooking pot sat. When I'd first seen the area, I'd mistaken the carbon as damage from our latest fight. The smell of wood smoke and the brown liquid Sendrei was pointing to inside the pot made me think otherwise.

"We're cowboys?"

"We sure are where coffee is concerned," he answered, tipping back his own cup. "I created an electrical arc to ignite flammable debris which boiled the water. I'm not sure where I went wrong; I added grounds and boiled until the granules floated to the top. I poured more water in, which the AI indicated would cause the grounds to drop. That didn't happen. I suppose we could find some filtration fabric to remove the grounds, but then we wouldn't be camping."

Sendrei had a quiet sense of humor that belied his warrior physique. "Well, if drinking coffee in a ruined ship is camping, I'm all in." I pulled a meal bar from a pouch lying next to the cabinets and peeled it open.

"What's on deck for today?" he asked. He'd already thought through the top priorities, but would give me the courtesy of speaking first.

"I was thinking. We lost five Piscivoru in the fight with that Kasumi. That means there are ten Iskstar crystals available from their staves," I said, pulling the crystal I'd retrieved from the pouch on my waist. Once again, I felt a connection to the crystal as I turned it over in my hand. "I know the staff crystals aren't the same shape, but I was wondering if we could make them work."

"Work with what?" Sendrei asked. "We only have one blaster turret and your crystal does the job pretty well."

Movement at the corner of my eye caught my attention. Jonathan, or at least the holo projection of their common physical form, approached from beneath the ship.

"Where have you been, Jonathan?" I asked, momentarily ignoring Sendrei's question.

"We have discovered reference to a planetary defensive weapon," he answered.

"That's perfect," I said. "Where is it and what will it take to get it fired up?"

"We have perhaps oversimplified," Jonathan answered. "We have only just learned of its existence. The status and even the location of the weapon is yet unknown."

"You didn't answer where you've been," Sendrei said. "As far as I can tell, you were gone all night."

"That is true," Jonathan said. "We returned to the underground city of the Piscivoru. In that our corporeal form is close in diameter to that of our guests and our speed over ground can be quite fast, we took it upon ourselves to establish communications between the two locations by placing repeaters within the tunnel."

"A planet-wide defensive array sounds like a great long-term answer," I said, "but if the Kroerak return before it's working, they could wipe us out. We need something now. We don't even have our Popeyes. A band of twenty warriors would likely take us out."

"Your concern is legitimate," Jonathan said. "According to Noelisk, five Kroerak were discovered within the city throughout the evening and were dispatched. There could be good news on the Mechanized Infantry suits, however. We have calculated that if the suits were sufficiently dismantled, they could be carried by Piscivoru through the lower tunnels."

"No way," I said. "We barely scraped through some of those passageways. The back plate would never make it."

"It is remarkable how you are capable of intuitive calculations of this nature," Jonathan answered. "And you are correct, the back plate and ammunition pack storage both have dimensions incompatible with the passage in its current form. There are, however, only eight locations that would require widening. To be specific, a total of twenty-seven cubic meters of material would need to be removed."

"If only we had someone who was familiar with mining equipment." Tabby's voice wafted down the hallway just before she appeared. Her tousled, long amber hair and puffy eyes were a good telltale that she'd just awakened.

"Coffee?" I asked, handing her my cup. "Sendrei says we're cowboys now."

"Cowgirl," she said foggily, as she accepted the cup and looked into it suspiciously.

"What would you require to remove that much material?" Jonathan asked, projecting the sideview of a tunnel onto the galley's bulkhead. The pinch-points were well identified, and I recognized a few of them from the scrapes the mech suits had left behind.

"Ideally, we'd have a mining laser. We would bore holes and pop 'em with a controlled gas expansion. That far underground, we wouldn't dare risk using direct explosives. A cave-in would be ... well, I think we all understand that would be bad," I said. "That Class-A replicator we were going to give the Jarwainians is too small to build anything but the bags. We'd need to get the Class-C going. I think we'd have to build a bore instead of a laser; build time on a Class-C for a halfway decent laser is at least twenty hours."

"How long for a bore?" Tabby asked. "Do you even know how to use a bore?"

I chuckled and raised my eyebrows at her. "Of course. Hoffens are, if anything, good at using even the most Luddite technology. Fact is, a quality hammer bore is almost as fast as a laser. It just requires more attention and leaves a mess. Lasers are pretty much point and shoot. Given that *Gaylon Brighton* isn't going anywhere anytime soon, we can scavenge her for material."

"Popeyes aren't much protection from ships," Tabby said.

"Agreed," Sendrei said. "First order has to be repairing *Gaylon Brighton's* turrets and power supply."

"Anyone think this ship will sail again?" I asked.

"No way," Tabby answered.

I nodded in agreement with her statement. We'd been lucky to sail her up against a Kroerak frigate. That luck had run out when she'd been impaled by a dozen lances.

"We should move the turret to a position worth defending," I said, "along with the med-tank and replicators. Like Sendrei's cowboys, we need to build a fort and bring everything inside the walls. If we're spread out when the Kroerak come, we'll have trouble putting up a defense."

"Move it where?" Tabby asked.

"To the bunker where the Piscivoru are holed up," I said. "Engirisk was excited to start looking through all the technology that had been left behind. How about this? Jonathan, you and Sendrei get *Gaylon Brighton's* turrets, Class-C replicator, and med-tank portable. We can use the stevedore bot to move them once you get them freed up. Tabby had the Class-A mostly removed. We'll take it over to the bunker and negotiate with Noelisk and crew. They already have power and hopefully we can just connect the Class-A."

"We have constructed a power regulator pattern for the purpose of connecting human technology with the Piscivoru," Jonathan said. "This part sits within the completed bin labeled 'A.'"

His statement reminded me that he was not a single entity but a community of 1,438 silicate-based sentients. The fact was, they'd likely already discussed everything and come to the same conclusions hours ago.

"What are we missing, Jonathan?" I asked.

The collective was generally unwilling to change plans we came up with. In some circumstances, like with the communications and arranging to disassemble the Popeyes, they would act independently.

"There is a matter of food for the Piscivoru," they said. "There existed an unusual symbiosis between Kroerak and Piscivoru. While the Kroerak hunted the Piscivoru, the Piscivoru in turn fed on the fallen Kroerak. The Piscivoru have become dependent upon Kroerak as their primary source of protein."

I shuddered, recalling the disgusting crunch of Kroerak shell. "I think Sklisk said there were supplies in the bunker."

"We estimate there is perhaps enough for sixty days with proper rationing," he said. "If the Kroerak do not return with ground forces, and if an effort to replace this food supply is ignored, the Piscivoru will starve."

"Anything else?" I asked.

"We think it likely an advanced guard of Kroerak will arrive as early as ten days from now. Whatever our preparations, we should execute them with due haste."

"Have you been in contact with Thomas Anino?" I asked.

Jonathan held a quantum crystal that allowed direct communication with Thomas Anino, the inventor of TransLoc. While no longer operable, TransLoc technology had originally given humanity access to the stars. Unfortunately, it had also given the Kroerak a way to invade Earth.

"Our communication has been limited," Jonathan answered. "We believe, as do you, that quantum communications may not be completely secure. Thomas Anino knows of Loose Nuts' limited success in tracking down that which the Kroerak most fear. The details of the utilization of Iskstar have been withheld, however."

"I appreciate that," I said. "I'm not sure what the Kroerak would do if they thought we were developing technology as powerful as Iskstar. If I were them and I believed that intel, I'd throw everything I had at the problem."

"We also believe this to be true," Jonathan said. "It is prudent to assume the Kroerak are aware of your victory and are indeed amassing attacks on multiple fronts."

"Time to stop talking and get to work in that case," Tabby said, stuffing the rest of a meal bar into her mouth before washing it down with scalding hot coffee.

Sendrei nodded in agreement. He would work on freeing the top turret and a power source while Tabby and I met up with the Piscivoru.

"Did you lose your brush?" I asked as we walked up the incline leading forward. Tabby's hair was always meticulously kept. As we walked she flipped it back, obviously annoyed.

"Did you see it?" she asked, pulling her hair over her shoulder and holding it in place. "It wasn't in our quarters."

"Probably fell out. I patched some pretty big holes in the head. It won't take even three minutes to make one on the Class-A," I said. "We can do that first if you want."

"I feel selfish, but yeah, we need to do that," she answered. "Otherwise, someone is going to get beaten."

"Why don't you grab a couple of blaster rifles and I'll get started on the replicator." Avoiding a Tabby beating, physical or verbal, was always high on my priorities.

"You're the best," she said, pecking me on my grimy cheek.

At the replicator, I punched in the plans for her brush. Technically, it was more than a brush as it kept a person's hair at exactly the right length in addition to styling it to specification. I personally didn't use the brush more than once a ten-day and was due. In the last few months, my normally reticent beard started to fill in on my chin and I was toying with the notion of growing it out. Tabby wouldn't love the idea, but it seemed a manly thing to do. Since I was generally the physical lesser of my peers, especially since Nick was no longer traveling with us as much, I figured I should give it a try.

"M-1911," Tabby said, joining me at the replicator, handing me the replica slug thrower I favored. I'd already extracted the power coupler Jonathan had programmed and was just pulling out her brush.

"Thanks," I said, affixing the holster to my favored chest position. "Grab an end."

Tabby had been working on the replicator, preparing to give it to the Jarwainians. She'd already installed handles so it could be carried easily by two people. Massing thirty kilograms, the device was bulky as well as heavy.

"I have it. Grab the material bags," She grasped both handles and lifted from the deck with her grav-suit.

We exited the ship into a rainstorm that had spent most of the morning intensifying. I had twenty kilograms of raw materials and Tabby had the replicator. As it turned out, our second crash site wasn't quite as conveniently located as our first had been. By the time we arrived at the building beneath which the bunker lay, my arms were tiring from the bag's weight. A younger Liam would have tasked a stevedore bot to carry the loads, not caring whether that was the lazy way to do things. Tabby, however, was my kryptonite in this. If she could handle the replicator, I would man-up and do my part.

Dropping through the rubble of a recently demolished series of floors, my eyes finally lit on the blue telltale of an Iskstar staff. One of the Piscivoru guards stepped out from the shadows. As soon as she saw who it was, she nodded and continued along her close-in patrol route.

"Liam Hoffen, welcome." The comm in my ear chirped to life with the unmistakable sound of Engirisk's voice. "You have brought machines. Is there purpose to this?"

At the far end of the hallway, which was still mostly obstructed by fallen building debris, a meter-and-a-half-tall hatch opened and Engirisk appeared. The height of the hallway – what remained at least – was far too short for either Tabby or me to walk upright in. Fortunately, our grav-suits allowed for horizontal travel and we glided through.

"Replicator machine," I answered. "I think we talked of this when back at the Iskstar grotto."

"So, this is a replicator. I would never have believed such a thing existed, although Tskir assures us that Piscivoru invented a similar technology before the fall of Picis."

"Do you have a place where it could be set out of reach of the rain?" I asked.

"There is a partially full cavern ... no, that is not the correct word according to the device that speaks to my ear and presents ghosts to my eyes. There is a warehouse beneath us," he said. "Not only does it have room enough for your machine, but it also has ceilings beneath which you would not be required to bend when walking upright."

"Sounds perfect," I said.

"What is it that you wish to create with your machine?" he asked as we settled on the ground in front of him, the debris now cleared from the doorway.

"It's probably a conversation for Noelisk and the other elders as well," I said. "It is our analysis that the Kroerak are likely to return with a considerably larger force. They will hope to capture us before we're able to escape Picis. We also think they'd make an even stronger push to eradicate your people."

"Noelisk and Ferisk rest now as do the other elders," he said. "I find I am unable to sleep. Technology I have studied my entire life has suddenly become available to me and I find I must use it. We also believe the Kroerak will return, if for no other reason than they have always been here. There is a faction that seeks to return to the mountain and hide within its depths."

"Why?"

"They would return to the nature of the first people, before language and society," he answered. "They believe it is only by living this way that they can truly be free."

"Sounds like hiding to me," Tabby said.

"It is not within our nature to seek battle," Engirisk said. "I have spent much time learning of how the Kroerak so easily murdered our people. In the beginning, we met the Kroerak with open arms only to be slaughtered by the billions, a number so large I cannot rectify its meaning. There were a few who resisted, but even with our advanced technology, we lasted for only a half a pass around our star."

"You lasted an entire half a stan?" I asked. While he spoke, my AI displayed that Picis had roughly the same orbital distance as Earth did around the Sun.

"The Kroerak were not well organized," he answered. "Our people, while trusting, were difficult targets for their warriors. Three cities constructed great weapons that fired upon the ships in the darkness above the sky. Dskirnss, the city where we now stand, was one of those three cities. Enough of history, what is it again that you wish to create with your machine?"

We'd need to work hard to keep Engirisk on task and I had to be careful about getting him overly distracted. "Defenses," I said. "We'd like to talk to the elders about placing the weapon that was atop our ship onto the bunker. It's not enough to defend against orbital bombardment, but we believe it would provide a significant deterrent to anything short of that. We'll need the replicator to make parts so the weapon can be moved."

"There is another entrance," Engirisk said. "One for which I can provide access, or at least so I am told by this Ay Eye." I smiled, the translator program had finally rectified Engirisk's 'kroo ack' as Kroerak, but was stuck on the acronym for artificial intelligence.

GLOSSARY OF NAMES

L*iam Hoffen* – our hero. With straight black hair and blue eyes, Liam is a lanky one hundred seventy-five centimeters tall, which is a typical tall, thin spacer build. His parents are Silver and Pete Hoffen, who get their own short story in *Big Pete*. Raised as an asteroid miner, Liam's destiny was most definitely in the stars, if not on the other end of a mining pick. Our stories are most often told from Liam's perspective and he, therefore, needs the least introduction.

Nick James – the quick-talking, always-thinking best friend who is usually five moves ahead of everyone and the long-term planner of the team. At 157 cm, Nick is the shortest human member of the crew. He, Tabby, and Liam have been friends since they met in daycare on Colony-40 in Sol's main asteroid belt. The only time Nick has trouble forming complete sentences is around Marny Bertrand, who by his definition is the perfect woman. Nick's only remaining family is a brother, Jack, who now lives on Lèger Nuage. The boys lost their mother during a Red Houzi pirate attack that destroyed their home in the now infamous Battle for Colony-40.

Tabitha Masters – fierce warrior and loyal fiancé of our hero, Liam. Tabby lost most of her limbs when the battle cruiser on which she was training was attacked by the dreadnaught *Bakunawa*. Her body subsequently repaired, she lives for the high adrenaline moments of life and engages life's battles at one hundred percent. Tabby is a lithe, 168 cm tall bundle of impatience.

Marny Bertrand – former Marine from Earth who served in the Great Amazonian War and now serves as guardian of the crew. Liam and Nick recruited Marny from her civilian post on the Ceres orbital station in *Rookie Privateer*. Marny is 180 cm tall, heavily muscled and the self-appointed fitness coordinator — slash torturer — on the ship. Her strategic vigilance has safeguarded the crew through some rather unconventional escapades. She's also extraordinarily fond of Nick.

Ada Chen – ever-optimistic adventurer and expert pilot. Ada was first introduced in *Parley* when Liam and crew rescued her from a lifeboat. Ada's mother, Adela, had ejected the pod from their tug, *Baux-201*, before it was destroyed in a pirate attack. Ada is a 163 cm tall, ebony-skinned beauty and a certified bachelorette. Ada's first love is her crew and her second is sailing into the deep dark.

Jonathan – a collective of 1,438 sentient beings residing in a humanoid body. Communicating as Jonathan, they were initially introduced in *A Matter of Honor* when the crew bumped into Thomas Phillipe Anino. Jonathan is intensely curious about the human condition, specifically how humanity has the capacity to combine skill, chance, and morality to achieve a greater result.

Sendrei Buhari – a full two meters tall, dark skinned and heavily muscled. Sendrei started his military career as a naval officer only to be captured by the Kroerak while on a remote mission. Instead of killing him outright, the Kroerak used him as breeding stock, a decision he's dedicated his life to making them regret.

Felio Species – an alien race of humanoids best identified by its clear mix of human and feline characteristics. Females are dominant in this society. Their central political structure is called the Abasi, a governing group consisting of the most powerful factions, called houses. An imposing, middle-aged female, Adahy Neema, leads

House Mshindi. Her title and name, as is the tradition within houses, is Mshindi First for as long as she holds the position.

Strix Species – A vile alien species that worked their way into power within the Confederation of Planets. Spindly legs, sharp beaks, feathery skin and foul mouthed, most representatives of this species have few friends and seem to be determined to keep it that way.

Aeratroas Region – located in the Dwingeloo galaxy and home to 412 inhabited systems occupying a roughly tubular shape only three hundred parsecs long with a diameter of a hundred parsecs. The region is loosely governed by agreements that make up The Confederation of Planets.

Planet Zuri – located in the Santaloo star system and under loose Abasi control. One hundred fifty standard years ago, Zuri was invaded by Kroerak bugs. It was the start of a bloody, twenty-year war that left the planet in ruins and its population scattered. Most Felio who survived the war abandoned the planet, as it had been seeded with Kroerak spore that continue to periodically hatch and cause havoc.

York Settlement – located on planet Zuri. York is the only known human settlement within the Aeratroas region. The settlement was planted shortly before the start of the Kroerak invasion and survived, only through considerable help from House Mshindi.

ABOUT THE AUTHOR

Jamie McFarlane is happily married, the father of three and lives in Lincoln, Nebraska. He spends his days engaged in a hi-tech career and his nights and weekends writing works of fiction.

Word-of-mouth is crucial for any author to succeed. If you enjoyed this book, please consider leaving a review at Amazon, even if it's only a line or two; it would make all the difference and would be very much appreciated.

FREE DOWNLOAD

If you want to get an automatic email when Jamie's next book is available, please visit http://fickledragon.com/keep-in-touch. Your email address will never be shared and you can unsubscribe at any time.

For more information
www.fickledragon.com
jamie@fickledragon.com

ACKNOWLEDGMENTS

To Diane Greenwood Muir for excellence in editing and fine word-smithery. My wife, Janet, for carefully and kindly pointing out my poor grammatical habits. I cannot imagine working through these projects without you both.

To my beta readers: Carol Greenwood, Kelli Whyte, Barbara Simmons, Linda Baker, Matt Strbjak and Nancy Higgins Quist for wonderful and thoughtful suggestions. It is a joy to work with this intelligent and considerate group of people. Also, to my advanced reading team, you're a zany, fun group of people who I look forward to bouncing ideas off.

Finally, to Elias Stern, cover artist extraordinaire.

ALSO BY JAMIE MCFARLANE

Privateer Tales Series

1. Rookie Privateer

2. Fool Me Once

3. Parley

4. Big Pete

5. Smuggler's Dilemma

6. Cutpurse

7. Out of the Tank

8. Buccaneers

9. A Matter of Honor

10. Give No Quarter

11. Blockade Runner

12. Corsair Menace

13. Pursuit of the Bold

13. Fury of the Bold (April 2018)

13. Judgment of the Bold (May 2018)

Pale Ship Series

1. On a Pale Ship

Witchy World

1. Wizard in a Witchy World

2. Wicked Folk: An Urban Wizard's Tale

3. Wizard Unleashed

Guardians of Gaeland

1. Lesser Prince